A Dubious Position
A Colton Banyon Mystery #7

Gerald J. Kubicki &
Kristopher Kubicki

3/24/17
To Sarah

Gerald J Kubicki

ISBN: 1489519564
ISBN-13: 9781489519566

Other Books by Gerald J. Kubicki

A Dubious Mission
A Dubious Secret
A Dubious Dream
A Dubious Terrain
A Dubious Plan
A Dubious Artifact

This book is dedicated to Ryder John Kubicki

Prologue

It was the middle of a hot Mexican summer in the war year of 1942. A heavyset man sat at a small table inside a tiny cantina in the dusty town of Guanajuato, Mexico. A bright sombrero clung to his back, held there by a thin leather strap around his thick neck. On the table in front of him sat a three-quarters empty bottle of the local tequila. There was a small glass, but nothing else adorned the scuffed wooden table. It had been a full bottle of tequila when the man first sat down. A huge Cuban cigar hung from his mustached covered mouth and smoke circled his big head. He paid little attention to the choking pollution.

He was in a foul mood and anybody who approached him found out very quickly. No one sat at the tables around him. The reason for his anger was that he had recently received some very bad news. He just heard from a contact, in the capital, that Mexico had declared war on the Axis that morning.

He, unfortunately, was a member of an Axis based organization, in Mexico. Although it had never been his intention, he was now on the side of the dreaded Germans. He pondered the impact this made on his organization. He was sure the hated Mexican President Manuel Avila Camacho would soon declare his organization illegal and they would lose much of their support in the populace. They currently had an army of over five hundred thousand members, scattered around the area, and it was growing. *How long before they will all be gone*? he thought.

The man, Alberto Alverez, was a member of the Sinarquistas. While he was not a top leader, he was an organizer in the streets and small towns of Mexico, where the organization had the most support. The organization in Mexico had started in 1937, as a right-wing Roman Catholic religious movement. The political organization was based on religion and nationalism. It violently opposed idealism, socialism, communism, and liberalism. True, it was closer to national fascism then democracy, but it was a Christian religious organization. Religion was very important in the Mexican culture.

The Sinarquistas movement gained strength quickly. Many people in Mexico felt that the government was too soft, easily pushed around, and too much control of the economy was in foreign hands, especially Spain. He muttered to himself as he got drunker. *How could we have been so stupid? How could our leaders trust those people?* he thought.

The movement was not just in Mexico, but was already strong in several European countries like France, and Spain. It had been around since the 1920's, but was more of a nuisance then a threat to the leadership in those counties. In 1936, things changed. A powerful new dictator named Francisco Franco took over the Spanish government by force. Franco's ideals matched closely with the Sinarquistas in Spain. The political party that Franco consolidated and then led was called the *Falange*. Their origin was the Sinarquistas, but new agendas now emerged. Soon the *Falange* was spreading the belief that Spain was a world power and would be even more important, if only some former Spanish colonies aligned with Franco. There was a compelling reason for Mexico to be one of those entering the fold of the *Falange*.

Much of the wealth and power in Mexico was still controlled by the Spaniards. They heavily influenced the politics of the emerging nation. In the 1930's, sixty percent of the land was owned by Spaniards and almost all the major industries were controlled by Spanish nationals. Mexico was even one of the few countries that had aided and supported Franco in his grab, for control, of Spain. The other was, of course, Nazi Germany.

And that was when the problems started for Alberto Alverez. The *Falange* poured into his country and soon had complete control of the Sinarquistas movement. Before the *Falange* involvement, Alverez had been one of the top leaders. He worked in the small towns and countryside of rural Mexico, enlisting the poor peasants into the movement. He was a grassroots worker. When the *Falange* stepped in, he was relegated to a low-level position. He was no more than a lackey. All of a sudden, he was not privy to the details and plans of his own movement. Priories had changed, as well. The movement seemed more concerned with spying on the dreaded, imperialistic, Americans than helping their own people. *I should have realized what was really happening*, Alberto thought, as he gulped down another shot of tequila. *I have let my people down.*

Suddenly, a tall man entered the dusty cantina. He wore a black suit and had blond curly hair. He recognized Alverez and made his way over to the table. Alverez swore under his breath as the man approached. It was his new superior. The man had arrived from Germany only two weeks ago.

"I have a job for you, Alberto," the man said in accented Spanish.

"I'm busy," Alverez said, with a swipe of his hand.

Undaunted the man continued. "I want you to take ten men and go over the border as soon as possible."

"And why would I want to do that? America is now our ally."

"All the more reason for you to protect us," the man retorted. "Word is that the Americans are planning to sneak some military into the country and attack our troops. The simple minded President of Mexico has given them permission."

"I'm to stop a military invasion with just ten men?" Alverez stupidly asked in his drunken stupor.

"Not stop it, but allow us to prepare for it," the man said reasonably. "You need to steal the plans from the military offices, over the border. I have all the information on where to look and I'm told the offices are empty at night. You and your men will easily pass as some of the cheap laborers, on the base." The German man spoke with an evil grin.

So, this is what it has come to, Alverez thought as he tried to look the man straight in the eye. *He wants me to become a spy for Nazi Germany.* Alverez knew the *Falange* was filthy with men of German origin. They came and went from the movement offices like flies. They both gave information and issued orders on a routine basis. He knew they were spies and there were thousands of them. He realized Franco and Hitler were friends and even though Franco remained neutral, so far, during the war, he still had Axis fascist motives. The *Falange* had become the conduit for Nazi German spy activities, in Mexico. Alverez had been approached by several other members of the Sinarquistas, who had told him the movement had become corrupt. Now he had real proof.

"And if I refuse?" Alverez announced.

"Then I'm afraid the movement has no further use for you," the German said as officially as if he was a General.

That cut it for Alverez. "Get out of here before I put a knife into your neck. I will not spy for Germany. You're a bastard Nazi," Alverez roared with as much machismo as he could muster. He quickly unsheathed his large knife and held it out for the man to see. People at the other tables scattered.

"No need to call me names Alverez," the German replied, as he got up and left, making sure that the Mexican was not following him. "This isn't over," he pointed his finger and said just before he passed through the doorway.

Alverez wondered what he should do. *Should I continue to work for the Cause, or should I disappear and do something else.* As he finished the bottle of tequila, he decided to find another vocation. His brother was a smuggler, which sounded like easy work. He realized the Nazis were in Mexico to stay. They would never be completely driven out.

He staggered out of the cantina into the bright sunlight. He didn't get very far when a man stepped out of the alleyway and thrust a knife into his back. Alberto Alverez died on the dusty street thinking, at least, he gave his life for the movement.

Part One

A New Position

1

Colton Banyon strolled casually down the sidewalk on Hubbard St., just north of the loop in downtown Chicago, Illinois. He was currently only a few blocks from the famous Michigan Avenue. He had decided to park his car at his son's house and walked the several blocks to his destination rather than deal with the exorbitant parking rates charged in the loop.

It was a bright late-spring afternoon, the temperature hovering around seventy degrees and there wasn't a cloud in the sky. It was a beautiful day. His black Tumi satchel slapped at his side as he walked, reminding him that he had work to do today. As he neared the restaurant, he noticed several people across the street milling around the Marriot hotel. Some had on Cubs hats and jackets and some wore Yankees hats and shirts. He immediately realized they were all going to the game scheduled at Wrigley field today. He knew a bus ran from the Marriot directly to the ballpark and the people were waiting for their ride.

It was rare for the Yankees, his favorite team, and the Cubs to play each other except in the World Series and that hadn't happen since 1902, but interleague play had changed that. The Yankees were in town for a three game series starting tonight at seven o'clock. He looked at his Movado watch and noted that it was only a little after one o'clock in the afternoon. The people had a long wait before the game started.

He suddenly realized the baseball fans across the street would spend most of their day just going to a baseball game. *How great it must be to have that much free time*, he thought. He was envious. Although, he was supposed to be retired himself, he was always busy and today he would be starting a new career. He was heading to a luncheon where the details would be explained. This was, however, no ordinary position. It had been arranged by the President of the United States.

As he neared the entrance to Shaw's Crab House he spotted a black Cadillac Escalade parked illegally on the street, right in front of the restaurant. Two men in black suits and dark sunglasses stood at both ends of the vehicle and scanned the surrounding area with watchful eyes. One noticed Banyon and kept him in a steady gaze as he approached.

"Good afternoon Mr. Banyon," he spoke with a slight southern accent.

Wondering how the man knew his name, he responded with, "Hello".

"The Secretary is waiting for you, but first we must scan you," the man said evenly and motioned for Banyon to move alongside the SUV and out of the line of sight of the fans across the street. He opened the back door of the SUV and produced a hand held scanner. The second man grabbed Banyon's bag and rummaged through it as the first man passed the device over Banyon.

Satisfied with the results, the first man announced, "Clean".

"I did shower this morning," Banyon joked, but it was lost on the serious Secret Service men.

"Follow me; I will take you to the private dining room," one said.

They entered the busy restaurant and weaved through the crowded serving floor. Wondrous smells of cooked fish permeated the air. They soon came to a closed door. The man opened it and Banyon walked inside.

The room was small, but there was only one person in it, The Secretary of the U.S. Department of Justice. The Secretary did not get up to greet him, she was a woman. Banyon stepped over to her and extended his hand.

"I'm Colton Banyon," he said.

The Secretary said nothing and didn't offer her hand. She was munching on a piece of bread. Instead, she motioned for Banyon to sit next to her at the small table.

She continued to chew for a full minute as she sized up her visitor using the corner of her eye.

Finally, she asked, "Want a drink?"

"I'll have a vodka and tonic with a twist of lime," Banyon told the waiter who had been all but invisible in the corner of the room.

"Do you have a preference for the vodka?" the waiter quickly asked.

"Stolichnaya," Banyon replied.

"I'll have a Jonny Walker Red, neat," added the Secretary. The waiter left to fill their order.

"It's a pleasure to meet you, madam Secretary," Banyon started, but was waved off by the DOJ.

"We'll talk after he brings the drinks," she announced dismissively and went back to eating more bread.

Banyon already knew a few things about her. The Secretary of the Justice Department was a cabinet level position. The DOJ was a political appointment made by the President. Her name was Marlene Moore and it was rumored that she was very close to the big man. It was also rumored that she was a control freak, an ice queen, and never said anything more than was absolutely necessary. As he studied her, he realized she had once been very attractive, but the weight of her position was taking its toll on her features. Her clothes were fashionable and sexy, but she looked more like a woman that had passed her prime, but refused to believe it. He was sure she recently had plastic surgery.

The waiter returned with their drinks and served them. "We will have our preordered lunch in exactly one half hour," she informed him. "Until then, leave us alone." The waiter hurriedly left the room.

Banyon took a sip of his drink and noticed her staring at him. She had dark green eyes and they were full of resentment. "Frankly," she started, "I don't like that you have been forced upon me and I want you to know that while working for me you will do exactly what I tell you. Do you understand?"

Banyon had been told that the DOJ would attempt to intimidate him and make an untold number of unreasonable demands on him. In the business world, he had run across many such women. They thought they had to be tougher than any man and used their positions of authority to keep their male underlings off balance. Good communications and terms never resulted in the relationships.

Fortunately, he knew what to do. "Excuse me a minute," he replied as he pointed into the air and opened his phone.

"No phone calls," she ordered.

"Don't worry, I'll soon pass the phone to you," he offered calmly.

"Who are you calling?" she suddenly demanded.

"I'm calling my real boss. I only report to you for political reasons and convenience, you know that, don't you?"

He noticed a sudden change in her. "No need for the call," she quietly replied. Banyon knew intimidation worked both ways on this type of bureaucrat. He hung up the phone and turned towards her.

"I believe you have some papers for me to sign and some information to pass on to me," he said smoothly with a smile on his face.

The DOJ studied his face for a minute, then her eyes narrowed, before she replied. "Who are you Mr. Banyon? Why do you have so much clout? What is it exactly that you do?"

"I'm afraid only one person can tell you that," he replied. "If and when, he tells you, I will fill in the blanks, until then everything is on a need to know basis. I'm sorry but those are the rules for now."

Suddenly, changing her tone again, she sweetly said, "Call me Marlene." She offered her hand and shifted her seat to be closer to Banyon.

"You can call me Colt," he offered, attempting to be conciliatory, as he accepted her hand. It was warm and silky.

"This is all so strange. Why does the President want you to report directly to him?" she asked as an inquiry.

"Because, I can do things for him that no one else can, Marlene. Sometimes these things are too sensitive for the general public. He is afraid of leaks, and so am I."

"But I'm in charge of the finest law enforcement agency in the world, the FBI. We can keep a secret."

"I know, sometimes, I've used the FBI to help me," Banyon replied. "I know they can keep a secret, but some of the other people in government can't. I expect I will continue to use them in the future," he said as he looked directly into her eyes.

"The President told me you are a 'finder'. What does that mean? I mean, I checked up on you and found out that you and your team have an excellent record of recovering artifacts and solving mysteries, better than the FBI. How do you find things so easily and quickly?"

"I may tell you sometime, but not today."

"But you said that you worked with the FBI before. We work together and yet I know so little about you."

"I have worked with the FBI many times, but there is no record. Agent Gregory Gamble was my main contact."

"Yes, it was a major tragedy to lose him," she quickly replied while shaking her head. "It happened during a shootout in Wisconsin, as I recall," she added.

"Yes it did, I know, I was there," he replied as he watched the shock fill her face. Agent Greg Gamble had been part of Banyon's team, he was also a full-time FBI agent, and was a member of a clandestine task force set up by the President to rid the government of an insidious evil force that had infiltrated deep into American politics. Banyon's team also hunted old-line Nazis and the new American version known as the Effort. The Effort had tentacles deep into several government agencies and tracking them required complete secrecy.

Agent Gamble, and others, had died while protecting Banyon and a defector at a safe house in Wisconsin. Word had leaked out through government employees. The President attended the funeral and recruited Banyon to help him in his fight.

Suddenly, Banyon's phone rang. He looked at the caller ID and said to the DOJ, "It's the President."

2

"Are you done yet?" the President said without preamble. "We haven't started yet," Banyon answered.

"Well, Godamnit. I have an urgent assignment for you. Call me back as soon as you are done with her," the President blustered.

"Yes, sir, I will do that" Banyon replied as he watched a suddenly nervous Marlene fidget in her chair.

"Now, give the phone to Marlene," he ordered. Banyon handed her the phone. Her eyebrows revealed her shock.

"Yes, Mister President," she said as she rose from her chair and began to pace the small room. Banyon found himself admiring her slim toned figure. She didn't just pace, she strutted as she talked. He heard many 'yes sirs' in her replies. Soon she was off the phone and handed it back to Banyon.

"Whew, that was fun," she exclaimed as she returned to her seat. Banyon noticed the slight shaking of her hands.

"He wants me to call him back very soon," Banyon told her. "So, let's get down to business."

Marlene was much friendlier now and seemed eager to please Banyon. "Colt, let's get all this paper work done right now, so we could have a nice lunch, okay?" she announced with a hundred watt smile.

Banyon took out a pen and said, "I'm ready."

Marlene reached below the table, brought up a slim attaché case and pulled out a folder, brimming with paper. She opened it and pushed the first page to Banyon. "This is your employment contract. It says that you are a contract employee paid the annual sum of one dollar. The money is to be paid to the LCH Detective Agency, LLC. There is also a list of bonuses that you will be paid for finding documents, artifacts, and people. If you succeed, you will be a wealthy man," she commented with a smile.

"I'm already wealthy," he replied.

"It also says that either party can cancel, at any time, with no penalty."

Banyon quickly read the document and signed it. "What about employment hours, etc?" He was very concerned about being roped into an impossible schedule.

"This document says you are not required to work on any schedule and you can work from anywhere you choose. But you are required to respond to the President, when needed. Good negotiating," she brightly commented as she smiled at him again.

"Where is my home base of operations?"

"We have made arrangements with the legal firm of 'Dewey & Beatem'. They have offices in Chicago, Washington, New York, Los Angeles, Dallas and Las Vegas. Chicago is the main office, but you can commandeer any office or staff you need."

"Do they expect me today? He asked.

"You can use their services effective today. When you go to their offices in Schaumburg, see Heather Vance. She is the office manager. You do not need to meet with the other principals unless you want to."

"I'll go there this afternoon and introduce myself."

"Heather will be your major contact for all the offices. Just call her and she will arrange everything anytime you are headed to one of their other locations."

"Good, I have a home in Las Vegas," he told her. "I spend much of the year there."

"I do need to warn you. They are not a conventional Law office."

"What do you mean?"

"I mean that while they do handle legal matters, they are also a rallying point for operations that the government does not want the public to know about."

"So, they have several offices that are used by people on a special assignment, like me." Banyon commented.

"Yes," she replied. "But the staff is rather unconventional as well."

"Thanks for the warning," he answered with raised eyebrows.

She selected another sheet and passed it to Banyon. "This is a Presidential letter. Do you know what that is?"

"Yes, I do. I can require any Federal employee do follow my orders, without question. I can also requisition any Federal assets as well."

"That's correct. Use it wisely," she told him.

"Most of the time, I prefer to use my charm," he joked. She just smiled at him.

"Here is a list of federal employees reporting to you. The list includes: Maya Patel. She is listed as an archeological field agent. She is Chicago based and has a regular job, but can take time off whenever you need her. It also says you can use additional contract employees as required."

"I have a team of people I use most of the time," he told her.

"I have met Maya, she is beautiful. She is currently on maternity leave, you know."

"I know, she is a good friend and part of my team," he replied.

"I also understand that most of your team consists of women. They must be very capable," she added as she blinked her eyes at him.

"They are," he replied without adding anything else.

The DOJ continued. "Did you bring your encrypted phone?"

"I did."

"I have a new one for you. It includes my private phone number as well as the Presidents private cell. Call anytime, if you need anything." They exchanged phones and Banyon put it in his satchel.

"There is another document signed by the President. It says that by Presidential order, no Federal employee is allowed to write your name on any document including any report on a crime. It seems you are to be invisible, Colt."

"Marlene, let's make sure it stays that way," he encouraged her.

"If I ever see your name on a report, for any reason, I will censor it immediately," she promised.

The process took another ten minutes and concluded just in time to have a good lunch of fresh fish. The DOJ was now very cordial. "I do know there is a problem with several government employees, but I am not in the Presidents confidence about who and why. I hope to eventually gain your confidence."

"I hope so too."

When lunch was finished, Banyon stood and gathered all the papers. He told Marlene he had to respond to the Presidents call immediately.

"You can call from here, it is secure," she invited.

"It's a private situation," he replied as he headed for the door.

"What does he want?" she asked as she left the table and strutted towards him.

"He will have to tell you that," Banyon responded. "At this point the less you know about me and what I do, the better."

She suddenly was very close, he could smell her perfume. She offered her hand again and engulfed his in both of hers. It was an intimate moment, and he recognized it. He then left the restaurant.

Her final remarks were sincere, "I hope we will become good friends."

As he walked up the street back to his car, he realized the President had met all of his demands and he became more confident in his new position. He didn't want anyone else to become aware of his capabilities and the President seemed to understand. The risk was just too much to allow.

He pulled out his encrypted phone and called the number for the President. He answered in two rings. "Mr. President, this is Colton Banyon"

"Thank God you finally called," the President nervously replied.

"What seems to be the emergency?"

"My granddaughter has been kidnapped. You have to find her."

3

Banyon immediately picked up his pace. He was five minutes from his car and the privacy he needed, to help the President.

"Mister President, I don't know if I can help you unless a Nazi or the Effort is involved." The President's request was Banyon's worst nightmare. The reason, for the need for secrecy, was once people found out about his abilities; he would be besieged with requests and demands to find things that didn't involve Nazis. He wasn't sure, he could get his source, to comply, nor if he himself wanted to.

"Please you must find my granddaughter," the President pleaded. "It's my entire fault. I shouldn't have let her go."

"I'll try my best," Banyon quickly responded. "I'll need some information, to find the historic timeline."

"Tell me what you need," he quickly responded.

"I'll need a place, a time, and a name, to start the search."

"Her name is Kelly Cable. She was in Cancun, as of three days ago. I sent three Secret Service agents there yesterday. The Mexican authorities have not been very helpful. They told my men the white sex-slave trade is very active in Cancun."

"White sex-slave trade?" Banyon repeated.

"Yes, they suspect one of the cartels is involved. She is a beautiful girl, and young too, only seventeen. They told my men she would be a prime candidate to be kidnapped. I can't accept that."

"Do you have the flight number she took for Cancun?"

"Why do you need that?"

"A historical timeline research has to start with a definite place and time. We can then follow the history and find out where she is today. Without a starting point, it will take much longer," Banyon replied.

Banyon heard a shuffling of papers in the background and suddenly, the President blurted out a flight number. "She was on US Airways flight 949. It left Washington three days ago at 9:00 A.M. Does that help?"

"That's what I need, sir," Banyon said as he tried to be cheerful. "I'll call you as soon as I have something."

"I'll have my men in Cancun stand by so they can rescue her," the President promised. "We can also bring in addition men, if needed. I have a SWAT team ready to enter Mexico. They are less than an hour from there."

"But   ?" Banyon began, but was interrupted.

"I know that it looks like an invasion, but they will have Mexican police uniforms. You can buy them on the open market in almost any border town in the U.S. We have done this before.

"I'll get back to you soon," Banyon promised and hung up the phone.

4

Banyon quickly called his son and told him to open the garage door. He told him he had an urgent meeting and he would not have time to talk to him, right now. His son agreed to open the door and wait for him. Banyon's son knew his father well and had dealt with Banyon's erratic behavior before. After he hung up his phone, Banyon started to run.

While Banyon was over sixty, he was still in pretty good shape and figured he could run the five blocks to his car. He thanked his parents for his good genes, as he ran. He was six feet tall and around one hundred and ninety pounds, on a muscular frame. If not for his loss of hair, he could easily pass for fifty. He credited his endurance to his girlfriend.

As he turned the corner, he saw his car running, in the roadway, with the door open. *Good kid*, he thought. He had left his keys with his son, who didn't own a car, in case he needed to go out. His son claimed he didn't need a car in downtown Chicago, but often borrowed Banyon's green Jaguar.

"I'll fill you in on everything about my new position as soon as I finish my meeting," he yelled breathlessly to his son.

"Where are you going?" the son asked.

"I'm heading to the Law offices of 'Dewey & Beatem', to my new office.

"Dewey & Beatem, really?"

"Yup," Banyon replied as he slammed the door and threw the car into gear. The big V8 engine effortlessly pulled the car from the curb. Banyon watched his confused son wave as he squealed around the corner. He drove several blocks and then turned into a small park. He stopped his car under a large oak tree. All he needed was privacy to make contact.

"Wolf, are you there?" he yelled out. Banyon's secret was that he could speak to a spirit. It had all been arranged several years ago, when a curse had been placed on, a then living man, named Walter Pierce. His real name was Wolfgang Becker. Wolfgang, or as he preferred to be called, Wolf, had arranged for the curse so he could hunt old Nazis, when he died. He had picked Colton Banyon as his conduit, because they had actually grown up in the same house on Eastern Long Island. The spirit could find anything by looking at history. He had once told Banyon everything that had happened on earth left an energy trail and Wolf could follow the trail until he found the object of his search. Sometimes, it took a long time because there was no starting point, but given a time and location, he had never failed. The only rules were Banyon had to ask a question and Wolf could not tell him about anything in the future.

"Yes, I am here," a deep, older, voice filled the interior of the car, although only Banyon could hear him. Even if they were in a crowd, Banyon was the only conduit.

"Did you hear my conversation with the President?"

"I have already located her," the spirit replied.

"So we can save her?"

"I normally can't help you unless a Nazi is involved, but fortunately one is involved with her kidnapping."

"A Nazi, in Mexico?"

"Colt, during World War II, thousands of Nazi's were located in Mexico. After the war, many stayed and started new lives. But the Nazi we seek today does not live there."

"So, where is he?"

"He works for the government in the U.S. and is a senior member of the Effort. That's why I can help."

"Not the Effort again," Banyon commented with a moan.

Banyon knew about the Effort, but not everything. The Effort was actually an organization established in the nine-teen thirties, in Germany. Its primary goal is to take over America and reestablish the Third Reich. It was well-planned and funded by German plunder, before and during World

War II. Several people were planted in the United States in the nineteen-thirties and, using the money, had taken over many industries in the USA and also worked themselves into prominent positions, even in politics. There were now second, third generations and even fourth generations, involved. They were a very strong and hidden organization. Banyon had faced them several times before.

"I'll need to know all about that, but right now, can you tell me where the President's granddaughter is, so that we can rescue her?"

"The President is correct; she is in the hands of a white sex-slave group. There are five other young women with her."

"What is her location?" Banyon had a piece of paper and a pen at the ready.

"She and the other girls are located in a cartel owned house. They have been there for two days. The address is 2243 Francisco May in North West Cancun."

"Is she alright?"

"She and the other girls have been drugged and are currently being trained to be sex slaves. I don't think you need any further description."

"How many men guard them?" Banyon asked through gritted teeth. Wolf was right, he needed no further description.

"There are six men. They rotate their responsibilities. Three are always on duty, watching the house; the other three train the girls. The President needs to hurry; the plans are to move the girls in six hours. They will be split up, then."

"Which cartel owns the house?" Banyon asked.

"They are a new group and call themselves the 'Machos'. They took over much of Danta Lopez's business." Banyon and his team had helped to bring down Danta Lopez, about a year ago.

"The President has only three men in Cancun. Can they use local police to help rescue the girls?"

"The Cancun police chief is on the Macho's payroll and arranged the kidnappings of all six girls."

"Damn, he'll want to know that. Why did they grab her?"

"It is all part of a bigger Effort plan, Colt. They want the President to be so despondent he takes his eye off of them.

"Why didn't they just kill her? Wouldn't that accomplish their goal?"

"Colt, these Mexican Mafia men are greedy, as well as, evil. The cartel expects to fetch as much as a hundred thousand dollars for the President's granddaughter. The Effort believes she is dead."

"That also makes them stupid," Banyon replied knowing Wolf would not respond without him asking a question. "I'll need to call the President now, but will you be available for updates as this unfolds?"

"I will be here, as always."

"I have one more question. What is the Efforts' plan?"

"Colt, it is very complicated and will take more time to explain. Why don't you call the President first, the plan can wait."

"All right," Banyon said with a measure of frustration. "At least tell me, who is directing all of this?"

"I'll tell you, but don't tell the President yet. He has enough on his mind and we don't want him to over react."

"I'll keep the name to myself. So, who are we after?"

"His name is Paul Slezeck."

"You don't mean the Paul Slezeck who is the Director of Homeland Security, do you?"

"Yes, he is our next Nazi to take down."

5

Banyon decided to collect his thoughts before he called the President. His main concern was Homeland Security might be involved in the rescue of the girls and it could wind up as a disaster. Homeland Security employed a fast attack strike-force that had unlimited powers over life and death. It had been established after the Katrina hurricane to help protect people in a devastated area. After hurricane Katrina had devastated New Orleans, many police and civilians had taken the law into their own hands, many people died. The fast attack strike-force was developed to institute law and order in disaster areas. It had also been used many times to reduce threats to America in several states and countries. It was top secret and tightly controlled. The individual, who had pushed for the attack force and currently commanded it, was none other than Paul Slezeck.

Banyon pushed the button on his encrypted phone and he was immediately connected to the President.

"Have you got anything?" The President immediately asked.

"She is alive and being held in a house in Cancun. You need to hurry, as they intend to move her in less than six hours," Banyon told the President.

"I'll have boots on the ground, in less than two hours," he quickly replied. "Give me the address. How many men are we dealing with?"

Banyon complied and quickly asked, "Who are you sending in? I can have my contact track them and keep us all informed."

"I'm sending in a Navy SEAL team from San Diego. They will leave in fifteen minutes. Is that enough information?"

Relieved, Banyon said, "yes sir. But there is more to this plot than you currently understand."

"What does that mean?" the President demanded.

"Get your men going first and then I'll explain," Banyon replied. The President put the phone down and Banyon could hear him giving orders in the background. Soon, he was back. "What else do you have to report?" he asked officially.

"The Cancun police chief is involved. They have actually kidnapped six young girls in total. Your men must rescue them, as well."

"Stop," the President ordered and dropped the phone again. Banyon could hear him ordering the demise of the police chief in the background. "What else?" he gruffly asked as soon as he picked up the phone.

"The Mexican Mafia is also involved. This new group is called the 'Machos'. Their men are the ones guarding the girls."

"God Damn, we are taking them out too. Tell me who the friggin leader is and where we can find him," the President ordered.

"I'll have to get back to you on that. It shouldn't take too long," Banyon replied.

"I'm headed to the situation room, so I can see everything. My phone will work there. Call me back as soon as you have the name." The President then hung up the phone before Banyon could respond to him.

Banyon leaned back in his car seat and said, "Wolf we have some more work to do. Who heads up the cartel and where is he located?"

6

Wolf complied with the Mexican Mafia man's name and location. Banyon called the President back to inform him. The President was angry and very agitated. "Call me back in an hour and a half with an update," he demanded. Banyon agreed and decided to call him from his new office in Schaumburg, Illinois.

As he drove to the offices of Dewey & Beatem, he found himself thinking about the Mexican Mafia. The term Mafia had only been added recently. They were still cartels, but now, because of the huge profits generated by the organizations, authorities had raised them to Mafia status. They had also invaded the United States.

The Mexican Mafia controlled about eighty percent of the marijuana sold in the United States. Much of it today, was grown on American soil, predominately in national parks. They smuggled in almost all of the cocaine, heroin, and most of the pill drugs. They now also controlled the illegal immigrant flood and had branched out to kidnapping, extortion, protection, prostitution, and even cyberspace scams. They could afford to hire legions of unemployed hackers in both Mexico and the U.S. They also employed a great number of police officials, judges, politicians, government officials in Mexico and a growing number of officials in the United States.

If you became a target of the Mexican Mafia, there was no place for you could hide. Their electronic capabilities matched law enforcement. They killed you and your family as well. Mostly they killed each other, just like the old time mafia groups, but a lot of innocent people died along the way. They were ruthless, uncontrollable men, who answered only to their leaders. Banyon wondered if they were the new Nazis.

He had to put his thoughts on hold, as he entered the parking lot of the Law offices of Dewey & Beatem.

7

The offices were located at the fringe of the Schaumburg mall, in suburban Chicago. It was one of the largest malls in the country. As he approached the front door, he realized the entire building belonged to the Law firm. A discreet sign said, 'Dewey & Beatem, Attorneys of Law'. While it was only three stories tall, it was very wide, almost half the size of a football field. The front was all dark tinted glass and curved in a quarter circle arc. He climbed the three wide concrete steps and pulled the main door open. It was also made of substantial tinted glass. He then stepped inside.

Banyon believed the reception area was at least sixty feet long. The first thing he noticed was a young girl in light blue spandex pants and a very tight top, sprinting across the lobby as fast as she could. It was very fast. When she reached the far wall, she touched it, turned around, and sprinted back past him. She came so close to him that he could feel a slight breeze as she zipped by him.

He heard her say cheerfully. "Hello, be with you in a second."

He started cross the marble floor, admiring the decor. The lobby was all glass, marble, and black leather, with a light-colored-wood reception desk in the back. It looked like a ticket counter. The entire area was very modern and sleek. The ceiling was three stories high with semi-circular balcony overhangs, for the second floor and third floors, jutting out from the back wall. He felt like he was in an airport terminal.

As he reached the reception counter, the young girl was already standing there. Because she was short, she stood on a platform behind the counter and no longer had on pants. Banyon realized her tight top was actually a speedo, skin-tight, light-blue, swimsuit. He also could see she didn't have an ounce of fat on her trim barely five-foot tall body. Her short chestnut hair was cut in a pixy style and when she smiled, Banyon could clearly see she wore braces. She looked like she was fourteen years old.

"Good afternoon Mr. Banyon. We have been expecting you. My name is Mandy," she said in a preadolescent voice with sexy overtones.

"How do you know my name?" he asked, a little flustered. Banyon felt like he could go to jail, just for looking at her.

"Why I have your wallet," she simply replied. "I have already checked your drivers' license and other identification."

"What?" Banyon stammered and put his hand into his suit jacket.

She held out his black, leather wallet. "Part of my job is to identify all of our visitors," she offered.

"You're a pickpocket?"

"Mr. Banyon, I do everything very fast," she replied in a sexy soft voice.

"But how..?"

"When I brushed by you, as you came through the door," she explained. "You were distracted. I'm good at distracting people," she smiled revealing her braces.

"But you seem so young?" It was all he could muster. She had indeed distracted him.

"I'm actually twenty-two years old," she said as an explanation as she stood up straight and tall. She then turned slowly around so Banyon could see that she was fully developed. A flush began to rise on his face.

"I see," he stammered.

"My young appearance generally catches people off guard," she admitted. "Then I swoop in and get what I want from them."

"But are you the receptionist?" Banyon asked. His idea of a receptionist was a lot different.

"Yes, of course I am." She said indignantly and nodded her head. "I'm also one of the fastest humans alive. I expect to someday be in the Olympics. I can train all day long on this job and help my country too," she said proudly.

"You do seem to have incredible speed and reflexes," Banyon commented as he attempted to make her feel good.

She didn't seem to buy his answer. "Let me show you more," she said. As a demonstration, she suddenly cartwheeled over the counter, landed in front of him, leaped in the air with her legs apart, twisted and landed softly piggyback on his shoulders. While sitting there, she handed him his watch.

"Wow, now that's impressive," Banyon managed and meant it. Her weight didn't bother him, the heat of her body did.

She quickly spread her legs and slid down his back. She leaped over the counter gracefully. "I hope I can help you someday. I often help the government," she said, as sweet as butter.

"I'll remember that," he acknowledged.

"Now what can I do for you today?" she asked officially but made it sound like an invitation.

"I'm supposed to see Heather Vance," he replied. Mandy reacted with a little too much emphasis.

"Oh, her," she ask with distain.

"Is there a problem?" Banyon asked. "I'm starting work here today, and was told to see her."

"I'm sure she is busy, but I'll check anyway." Mandy pressed a button under the counter. She raced to a door, flinging it open. Before it was able to reclosed, she was back.

"That was fast," Banyon commented.

"She'll be another ten minutes, but I've found Edgar to take you to your office. Timmy is setting up your computer, as we speak." As she spread her slender arm towards the doorway a man made his appearance. He looked like a ferret to Banyon. He was of average height, skinny build, with black greasy hair that covered his face as well as his head. His dark black eyes were set close together. He also had a severe overbite. He walked in small halting steps towards Banyon with his hands close together.

"Hello," he said with a Midwestern accent. "I'm Edgar," and offered his hand for Banyon to shake.

"Hello, I'm Colton Banyon."

To qualify, Mandy said, "No last names here Colt. Edgar is our language expert. He speaks eighteen different languages, along with all the dialects. He is also our main document forger. He will show you to your office."

"Follow me," the ferret said. They passed through the door and entered a long hallway. They passed many closed doors before they reached a spiral metal staircase. They proceeded up to the second floor and back down another hallway. Edgar finally pointed to an open doorway. Both he and Banyon entered. The big room was almost twice as long as it was wide. The back wall of his office was floor to ceiling, sliding glass doors that lead onto a small patio. He realized it was one of the overhang balconies. The sliding door was open and Banyon stepped through and looked down. He could see Mandy sprinting back and forth in the reception area. She waved to him.

Pointing down, he said to Edgar, "Mandy is an unusual character."

"You'll find that all of us are unusual," Edgar replied mysteriously. "We all offer different talents the government needs from time to time. I assume you have a talent too. If I may be so bold, what is your talent Colt?"

"Oh, ah... I find things," Banyon offered, but said nothing more.

"So you're a 'finder' then." The ferret noted as he nodded his head in acceptance. "They have set you up here, on the second floor, which means you are an Alpha and can request any of us to assist, anytime. Heather will get you a list of our capabilities. She'll be here in about five minutes," he said as he looked at his watch. "She is just finishing up a routine task in one of the offices." He turned to leave.

"Thanks," Banyon managed before he was gone. Banyon now turned to survey his office. He had a large oak credenza, on the wall, and an elbow shaped desk. The desk was located in the very back of the office near the sliding glass doors and faced the office door at the far end where they had entered. There were also two couches with a coffee table between them at the far end, from where he stood. It was large, measuring roughly, thirty feet by twenty feet. The chair for the desk was big and brown in color. As he studied it, the chair moved.

Soon, a large lump of brown, curly, frizzed, hair came into view, followed by horn-rimmed glasses and a slender male face. The face spoke. "Hi, man, I'm Timmy. I just finished setting up your kick ass computer, dude."

"Thanks," Banyon said brightly.

Timmy extracted himself from under the desk. He was tall, over six feet, very slender in build, and his skin was almost opaque. Timmy didn't get outside much Banyon figured. He was young, maybe twenty, and had on jeans and a tee shirt which said in bold letters, "World's Best Hacker".

Banyon noticed Timmy had a Bluetooth phone connecter in his left ear. Timmy began to explain the computer system. "I got you a bong, 25 inch monitor, because you're old," he explained.

"I see," said a slightly annoyed Banyon.

"Boise speakers, so you can hear better. Your tower is state-of-the-art. You'll have access to every data base available in the world from this machine."

"Thanks," Banyon said.

"You can work the internet, can't you?" Timmy talked like a person who was used to people not understanding him.

"Yes, of course I can," Banyon replied a little peeved that Timmy thought he was not computer savvy.

"Well, let me explain the capabilities of the tower," Timmy said with enthusiasm, but Banyon interrupted him.

"We can cover that at a later time."

"Toss me your cellphone, man. I'll connect it to your computer and you can download everything to your phone." He held out his hand in expectation.

"Not going to do that," Banyon countered as he shook his head.

Appearing very disappointed, Timmy said, "Why not man. This is cool stuff."

"Timmy, if I connect my phone to the computer, you will be able to see everything on my phone and everything on my computer. You do record everything don't you?"

Reluctantly Timmy admitted they did. "But no one cares if you go on porno sites or download movies, man."

"Well, I care about my privacy," Banyon said.

"Up to you man, you're an Alpha," Timmy shrugged his shoulders in defeat.

"Just what does an Alpha mean?" Banyon was confused by what Edgar had told him. He hoped Timmy would explain.

"You're a boss. You can order us around like cattle, dude."

"I see." Banyon realized everything in the building was need-to-know, by position level, including the talents of the people.

"I work for you, whenever you need my help."

"So you're the resident Geek then?" Banyon asked.

"Man. I'm so past Geek status," he waved his hands at Banyon. "I am the world's best hacker," he pointed to his shirt.

"Isn't that illegal?"

"Nothing is illegal in this building," he replied casually. He suddenly acted like he was listening to something. "Uh oh, I've got to run," he said as he pressed his Bluetooth in his left ear and stared at the door opening. He then moved past him to the door.

"Why?" Banyon asked.

"The witch-bitch is coming."

8

Banyon barely had time to set his satchel on the floor, behind his desk, and sit down before a stunningly beautiful woman entered his office and slammed the door loudly. She then took up a sexy pose and threw back her head in defiance. She looked like she had just showered, as her long auburn hair lay flat against her back. She wore no makeup on her Euro-Asian face and didn't need any.

Oh my God, the thought. He recognized her immediately. He had seen her several times before. "You must be Heather?" he forced himself to say, even though he knew it was not her real name. He sat rigid in his chair, with both hands on the desk top.

"Heather will do," the beauty said dismissively. "Judging by your reaction to seeing me, you are a fan," she stated through large pouty lips.

"Yes, I have seen you before," he answered like a robot.

"Good, then we understand each other," she hissed. She took two large steps closer to his desk, but stayed far enough away from him so he could see her complete body. She was about five foot four inches tall, with a perfectly-shaped figure and flawless skin. Her eyes were a deep-ocean blue and all but smoldered with intensity. She was dressed in a red, very tiny, micro mini-skirt, and a matching red tube top which barely covered her pear shaped breasts. Her shoes had six inch stiletto heels, also red in color. She carried a clear plastic bag with several things visible inside. She looked just like a porno star, which of course, she was.

Colton Banyon had one fatal weakness. He, like many men, was helpless around gorgeous, sexy, women. They could intimidate, manipulate, encourage, discourage and control him with just a look or a flip of their hair. He quickly understood this woman was a grand master of the art. She

Gerald J. Kubicki & Kristopher Kubicki

could also offer many physical enticements. He had never actually met a porno star before. He wondered if he could control himself as he stared at her. He was in a dubious position.

"You're the office manager?" he said with disbelief.

She looked at him like he was an idiot. "We can do this one of two ways," she growled with a deep throaty voice. "The hard way or the easy way, which do you prefer, Colt. I have another appointment in ten minutes," she said as she slapped her bag against her leg.

"I'm not sure what you mean?" he admitted.

She moved quickly around his desk and stood next to his chair. He now smelled fresh soap and a hint of perfume. She was intoxicating. "Okay, I'll make it hard for you," she said in a determined but sexy voice.

"But, I...," was as far as he got, before she interrupted him.

"You have been assigned Alpha status, so you have the privilege of my services three times per week. I do not provide services before eight o'clock in the morning and none after five o'clock at night. What times would fit your schedule. I'll see if I am open then." She pulled out a small black book and a pen from her clear bag.

"But Heather," he muttered. "I don't think I can do this. I have a committed relationship," he blurted out.

"Come now, you want me, every man does. In this building nothing is illegal or even immoral. Give me your times," she demanded as she opened her black book and clicked her pen open.

"I can't do this," he whispered, but found he could not move his body. His face flushed and suddenly his was very warm. *This woman is offering me sex*, he thought.

"Maybe you need more convincing," she announced and slid her tight, rear end, onto his desk. Her shapely long, beautiful, legs were now inches from his hand and slightly spread. She stared at him with eyes containing pure lust. A small moan escaped her lips.

Sweat dripped from his brow, "All I want to do is find things," he croaked.

"Ah, so you are a voyeur," Heather quickly replied. "We have several of them in the office including Timmy, who you have already met." She then repositioned herself on his desk, like she was a display.

"You are beautiful and very sexy," he muttered. "But I still can't do this."

"You ain't seen nothing yet," she commented. He heard himself gasp, as she raised her legs over his head, placed them on the desk, and turned on her side. She then smiled at him. Banyon was beside himself.

"Heather," he started. "If we have sex, then you would have power over me. You could blackmail me, extort money and favors, and keep me off balance forever. I can't allow that to happen."

"Dear Colt, don't you realize that every woman does the same thing. I'm just a little better at it."

All his life, Banyon had fallen prey to the sexual advances of beautiful women, but he had Loni now. He wasn't going to spoil their relationship.

"No," he yelled in a determined voice and slammed his fists on the desk. Heather's reaction was immediate. She swung her legs back over his head, stood up, and began to put her book back in her bag.

"Good, you passed the test," she said cheerfully.

"What test?" he demanded with confusion. Sweat was running down his back.

"The test to find out how susceptible you are to 'honey traps', of course," she answered, as she wiggled in her clothes. Banyon knew honey traps were usually female spies who used their sexuality to gain information.

"Your job is to test men, to see, if you can convince them to have sex with you?"

"You would be surprised how many fail," she told him. "I work with the men here, to teach them how to resist. Some are slow learners, like Timmy. I make his life miserable. I also teach the women here how to entice men. It's a fun job."

"You're very good," he admitted as he wiped the sweat from his brow.

"I sometimes work in the field as well." She suddenly offered her hand.

"Doing what?"

"Draining men, of course," she replied with a double entente.

"Oh," he replied.

"I think we will be friends," she offered.

He took her hand and felt a jolt of electricity pass between them. "I'd like that," he found himself saying.

"The managing partner will be here in a couple of minutes. He will fill you in on the rest of the operation and answer any questions."

"So, we are done?"

"Yes, we are, and I'm actually the office manager. I can supply anything you need. Just page me by pressing this button." She leaned over him, brushing his body with her hair, and pointed to a red button on his phone. "I'm usually busy working on some man in the building, but I'm never more than ten minutes away. I will also deliver you a Bluetooth to keep in touch in the office. We all wear one."

"That's good to know," a relieved Banyon told her.

"Oh, and Colt, many of the other girls in the office are taking lessons from me. They'll want to try out their lessons on you, so watch yourself around them."

"Okay," he answered. "Can I ask you one question?"

"Of course," she brightly replied, showing a perfect set of white teeth.

"When did you...er...retire," he delicately asked.

"When I received a master's degree in Psychology from Berkley," she quickly replied. "That other job was temporary until I got an education."

"So, you're like the resident shrink here?" Banyon asked.

"Amount other things," she evasively answered.

"I'll probably not use your services. I'm mentally sound," he said, not really believing that he meant it.

"But if you find that you are overstressed, or need to relax, or even just talk, I hope you will call on me. I am really quite satisfying."

"I'll remember that," he said as watched her sashayed out the door.

9

While he waited for the managing partner, Banyon fired up his computer. It was up and ready to go in seconds. While, he didn't visit any of his personal accounts, he surfed the web and discovered that Timmy was right. His computer was extremely fast. He noticed many shortcuts on his desk top, but before he could explore them, there was a knock on his open door. "Come in," he said.

The man that entered the room was a throwback to a Raymond Burr movie from the fifties. He wore a blue-pinstripe suit, complete with pleated pants, a three button vest, and a bright blue bowtie which accented his white on white shirt. A gold chain hung from one of the buttons and disappeared into a small pocket on the vest. Banyon believed it was connected to a gold watch. But that wasn't the most startling feature of the man. He was also rotund. While, he was over six feet tall, he was about six feet around as well. He looked like a big balloon as he waddled up to the front of Banyon's desk. Banyon immediately stood.

The man spoke in a deep baritone voice. "Hello, my name is Bart Longwood. I'm the managing partner of Dewey & Beatem. Welcome aboard Colton," he said using Banyon's complete first name to be formal. "I'll only use my last name once. We do not use last names here, for security reasons."

"Hello, Mr. Long...I mean Bart," Banyon said, as he held out his hand. "Please have a seat."

Bart looked at the small arm chair and declared, "I am quite comfortable standing," he replied. He then shook Banyon's hand precisely three times, then dropped his hand like it was a hot potato.

"Quite an operation you run here," Banyon opened.

Bart ignored Banyon's comment. "I have four things to tell you," Bart said formally. "Do not take notes."

Banyon quickly realized Bart was a no nonsense manager. He wanted to get right to the point. "I'm sure you are very busy," Banyon said graciously.

"First, I want you to know this office handles many legal cases for our clients. The United States government is just another client, to us. There will not be any hijinks or inappropriate behavior in the lobby or in the hallways, when clients are in the building. What you do in your closed door office, is your business. All the offices on this floor are equipped with counter surveillance devices. No one can hear or see anything going on in your office. Do I make myself clear?"

"Perfectly," Banyon answered. "But how do I know when clients are in the building?"

"Heather will supply you with a Bluetooth connecter in a few minutes. It is to be worn, at all times, while you are in the building. Whenever a client enters the building, Mandy will beep everyone."

"Okay," Banyon said as he tried to recall if Heather wore a blue tooth. He had seen Timmy's, Edgars and even Mandy's, but while he recalled several things about Heather, he didn't notice a Bluetooth.

"By the way, the doors open at eight o'clock in the morning and close at five-thirty at night. If you stay any long, Heather will have to be present."

"I don't think I'll ever be here after five o'clock. She is too distracting," Banyon muttered.

"Yes, she is a very talented girl," Bart observed. "That brings me to my second bit of information." Bart stopped for emphasis. Banyon knew he had to say something, but was still trying to remember if Heather had a Bluetooth.

"I'm listening," he replied.

"Most of the people here have unusual skills. We employ them for their legal abilities, but they often are asked to perform services for outside contractors like you. Whatever need you have, we can supply an expert."

"I've already met Mandy, Edgar, Timmy and of course Heather," Banyon recapped for him.

"Yes, Mandy will be a superstar someday, once Heather fully trains her." Bart commented. "If you need an expert driver, we have one. If you need a climber, an explosives expert, a safe cracker, or any other skill, please check with me. We can supply your every need. We also have people in other offices to draw from."

"I usually work alone, or with my own team," Banyon said. "But I'm sure there will be times when you can help."

"Good," Bart said as he extracted a sheet of paper from the inside of his suit. "The employees here all work by contract. Here is the price list for their services. It can never leave this room," he added. Bart then tossed the paper onto Banyon's desk.

Banyon quickly scanned the two paged list. No abilities were stated, but prices for time, on an hourly basis, and percentages of contract fees were listed. On the second page, Banyon found several names. Higher prices were listed for their services. He was not surprised that Heather commanded the highest fee. Mandy was listed near the bottom. Suddenly, he saw the name of Bart Longwood. He snapped up his head to ask Bart what he did, but Bart was gone. Instead a diminutive balding man stood across the desk from him. Now he looked like a college professor. He smiled at Banyon.

"I'm an illusionist," Bart said as an explanation.

Banyon sat down with his jaw open. "How did you do that?"

"This is the third thing I have to tell you. I am also for hire."

"Well you certainly had me fooled," Banyon commented.

"You will find, I have many personas," Bart noted.

"Which one is the real you?"

"You may never find out," Bart said sincerely. "By the way, you are entitled to carry a company gun in your position. Suddenly, a puff of smoke appeared before Banyon and a hand gun materialized on his desk.

"I never carry a gun," Banyon said as he pointed to the weapon.

"As you wish," Bart said. Immediately, there was another puff of smoke and the gun disappeared.

"It would have been easier to just pick it up," Banyon dryly noted.

"But not as impressive," Bart replied with a smile.

"What's the fourth thing you have to tell me?"

Another puff of smoke produced a credit card. "All your expenses will automatically be posted to this credit card. It has a limit of five hundred thousand dollars. You will be expected to pay it off after every mission. The company charges a one percent processing fee."

"And everything I do is an expense right?" Banyon knew how lawyers worked. "Every pencil will be charged to my account."

"Right," Bart nodded his head.

"Figures."

"Do you have any questions?"

"I have only one," Banyon pointed to the price list. "Down at the bottom of this price list, there is a little statement which says, and I quote, 'Any project undertaken from this office must have at least one employee under contract and two percent of any monies collected belong to the firm of Dewey & Beatem, LLP'. What does that mean?"

"It's quite simple really. You must understand, we have to cover overhead for the building, the firm, and we must keep our employees satisfied. You get to choose anyone you want to use for the mission. But you must choose at least one. What could be fairer," Bart said like a true lawyer, as he spread his arms. *This is their version of padding the clients' bill*, Banyon thought.

"And the President wants me to work out of this firm, right?" Banyon was beginning to understand the true rules of politics. Rub my back and I'll rub yours.

Acting a little flustered, Bart replied, "Well, he has referred clients to us on occasion. But we provide a much needed service."

"And how do you know the President?"

"Ah…well, we were college roommates," Bart admitted.

"Figures," Banyon muttered with a small feeling of being manipulated, once again. This time it was by his friendly government.

Suddenly, looking at his watch, Bart said. "Which reminds me, don't you have an operation going down in the next fifteen minutes?"

"Oh God you're right," Banyon spoke out loud. Everyone seemed to know about his business, but him.

"I'll have Timmy plug you into the situation room right now," Bart declared. He moved his hand to his Bluetooth.

"On my computer?" Banyon asked with surprise.

Bart held up his finger to stop Banyon from talking. "Timmy can you give Colt access to the President's situation room immediately," Bart said commandingly into his Bluetooth.

Within seconds Banyon's screen started to change. He just stared at it in disbelief. "He can get me into the situation room that quickly?"

"Of course he can," Bart announced cheerfully. "Now which of our contract people will you hire today?"

"You mean I have to pick one right now?"

"It is required," Bart said evenly.

"Do they have to be here? I prefer to work alone," Banyon asked wondering how he was going to talk to Wolf with someone else by his side.

"They must be with you," Bart clarified. "Otherwise, there might be some minor misunderstandings, you understand. Don't worry they all have top-security clearance. You must choose now, Colt, before the President comes on." Bart ordered.

Feeling like a trapped rat, Banyon finally responded. "Send me Mandy. At least she can exercise while I work and I can watch her."

"Excellent choice," Bart grinned and pressed his Bluetooth.

"Mandy, your services are needed in Colt's office. Wear your speedo."

10

Bart continued. "The monitor will automatically open at precisely three o'clock and you will be connected to the situation room. The President does not like people to be early and snoop around. You will get a two minute warning. So please be ready. Keep Mandy out of the picture, as well," Bart added with a point of his finger at the monitor.

"The President will not even know she is in the room," Banyon countered. "I'll make her stay over there," he pointed to the open office area.

"Good, now if you want to go off screen for a minute, just hit the escape button. When you want to return hit it again. When the operation is over, the screen will automatically go blank. Any questions?"

"No," Banyon replied.

"The time is now two forty-seven. You have thirteen minutes before everything starts. Are you ready?"

"I'm good," Banyon replied as he studied the icons on his desk top.

Bart then told Banyon he had other pressing business issues and turned to leave. Before he got to the door, Banyon noticed movement out on the balcony. Mandy had just leaped over the railing and was opening the sliding door. She had on her light blue speedo and carried a large white towel across her neck. She struggled with the big door but finally got it to move, then sprinted into Banyon's office. She stood at attention at the edge of his desk, just as Bart closed the door.

"Agent Mandy reporting to duty," she said with nervous excitement and saluted him like he was a general.

"You may be at ease," an amused Banyon said smoothly. She assumed an 'at ease' position with her legs apart and her hands behind her back. Her body all but vibrated with enthusiasm. A broad grin was plastered on her face.

"How shall I serve you Colt. I am ready to do whatever you want. Do you want me to chase down someone, steal their briefcase, or crawl through some ductwork maybe? I'm ready for anything."

"Relax Mandy, you won't need to chase or steal anything, for this assignment," Banyon told her.

She seemed perplexed for a minute, then suddenly her eyes widened, "Oh," she uttered. "It's a personal services mission, I get it. I've been training with Heather, I can do this Colt," she said unconvincingly. A slight bit of fear showed on her pretty face. "Who is the target?" she asked, to cover her concern.

"There is no target," a slightly annoyed Banyon responded.

Her eyes widened further. "Oh, it's for you then," she whispered and suddenly appeared more confident. "I'll need to get the plastic bag Heather gave me," she quickly added and got ready to take off.

"No," Banyon ordered as he realized Mandy thought she was summoned to provide sex for him. Before he could say more, Mandy reacted.

She threw out her short arms, with her fingers splayed in the hold on position. "Okay, your right, I don't need it," she said quickly. Her hands went nervously to the shoulder bands of her suit and quick as a flash, her speedo fell to the floor. She immediately struck a pose like Heather had done earlier.

Banyon was shocked, but couldn't help but look anyway. Mandy was fully developed, but smaller than he had first realized. His mind quickly filled with shame for staring at her naked body. "Mandy, I don't need..." But she was already on the move.

She grabbed her towel flung it across the desk and was laying on her back on the towel before he could continue. "I'm ready Colt," she said nervously.

Suddenly, it all became clear to Banyon; Mandy thought that she was required to have sex with Banyon.

"Mandy, please sit up for a minute so that I can see your face and not your other parts. I want to talk to you." She sat up and dangled her legs over the side of the desk.

She gave him a perplexed look. "Have I done something wrong?"

He ignored her question. "How many lessons have you had with Heather?" he asked.

"Just one," she sheepishly replied, with her head hung low. Her thick hair covered her face.

"And how many contracts have you completed for the firm?"

"Please don't fire me. I'll do anything you want, Colt," she whined. Her perfect posture was now slouched in defeat.

"So, this is your first assignment, right?"

"Yes," she hissed. "Heather seems to get all the business. But I need money too," she added.

"I have no intention of firing you," he quickly replied.

"Really," she exclaimed as her head raised and she looked directly into his eyes.

"Do you have any idea how much money you will make, if we can complete our mission?" Banyon asked.

"No, I assumed that you will pay me by the hour, so maybe a thousand dollars. I could sure use the money."

"Mandy, based on the percentage rate, you stand to earn fifty thousand dollars, when this is done," Banyon informed her.

Shock filled her cherub face. "Colt, that's more money than I have made in my entire life so far," she exclaimed excitedly. Before Banyon could react, she dropped to the floor, bounced high in the air, when she came down to the ground, she was suddenly very serious. "Colt please tell me that you are not trying to mess with me or fool me," she pleaded.

"The money is yours, if we can complete the mission, it will start in five minutes, put your speedo back on please. You are too distracting."

Her body shuddered, "Wow, that gave me a jolt," she announced. "Glad to hear that. She grabbed his hand and shook it rapidly and then attempted to hug him, but a voice came over the sound system.

"Connection in three minutes," a female voice announced. The spell was broken.

"Oh, my God," Mandy exclaimed. "What should I be doing?" She said in a panicked voice.

"You need to do your exercises while I do this mission. I can handle everything, but you also need to be quiet," he told her. Banyon then reached into his satchel and handed her his I-pod and ear plugs. "Wear these," he ordered. He didn't want her to hear him talking to Wolf.

"Yes, sir," she replied and saluted him again.

"And please put your swim suit back on," he added as he pointed to the very small clump of shiny cloth near his desk.

"Maybe I don't want to," she teased. "Just knowing that you are watching me exercise excites me."

"I'll be watching the monitor," he said dryly.

"But not all the time," she quickly replied.

"It's an order," He said sternly. After making a little girl face, she complied and proceeded towards the open area in his office, while inserting the ear plugs.

11

Mandy was, of course, right. Banyon could not keep his eyes off of her. She now appeared to be doing some sort of cheerleader exercise. She kept her hands on her hips as she performed high leg kicks, squats and even splits on the rug in front of his desk. At one point, she moved to the front of his desk and shook her hands like she had pom-poms in them, but it was her upper body that jiggled. Banyon could see she was very excited and so was he. A broad grin dominated her young face. He knew he wouldn't touch her, but she sure was fun to watch. *You'd better watch out when I get home Loni*, he thought. *I'm going to twist your little body into a pretzel.*

Suddenly, Banyon's computer screen came on. He was now looking inside the situation room. He had a clear view of a large seven foot by seven foot monitor divided into four boxes. In a row, running down, on the right-hand side of the main monitor, he saw several smaller monitors with several faces visible, including his own. He realized there were many people involved in this extraction and they were all watching from remote locations. No one from the room was visible, but he could see movement in the shadows and hear people talking in the background.

"Nice to see you could make it," he heard the President say. "Do you have any updates for me?"

"Let me get back to you in a second," Banyon told him. He had been so busy, with the provocative Mandy; he had forgotten to check with Wolf. Banyon quickly pressed the escape button and addressed Wolf.

"Wolf, are you there?"

"All these women around you are going to get you into trouble someday," Wolf reprimanded him.

"I understand, I don't need a lecture right now," answered a frustrated Banyon. "Do you have any updates?"

Gerald J. Kubicki & Kristopher Kubicki

"Only that there are seven man at the safe house now," Wolf answered. "The seventh man is a Mexican official from the immigration/travel department. He is the one who provides the names of the girls to be kidnapped."

"I'll pass it on to the President," Banyon told him. He noticed that Mandy was still exercising, but now she had a slight pout on her lips. He waved to her and quickly hit the escape button, reporting to the President on all he had learned.

"We are taking him out, too," the angry President ordered. "I want as many of these scumbags eliminated as possible."

Banyon watched the four split-screen monitors. One was an overhead view from a drone or satellite. It showed the building to be invaded. The second monitor was a side view of the front of the house, clearly taken from a surveillance vehicle across the street. The third view was from the head cam of the lead SEAL. Banyon could see he was on the move by the constant jiggling of the camera. His view was of the back of the house. It was clear the SEALs would access the building from the back. The camera stopped as a small wall came into view. Across the opening Banyon could see five other SEALs crouched by the wall. The fourth view was actually a picture of the heat signatures of all the people in the house. It was a downward looking view, and could only have been taken from a drone.

There were thirteen signatures in all. Some appeared prone on beds, he was sure they were from the girls. In the background, Banyon could hear several people talking; the commanding voice of the President was giving orders. The President had a military background. He knew how to run an operation.

"We go on my mark," the lead SEAL said. He had ten highly trained men all wearing Mexican police uniforms, but they all had on Kevlar vests and utility belts containing unique weapons, if needed. Their main weapon was a silenced machine gun just like the type the cartel used. The guns had been confiscated during previous drug raids and had only the prints of gangsters on the handles. The SEAL team all wore special gloves.

Banyon heard, "Roger," ten times.

"Ready, and go," the leader said.

As the SEALs entered the backyard, Banyon could see a man sitting on the chair, by the back door. The Mexican was only semi-alert, with his gun by his side. Banyon could now see over the tip of the lead SEALs gun, the silencer was attached. As soon as the Mexican went for his gun, the leader spoke.

"Hey Poncho, it's time to meet your maker." The gun suddenly spit out a bullet and the Mexican went down. "First target down," the SEAL said, "six more coming."

The leader quickly reached the back door, quietly opening it. Banyon could clearly hear the shuffle of several feet in the background. As soon as the door opened two of the screens on the big monitor changed. Two other SEALs activated their head cams. Banyon watched as they crowded through the open door.

Three men went left, three men went right; the leader went straight down a hallway with four men in tow. Everyone seemed to know their job. The camera on the right, found a closed-door. It was thrown open. Inside were two Mexicans sound asleep, on filthy cots. Two shots prevented them from awakening.

"Two more hostiles down," one of SEALs reported.

Meanwhile, the SEAL leader was working his way up some rickety stairs. Upon reaching the second floor, his men spread out. There were four doors closed along the upstairs hallway. Each SEAL took up a position at a door. The leader took the first door. Banyon could see down the hall as each man acknowledged that they were ready. A hand signal told them to break into each room. The SEAL leader kicked his door in, entering a shabby looking bedroom. There were two beds; strapped to the beds were two young girls. An older man with a beard, a very hairy, naked body, and a grin, was attempting to get on top of a young girl. The SEAL leader grabbed him by his neck, throwing him against the wall. He then shot him between the eyes. Banyon quickly heard three more muffed shots telling him, all the hostiles were dead. This was now a rescue mission.

"All hostiles down," the SEAL leader reported.

Banyon heard more men running up the steps. Soon, all three cameras showed SEAL members cutting the ropes which tied the girls and placing blankets around their naked bodies. The girls were then slung over shoulders and were rapidly taken outside the back door, where a van now stood, with the side door open. The SEALs deposited each of the girls gently on the floor of the van. As soon as all six were safely on board, a medic appeared, pulling the door shut.

"Get them to the plane as fast as possible," the SEAL leader ordered. The van disappeared in a cloud of dust, as it headed back to the plane. With everybody watching the monitors, the SEAL leader spoke, "we go after the cartel leader next."

Banyon pressed the escape button and whispered, "Wolf update?" he looked over his computer screen to see if Mandy was watching him, but she was busy doing yoga. He realized she was very flexible.

Wolf replied immediately. "The cartel leader is at his home. It is just three blocks away. He has two personal body-guards and six men guard the exterior of his estate. They all have machine guns. Colt you might want to pass on that the cartel leader is just finishing up a call with someone from the United States. That person gave the cartel leader the assignment of capturing the Presidents granddaughter."

Banyon quickly pressed the escape button. "Mr. President," Banyon interrupted the subdued celebration going on, in the situation room.

"Yes, Colt," he said. "Do you have something more to add?"

Banyon quickly told him what he had just learned. The President placed orders with the SEAL team to make sure to get the cell phones of the cartel leaders. He desperately wanted to know who had planned the kidnapping of his granddaughter.

"Roger that," came the reply.

The monitors, suddenly, refreshed, there were four new boxes. One was a satellite image. It showed the estate of the cartel leader. It was a walled compound with a sturdy iron gate in front. The villa was a large, two-story, pink stucco building, with red roof tiles. Everyone knew there would be many places to hide in the house. Also many places to set up a defense. And, if, someone hit an alarm, the SEAL leader understood it would only take five minutes for help to arrive. The infrared image monitor showed nine men in the villa complex. The third monitor was an additional shot of the front entrance to the estate. The SEAL leader's camera had been turned off, as he was now inside of a van, being transported to the new site.

While the SEAL team was in route, the President spoke. "What's the status of the takedown of the corrupt police chief?"

Another voice replied from inside the situation room. "Our female decoy has gotten him to leave his office and walk with her, in the park. He thinks she has damaging information about the cartel and wants to hear what she has to say. Our sniper is about a half a mile away, with a clear view of the park. When the sniper has a clear shot, he will notify her. She will enter the concrete bathroom in the park, leaving him completely exposed, for the shot."

"Make sure it happens that way," growled the President. "I want no slip ups on this one. He must go down. There is nothing worse than a corrupt police official." Everyone in the room quickly agreed.

The voice continued. "We have a van onsite. They will recover his body and bring it to the home of the cartel leader. He will be dumped inside the front yard near the house. There will also be a bank statement, in his pocket, that will make a connection between him and the cartel very clear. When the Mexican police investigate the murders, they will think a rival cartel did the damage."

"I want to send a message to all the scumbags in Mexico, The United States will not only protect itself, but will also take revenge on those who threaten us," the President slammed his fist to emphasize his determination.

The SEAL team's leader's camera came to life as he exited the van. His men spread out to their assigned jump off positions. Four of the six cartel guards were targeted in seconds. Everyone was ready, they just needed the go-ahead.

Banyon whispered once again, "Wolf, any updates?"

"The guard on the right wall has spotted one of the SEALs. He is about to pass on the information to the cartel leader."

"SEAL on the right wall location has been spotted by the guard. You need to take him out now," Banyon screamed.

"Take out the guards," the SEAL leader calmly ordered. Within seconds he began to receive acknowledgment from each of his men, as they took out the guards with their silenced machine guns. All four guards had died without making any noise.

"Four hostiles down. Five more coming," the SEAL officially reported to everyone listening.

When the SEAL team regrouped along the front wall, one of the SEALs attached an acid mixture to the front lock, on the gate. Within seconds the acid had burned through the mechanism. The SEAL leader was able to push open one door. Ten SEALs rushed the front door knowing they could face enemy fire at any time. But nothing happened, all was silent. Another mixture of acid was applied to the large double-wooden doors of the villa. Soon the SEALs pushed it open and peered inside. Once again two additional head cams came on as the men stealthy slipped into the house.

Suddenly, Banyon heard, "the police chief is down and currently in route to the villa. ETA is five minutes."

"Set up at perimeter at position A. Stop any cars that get within six blocks of the villa," the SEAL leader ordered.

"Roger that," came the response.

12

Inside the house, as before, three men went right, three men went left; the SEAL leader went straight down the hallway towards the large great room, in the back of the house, where they knew, the cartel leader was located. They must have tripped a silent alarm, because machine gun fire suddenly erupted. Everybody went to ground.

"Report," Banyon heard. The airwaves were suddenly full of reports. But none of the men could see any hostiles. The SEALs were trapped. They were unable to move forward from their cover. Something had to be done soon, or the mission would be a failure.

Banyon sang out. "They are all in the kitchen hiding behind the marble counter tops. The teams on the right and the left should be able to outflank them and get clear shots.

"Roger that," the SEAL leader replied. "I'm setting the charges now" The leader opened a closet door. He threw in the satchel he had carried into the house. He had the remote detonator in his pocket.

Banyon watched the second screen on the large monitor as the camera moved forward slowly, eventually rounding a corner. He could now clearly see five Mexican-looking men, with machine guns positioned behind a kitchen island. Their guns were trained on the hallway but could only see a portion of it, as the island was off-center. They didn't sense any movement to their right as the SEALs took up positions. On the Leaders orders, the SEALs quickly opened fire and all five of the Mexicans were dispatched.

"Five hostiles down," a SEAL reported. The three cameras started to jiggle as the SEALs ran to the kitchen to make sure the men were dead. They began to collect cell phones and any other cartel related materials.

"Got some papers and ledgers here," a SEAL reported. "Found them on the coffee table in the great room."

"Look for more evidence. Team one, you check out the office, team two go and toss his upstairs bedroom. I want to be out of here in three minutes," the leader said, as he rifled through the pockets of the five men.

"We have three Mexican police cars heading our way," the lookout announced. "They are about two minutes from the entrance."

"Stop those cars," the leader shouted into his communications gear.

The lookout was the same sniper who had taken down the police chief. He was set up on top of a building, about two blocks from the villa. He had a clear view of the two roads leading to the compound. He quickly took aim and shot out the right front tire of the first police car. He then repeated the process, all three cars ground to a halt. He had no desire to kill policemen, even if they were corrupt.

Nine Mexican police officers poured out of the cars searching the skies for the sniper, but he was too far away for them to see. Realizing the sniper only meant to slow them down; the policeman began jogging towards the compound. It would take them some time to cover the distance. By then the SEALs intended to be gone.

"Mission accomplished. It will take them at least ten minutes to reach the villa. I'm bringing in the police chief now," announced the sniper.

"Roger," the SEAL leader acknowledged. He took one more look around the house, he then said, "Okay, everybody out."

The SEALs exited the front door, just as a black van pulled up. It was driven by the attractive woman who had actually been the decoy for the police chief. The side door flew open and the sniper dragged the body of the dead police chief inside the grounds of the villa. Three of the SEALs dropped their guns on the ground, around the entrance. There were blood stains on two of the handles. The blood belonged to Danta Lopez and one of his henchmen. Lopez was the former boss of the cartel. He was in FBI custody, but no one in Mexico knew that. It was meant to lead the Mexican police on a lengthy, wild goose chase.

A second van followed immediately to extract the SEALs. As they cleared the gate in the front of the villa, one of the SEALs turned to look up the street and noted the policeman were still two blocks away.

"Initiating the final phase," announced the SEAL leader. He then extracted a remote from his pocket and unceremoniously pressed the button. The explosion was relatively small, but it had been a device designed to create a fire, not blow up the neighborhood. The entire house was now in flames.

"Home James," the leader said to the female driver, who didn't think he was very funny.

"You're not out of the woods yet," reminded a voice over the speakers. "Let's not be too jovial until you are over international waters. It still will take fifteen minutes to reach the private airport and another ten minutes until you are safely out of the country."

"Roger," replied a more subdued SEAL leader.

Now, Banyon observed the real workings of the federal government. In the situation room there was some clapping, some high-fiving and some cheering, but it only lasted a few seconds, as the President began to speak.

"I want a complete communications blackout of all the events which have taken place in Mexico," he said to everyone in ear shout. He then spoke to the Press Secretary. "Neil, prepare a statement which says, we are shocked and outraged by the events of today. We do not condone the use of violence, in any form, for any reason, other than our national security."

"I'm on it Mr. President," the Press Secretary replied, but then sheepishly asked, "But don't you think the wording is a little strong? It almost sounds like a veiled threat," the Press Secretary questioned.

"I want it to sound that way, Neil. We have the perfect opportunity to strike deadly blows to all the scumbags in the cartels. Let's hope they think we have a phantom, former drug cartel leader, taking out his competition for revenge. I want each of the cartels to know, they may be next. We have the perfect platform to make that happen," the President slammed a desk with his fist to emphasis his determination.

"I'll have it ready in fifteen minutes," the Press Secretary quickly replied.

"Heads will roll if there is a leak from anyone in this room," the President threatened again.

"Yes, sir," Banyon heard several people reply.

"Have we got the names of all of the girls yet?"

"I have a complete list, sent in from the medics, in the van. By the way, all the girls are in good shape, with only a few bruises, but scared out of their wits," someone answered.

"I want an FBI team on each of the girl's families immediately. There is to be a complete blackout. Make sure the families understand we rescued their children, despite great risk, to the men who saved them and also to the United States. Have each of them sign documents saying they will never discuss anything about what happened in Cancun, with anyone. Offer some compensation if necessary."

"I'll make the calls," someone off screen offered.

The President was giving orders at break neck speed. Banyon liked his style. "Contact our ambassador in Mexico City. Have him visit with and notify the President of Mexico that Danta Lopez has escaped prison. Tell him he is seeking revenge on his old cartel buddies," the President said, closing the final loophole in the rescue. Danta Lopez was actually still in maximum security federal prison, with no chance of ever seeing the light of day, but the Mexican President would never know that.

Banyon continued to watch the big monitor. The vans were quickly approaching the private airfield. He noted all the smaller side screens were blank except for his. He was the only one watching the escape. Suddenly, he saw a hand point at his screen. "Someone is still watching," a voice said.

The President's face quickly filled the screen in front of Banyon. "Ah, Colt your work is done, for today," he smiled. "You did a great job. We would not have been successful without your help. I will send a message to Bart immediately to cut you a check for $500,000. It will be delivered to your office before the end of the day. I trust everything you heard and saw today will not be shared with anyone. Do you understand?"

"Of course Mr. President," Banyon said as graciously as possible. His monitor suddenly went blank.

13

Banyon now leaned back in his chair and placed his feet on the edge of his desk. He could feel the tension drain from his body. As he looked around his monitor, he saw Mandy jogging in place, but staring intently at him. She quickly pulled out her earplugs and said. "Are you finally done?"

He nodded.

"Oh, goody," she exclaimed and clapped her hands.

Mandy flew around the side of his desk and stood next to his chair glistening with sweat. She leaned in towards him while her eyes searched his face for information. He finally realized she wanted to know about the money.

"Well, Mandy, it seems today is your lucky day, you will be receiving a check for $50,000."

She squealed like a teenager and quickly started bouncing up and down with her arms stretched over her head in victory. Banyon was suddenly aroused, again.

"I'm going to give you a huge hug and then a big reward for choosing me," she exclaimed.

Suddenly panicked, Banyon quickly stood up and put out his hands to stop her from jumping on him again. "Mandy you are all sweaty from your exercises. Your scent will get on my clothes. My girlfriend, Loni, will know immediately. She has an excellent sense of smell. I can't deal with that right now," he said defensively.

"But don't you see," she pleaded. I want the people in the office to believe I can seduce any man I choose, even you," she countered. "I want to be like Heather and make more money."

"You are very seductive," Banyon quickly told her. It will be our little secret, nobody else needs to know the details. Now towel off," he ordered. He watched as she reluctantly

Gerald J. Kubicki & Kristopher Kubicki

grabbed the big white towel and sensuously rubbed it all over her body.

"Satisfied," she said sarcastically, as she stood in front of him with a pained look on her face.

"Yes," he replied in a husky voice. He was about to say more when a knock at the door broke the tension between them.

"Come in," said an annoyed Banyon. The door flew open and Heather runway walked her way into his office and up to the front of his desk. She looked at Mandy and smiled, then looked at Banyon and frowned.

"Mandy you look excited, and Colt you look scared. I think both of you need some lessons from me," she grinned.

"What do you want Heather?"

"I'm here to deliver your Bluetooth connector," she said as she dangled it from her manicured index finger. "Wear it inside the building. It is not to ever to leave the office," she warned.

"That's it, that's the only reason you are here?" Banyon was suddenly suspicious that someone could listen in and see everything that went on in his office. He decided to ask Wolf about that later.

"Unless there's something else I can do for either of you," she offered while she batted her attractive eyelashes.

"I think I need your help Heather," Mandy moaned like she was hurt. "I think you need to give me some more lessons," she said as she looked at Banyon with sorrow.

"Well, I could do better than that," Heather brightly said. "Why don't we head to the shower room and I will help with your current problem," she looked at Banyon as she said it. You'll feel a lot better."

"Okay," Mandy replied brightly.

"Colt you can come and watch if you like. It's okay, men watch me shower all the time. Remember nothing is illegal or immoral in this office." "Almost all men are voyeurs, you know," she added.

I'm one too, he thought.

"You two go ahead and get started and maybe I'll catch up with you later," Banyon promised. Mandy's face quickly brightened as Heather stepped near, wrapping a delicate arm around her waist. She guided Mandy towards the door, away from Banyon.

He collapsed into his chair, realizing he was completely exhausted, drained, and very aroused himself. He couldn't wait for his check to be delivered, so that he could run to the bank and make a beeline for Loni. *She is in trouble today,* he thought.

He didn't have to wait long. His door was still open when he heard the sound of cloth rubbing together coming down the hallway. Suddenly, a Catholic nun dressed in a complete nun's habit of black and white, passed through his door. Her attire included a coif to cover her hair. She was older, maybe forty-five, but was still attractive, with high cheekbones, and a brilliant smile. She glided up to his desk and produced a check from inside her sleeve.

"Bart has sent me to deliver your check, Colt," she announced. She then ceremoniously presented it to him, over the desk.

Banyon grabbed the check stared at it for a few seconds then turned his attention to the calmly standing nun. She had her hands steeped for prayer and a Mona Lisa smile covered her face. She stared straight ahead. She didn't seem to know he was in the room. She made him feel very peaceful.

"Are you really a nun?"

"My name is Sister Teresa, and I am most certainly a nun in spirit and practice. I am very good at comforting people," she replied without hesitation.

"But you must have some sort of special talent to be employed by this firm, what is your special talent?"

"Well actually I am fully trained nuclear scientist, but there isn't much work for my talents, so I have adapted to a new persona," she said as she spread her arms producing an angel like pose.

"That might be useful in dealing with people who are Catholic, by religion," Banyon, the born and raised Catholic, noted.

"I also have a photographic memory and am an expert at deciphering codes and puzzles," she humbly admitted.

"I'll remember that," he said cheerfully.

"And, I have also completed all the training offered by Heather. Shall I demonstrate for you?" Sister Teresa asked as she tilted her head and looked into his eyes.

"No," Banyon yelled in a panicked voice.

Before Banyon could protest further, Sister Teresa stepped up on the chair in front of his desk and was suddenly standing over him with her legs apart on the desk. She began flipping her hips from side to side, while quickly raising the dress of our habit. Within seconds the bare thighs of her long legs were visible. Her Mona Lisa smile stayed plastered on her face.

"Stop. Please stop," Banyon protested.

Part Two

More Stress

14

The trip home, took way too long, but it gave Banyon time to think about his long day. He thought he did pretty well for his first day at Dewey & Beatem. He had been apprehensive as he had not worked in an office for over ten years. But in a nutshell, he had earned a net total of $440,000, after expenses for Mandy and the firm. He had already deposited the check in the bank. It was a good start.

Along the way, he helped rescue six innocent young women, helped destroy a white-slavery ring, put a corrupt police chief out of business, and pleased the President of United States. He had made some new acquaintances; even if they were a bit strange and extreme, and had developed new contacts he was sure could help him in the future. He also had lunch with, and was now on a first name basis with, the Secretary of the Justice Department. The DOJ. Not a bad day at all.

He realized he had quickly become somewhat of a celebrity at the Law firm. He knew this, because, as he was leaving the building, doors opened and several heads peeked out at him as he walked down the hallways. People stared at him as he left the building. He understood, word had quickly spread of his immediate success, many of the people were jealous. He knew that in an office environment, few secrets were kept hidden for long. He speculated the leak probably came from the highly-charged Mandy, and was probably coxed out of her by the intoxicating Heather.

He wondered how many people would visit his office tomorrow and what new talents they might have to offer. He reluctantly admitted to himself, he secretly enjoyed the sexual encounters as well. He wondered how long his celibacy policy would last in the office. He also wondered what affect it would have on his relationship with Loni. He really didn't want anything to change. She always seemed sexually charged and ready to go, but today Banyon was sure he would be the aggressor.

He suddenly was thinking about Loni. Since she had walked into his life several years ago, his world had completely changed. Everything now revolved around her. She was his live-in companion, his business partner, his best friend, and without question the best lover he had ever encountered in his life. The women he had met today were definitely intriguing, but no one could quite measure up to the standard set by Loni. They had a near-perfect relationship. He never wanted to lose that.

He could not help but think about her, on the seemingly endless trip home. Loni was a petite Asian woman, the only child of former main-land Chinese parents. They had expected to have a boy. She had been born in Hawaii and she was 100% American. She was 5'2", less than 100 pounds soaking wet, with long, black, hair that reached the middle of her back. She possessed dark penetrating almond eyes, and the athleticism of a gymnast. She had keen intelligence, did everything at 100 miles an hour, but still believed in the ancient Chinese values for women and men It had been drummed into her by her parents. She was an exotic female, who sometimes acted like a man.

She was trained by the FBI and was a ferocious fighter when she needed to be. She also looked to be about 25 years old, even though, she was actually nearly double that age. Banyon understood that she felt he was her last chance at having a long term relationship with a man. He was very thankful for that. She always tried for him.

To be sure she had faults. Her major fault was, she was so impulsive; she often misread the situation and jumped in feet first without knowing the full story. This sometimes led to a variety of problems. Sometimes, they were comical, sometimes they were dangerous, and usually they created situations for Banyon to fix. She was also, the most jealous woman in the world. She had gone so far as attacking a woman who had just looked at Colton Banyon the wrong way. In addition, she couldn't cook, didn't clean house, and was completely disorganized in her personal life. She thought money grew on trees. All of these things kept Banyon on his toes, but frankly he didn't want it to be any other way.

He did still have some long-term questions about her as well. Her background was very mysterious and she rarely would discuss it. All he really knew was that her mother had been some sort of magic-healer back in the old country and had passed on a green jade charm ring to Loni. The ring allowed Loni to produce any object Banyon asked for, at any time. It was truly magic.

Loni also never showed fear, even when bullets were flying all around her head. It was like she believed she was meant to have a very long life. These questions always bothered Banyon, but he was enjoying life so much, he had not pursued the answers. To him, she was that captivating.

Banyon now turned off the highway onto Barrington Road and headed to his home in the affluent Chicago suburb of South Barrington, Illinois. He bought the sprawling ranch just before he met Loni and had decorated it to be the home of a bachelor. Once Loni moved in he was surprised that she didn't attempt to change the style of the décor. Instead she complemented it and added only a few pieces of furniture. Of course, Elizabeth, Banyon's long-time housekeeper, had gone from a part-time employee to full-time, just to keep up with Loni's whirlwind nature.

Banyon entered the large circular driveway and pulled straight into his five car garage. He was happy to see Loni's small red Porsche parked in the slot next to his. This meant that she was home. He exited the garage through a door which opened inside the kitchen. He set his bag on the kitchen island and went off in search of Loni. He knew she was in the great room just off the kitchen, because he could hear sound coming from the new 80 inch flat-screen TV that she had purchased just last week.

He found her curled up on the big couch intently watching the news. She was dressed only in one of his white T-shirts. She had the TV volume up so loud she had not heard the alarm beep or the door slam, as he entered the kitchen. He was just about upon her when she suddenly turned her head and smiled at him. She then gracefully got up from the couch, hugged him, and then kissed him deeply on the mouth.

"Where have you been?" There was annoyance in her voice. "Elizabeth went home early today and I'm starving."

"I'm home from my first day at the Law firm of Dewey & Beatem," he beamed with spread arms.

"Make me something to eat," she demanded. When Elizabeth was not there, Loni relied completely on Banyon to be fed.

"Don't you want to ask me how my first day went?"

"Tell me while you're making salad," she countered as she rubbed her small stomach while continuing to watch the news.

"We made $440,000 today," he proudly announced, expecting her to leap into his arms, so he could carry her into the bedroom.

"Should we have steak or pork chops," Loni said with a one track mind, as she put her small finger to her lips, in thought.

Banyon decided things were not going his way and changed tactics. Suddenly, he became serious. "Loni I need you to give me a back rub first. I have a couple of muscles that need stretching. It is been a long day," he told her.

"Colt, are you hurt?" she blurted out with only modest concern. She seemed glued to the TV.

"No, but I feel some muscle strain."

She quickly ran around behind him and started rubbing all the muscles in his back. "There, is that better?" She asked as she continued to watch the TV. She seemed only slightly interested in satisfying him.

"No, it's not. I need to lie down on the bed with my clothes off."

"Maybe later," she said.

He grabbed her by the hand and began pulling her to the bedroom. At first she resisted, but when he said, "Loni please help me," she became docile, following him into the bedroom. She acted like he was asking her to do the laundry.

"Colt, what has come over you, you never act this way?" she stated with her hands on her narrow hips when they had reached the bedroom.

"Let's just say that I am over-stimulated," Banyon countered with an innuendo that seemed lost on Loni today. Normally, she picked up on everything he said. Today, she seemed to have other things on her mind. But Banyon didn't care, what she was thinking about, at the moment.

"Are you sure you need this right now? I'm hungry," she pleaded.

"Yes, now, hurry up and start massaging."

"Okay," she said without enthusiasm. She climbed up on the bed and straddled his buttocks like she was riding a horse.

"I don't feel much tension in your back muscles," she soon announced as she stopped rubbing his back.

"Well, I have one muscle that is throbbing," he confided.

"Oh," she replied in her small singsong voice. "I think I know which one."

"You're a smart girl," he replied lecherously.

She was suddenly, the Loni he knew and loved. She suddenly, didn't care about dinner.

15

It was an hour and half later, well after 7:30 P.M., when they decided to get out of bed. They both took a quick shower, dressed, and now stood in the kitchen preparing dinner. That meant, Banyon did all the work and Loni did all the talking. She had her usual list of a hundred questions about his new position.

They decided to have Caesar salad and an omelet for dinner. Banyon carefully cut the romaine lettuce and placed it in a wooden bowl. He then opened a can of rolled anchovies and began smashing them into a paste. He selected one of the anchovies, popping it into his mouth. It was part of the ritual he followed when making Caesar salad.

"How can you eat those things whole?" Loni protested.

"I have to make sure they are fresh," he quickly replied. "Otherwise, the salad will be ruined, and my reputation as a gourmet chef, as well."

"Did you really make $440,000 today?"

"Yes little lady, I did," he replied cheerfully as he added olive oil, garlic and several more ingredients to the Caesar salad dressing.

"Did your mission have anything to do with the news I was watching on the TV?" Loni asked.

"I'm not supposed to discuss my missions with anyone," he told her knowing it would not stop her from asking more questions.

"The news said, there had been a major battle in Mexico. It was between some drug cartels in Cancun, Mexico. More than fourteen people died, including the police chief of Cancun. The Mexican president is very upset, and vows to bring the killers to justice, even if they are Americans. What does he mean?"

"I believe, he thinks some Americans came to Mexico and did the killings." What Banyon didn't say was that the police chief was involved in a white-slavery ring and the rest of the men who died were part of a drug cartel. They were also involved in the slave trade. Banyon knew it was better to give her some information, than to deny everything.

"So, how did you earn the money?"

"We helped rescue six young women from a life in slavery," he said as he poured the Caesar salad dressing over the salad, added some grated cheese, and pushed the bowel towards her to serve.

"Who is we?" She asked as she tasted the salad directly from the bowel. Loni had a legendary suspicious nature.

"My contract employee and me, of course," he said evasively.

"Who is this contract employee? And what did they do for you?" Loni asked as she ramped up her interrogation. Banyon could hear concern in her voice.

"Oh, she is just the receptionist," he replied with a wave of his hand. "By contract, I have to pay at least one person at the firm whenever I am working on a case. I chose her because she didn't get in my way." Banyon had already decided to not discuss any of the more personal issues he had dealt with at the firm during his first day.

But Loni dug deeper. "She huh, what did she look like?" Loni quickly demanded.

"Loni, she is practically a teenager, she even wears braces. Her main goal in life is to be in the Olympics."

"So, is she athletic looking?" Loni asked.

"Not nearly as athletic looking as you are, babe," he said to deflect where she was going with her questions. To Loni athletic meant good looking.

"Well, I'll just have to go there and see for myself," Loni threatened.

"Don't bring your purse. She is also a world-class pickpocket," Banyon said nonchalantly.

"Tell me about the other people you met at work, then?" She said as her eyes grew narrow with suspicion.

"Well let's see," he started, as he looked up from his work and directly at her. "The managing partner is an illusionist, the IT guy is a world-class hacker, and they have a guy on staff that speaks dozens of languages and can forge most documents, but looks like a ferret."

"Specifically, did you meet any other women?" Loni demanded, as her jealousy grew. She didn't believe that Banyon was telling her the whole truth.

"Well, there is the Catholic nun, who has a photographic memory, and the office manager who is real good at psychology," he responded. "They are all business," he added.

"I want to meet them, as well," Loni demanded.

"I don't think anyone is allowed in the building, unless they are client," he said.

"That sounds awfully convenient to me," Loni huffed.

He quickly changed the subject. "Loni you seemed very distracted when I came home today, what's on your mind?"

"Oh, nothing," she lied. Banyon knew Loni never gave up any information without fight, but expected him to tell her everything.

"Could you be a little more specific? You were clearly thinking about something else when I came home. What was it?"

"I just have some concerns," she admitted.

"Well, are you going to make me guess?" he replied a little sarcastically.

"It's those damn Patel women."

With a little panic in his voice, he asked. "What's happened now?"

"Colt, they are always here, at the house. It's just that I don't want them in our house all the time," Loni pleaded.

The Patel women, all three of them, were part of Banyon's team. He had actually met them before he met Loni. They had a lot of history with Colton Banyon. Loni was insanely jealous of the beautiful, Indian, women, and actually, he knew that she had a right to be concerned.

"I thought you were friends now?" Banyon responded.

"Colt, we are," Loni replied. "But I can't help these feelings that I sometimes get when they are around. I think they want you back into their lives full-time and I don't like it. Our private life should be private."

"But Maya is pregnant, Pramilla is married, and Previne is completely dedicated to her work," he reasoned.

"Do they have to be here, in my house, all the time?"

By this time, Banyon had finished making the omelet, put it onto plates and proceeded around the kitchen island. He served the meal and plopped down next to her. It had given him a few seconds to think of something to say.

"Why don't you take some of the money I earned today and use it to redecorate your office in Hoffman Estates," he said. He knew that spending money was one of her favorite pastimes.

"Why?"

"You could add a couple of desks. Then tell the Patel's you made the workspace for them to use, any time, they wanted. That way they will be obliged to come to the offices of the LCH Detective Agency, LLC, to do their work. You could also keep an eye on them there, and get away from them, if you want to."

Loni face quickly lit up, "Colt you are brilliant," she beamed. "And I get to spend some of your money." She vibrated with happiness.

"I know," he replied sincerely, but with a smile on his face. "Besides, it is also your money."

Suddenly, the front door bell chimed. Loni, who was only attired in a terrycloth robe, leaped from her chair and ran down the hallway to peak through the eye hole.

She ran back into the kitchen with a look of exasperation on her face. "It's the Patel Clan," she screamed at him, like it was his fault. She bolted to the bedroom to get dressed.

16

Banyon left his meal half-finished and headed down the hallway to the front door. He wondered what the Patel women wanted, as it was already late in the evening. He knew Loni was upset, and he felt she had a right to be. These women intruded into their lives, a little too often, especially lately. He knew Loni had attempted to be friends with them despite her uncontrollable jealously. But the friendship was strained, as Loni knew, all three of the Patel women were ex-lovers of Colton Banyon. She suspected they might try to rekindle their sexually based relationship with him, at any time. But what she didn't understand was that Banyon had completely fallen for Loni, even though she didn't really believe it. Since they had become lovers, he had been able to resist the Patel's temptations.

Banyon had actually met all three women while solving his first mystery. Pramilla and Previne were exact twins and Maya, six years younger, could easily pass for either of her sisters. They had been sent by Walter Pierce, now Wolf, to guide and protect him. Their Grandfather Abu Patel had placed the curse that allowed Wolf to speak to Banyon.

An additional curse had been placed on the women, so that they could use their well-developed sexual powers to motivate Banyon, or actually, any good man. The grandfather had placed the curse so that his granddaughters could identify the right man to marry. At the time, Banyon was without a woman and was easy prey for the sisters. He also discovered they liked to share and were totally uninhibited around him. The second curse had ended when Pramilla married Eric. But Banyon wasn't sure about the curse ending, as sometimes they continued to attempt to seduce him. Eric, who was actually Wolf's grandson and looked like a tall surfer, once confided that he sometimes didn't always know which one of the sisters was in bed with him. Banyon knew the sisters shared everything, even their men.

But there was a reason for their behavior. The Patel's had been raised and still lived in central India. Their parents had died in a plane crash when they were very young. They went to live with their Grandfather Abu, who passed on some of his *Shaman* knowledge, but also trained them to use their sexual abilities to get what they wanted in life. He believed that a woman had only one purpose, to serve a man, and they had a lot of material to work with. Each girl was tall, slender, like models, with high cheek bones, and light brown soft skin, the color of mocha. They had long, silky, black, hair, and captivating dark eyes. They had learned how to seduce men as young teenagers when Abu decided they needed to learn the practical art of strip teasing in a local club. While they became highly educated and received advanced degrees in archeology, curating and diplomacy, they also were very capable of manipulating any man, including Colton Banyon.

A few months ago, things had changed. Maya had been dating an agent of the FBI and had become pregnant. Agent Gregory Gamble was killed during the line of duty. Maya was now alone and barely a few months into her pregnancy. The twins decided to take a leave of absence from their regular positions in India and stay in America, with Maya, at least until she had her baby. They had purchased a big house in Banyon's neighborhood and were all of a sudden fixtures at his doorstep. This, of course, made Loni very nervous and somewhat irritable.

He opened the door and saw the three Patel women smiling broadly. They were standing in a row and barely filled the doorway. Eric stood just behind the women. He towered over them. They were all dressed in white shorts, displaying their beautiful legs with different colored loose blouses, tied in knots, just above their flat navels. Banyon, as usual, could not tell them apart. So, he addressed Eric.

"What brings you guys out this late at night, Eric?"

"Two things really," one of the women spoke with the precise English accent that reminded him of the British influence on India.

"Oh?" he replied.

"Yes, Colt," another replied. "We wanted to find out about your first day at the Law firm and also we have a project you need to help us with."

"May we come in?" the third women asked as she batted her shining eyes.

"Of course," Banyon said and stepped back. He opened his arms in welcome, waving them to enter. The women walked inside three abreast, proceeding down the hallway, to the big kitchen. Banyon and Eric followed. He watched the synchronized, rhythmic roll, of their tiny bottoms as they headed deep inside his house. They were about halfway down the hallway when Banyon spied an old book in the arm of one of the girls. It looked like an old ledger and also looked very familiar.

"I think I have seen the ledger before, haven't I?" Banyon commented. "Why is it here?"

"Don't you remember?" the sister said over her shoulder. "We took it from Kammler's cave in Death Valley." Banyon now knew the sister dressed in the blue blouse was Maya. She was the only one of the girls who could read German.

While attempting to solve the mystery of Hans Kammler's cave, about a year ago, they had discovered on old ledger. It seemed to contain names and addresses of several of the founding members of the Effort, the modern day version of the Third Reich. Maya had taken the ledger to translate the information. While, it had been written in the nineteen-thirties, they hoped to find some names they could trace to current members, but Maya had never mentioned the ledger since.

"Actually, I had forgotten about it," he replied.

"Well, I haven't," she said. "I've had a lot more free time, since Greg died. I found something else in the ledger but didn't want anyone to know about, it until I checked it out," she explained.

"But do you have any information about the names in the ledger?" Banyon quickly asked.

"Yes, I do," Maya sweetly replied.

"Now you have my interest," he said. They had entered the kitchen were gathering around the kitchen island. Banyon quickly grabbed the dishes and threw them in the sink, for Elizabeth, the housekeeper, to wash the next day.

Maya set the ledger on the marble top and began flipping through pages. "Where is Loni?" another of the sisters asked.

"She'll be along shortly," he smoothly replied.

"She needs to be here," Maya noted.

"I thought you needed my help?" Banyon asked.

"Yes, we do. But Loni is the one that is going with us."

17

"Where am I going and why am I going with you guys?" Loni asked as she skidded to a halt at the kitchen island. She was now dressed in her traditional garb. It consisted of black skin-tight leotards and a loose white top. She had pulled her hair back into a ponytail, and it bobbed as she spoke. She didn't wear any shoes and was a full head shorter than the Patel sisters. Banyon was glad to see that she was in a better mood.

"I'll get to that in a second, okay?" Maya pleaded with Loni. "I need to finish with Colt first."

"Tell me about the names?" Banyon pressed Maya.

"There are ten names listed in the ledger. Many of them have been dealt with already. They are already dead. The first name is Hal Jones, who was really Klaus Gerut. He was killed by a fellow white-supremacist."

"Yes, that was when we were hunting for the rightful owner of the Mein Kampf book," Banyon remembered.

"Next, we have his brother George Gerut, who was the original head of the Effort in America. He died some time ago, but we faced his son John Gerut. Remember, he stole the artifacts from Area 51."

"Yeah, he turned to dust right in front of our eyes," Previne chuckled and elbowed Pramilla, who was also there.

"We also encounter the political family of Randolph and Sarah Sanders and ended their presidential aspirations. They are the children of two additional members, Adolf Sanders and Franz Hamburg. They both died several years ago," Maya said.

"And I found my loving husband, Eric, in the process," Pramilla pointed out. Banyon now knew which sister was Pramilla. She had on the red blouse.

"Then, when we found the old German plane in the desert, we had to deal with Adam Dunne," Maya continued.

"Yuck, what a creep he was," Loni said as she made a face.

"The final two names are also dead. They are Henry Fogel and Albert Spitz. They both died during our last caper." Maya suddenly became chocked up and started to cry. It was during the last mystery that Greg Gamble had also died. No one said anything for a few minutes as they each relived the tragedy.

Banyon then recapped. "So, we have run across these men or their children in each of our mysteries."

"Wow," Loni quickly remarked. "We had a hand in the demise of all of them. We must be pretty good."

"And solved the mysteries that surrounded them too," one of the twins pointed out. "Not to mention the money that we made."

"And Previne, you have several artifacts we collected, secreted away in your museum in India, don't you?" Banyon added.

"Yes, I do," Previne admitted. Banyon congratulated himself for solving the mystery of which twin was which. Previne had the blue top.

"I'd say we have had a pretty good run, so far," Banyon told them. "We have also put a serious dent in the Efforts plans."

"You guys are my best friends," Previne gushed. She turned and hugged her sister. Soon everyone was hugging each other as emotions ran high in the room.

The spell was broken by Colton Banyon. "But that still leaves three names," Banyon pointed out to everyone.

"That's right," a sadder Maya responded as she wiped her eyes with a tissue. She looked down, at a sheet of paper and continued. "Two of the people in the ledger have simply disappeared. I'm having the FBI trace the names, but so far no luck."

"Give me the names, Maya and I'll have Wolf find them," Banyon said as he opened a draw and rummaged around, with his hands, for a pen and paper.

"Loni, where can I find a pen and paper?"

"I thought you would never ask?" She remarked.

As he looked up, Loni handed him both. She then showed him her hand, where her green jade ring glistened in the kitchen lights. She had a wide grin on her face. Banyon smiled back and grabbed the items, preparing to write.

"The first name is Bernard Schultz," Maya then spelled out the last name.

"Wolf has mentioned his name before," Banyon announced, but it was a month ago, when everything was going down with the Chinese and Albert Spitz. I've been a little busy since then. I have not followed up with Wolf on him," Banyon admitted.

"Why haven't you?" Pramilla asked.

"You need to pay more attention to us," Pramilla said sharply as she pointed at each of the people at the island.

"What?" Banyon said in confusion.

"We can't solve these mysteries without knowing the details, especially if you keep them in your head," she added.

"I'm sorry," he replied sincerely.

"The second name is Werner Koltz," Maya read from the paper.

"Okay, I'll check on him too, when I talk to Wolf," Banyon promised. "That still leaves one name."

"I know and it gets a little more complicated here," Maya said.

"How so?"

"Her name was Hilda Brand," Maya said.

"A woman?" questioned Banyon. He knew it was very uncommon for the Nazis to include a woman in their plans. To the old-line Nazis, a woman was meant for one thing. They were meant for breeding. "Why would she be listed?"

"I think I can answer that," Maya told him. "Her first husband was named Wilber Brand. He was a high-ranking Nazi General, but was killed fighting the communists, in Spain, around nineteen-thirty five. He must have drawn her into the Effort before he died." Maya said as speculation.

"That's possible," Banyon admitted.

"You said was," Loni interrupted.

"That's right, she is also dead, but has left a legacy. According to our research, she married a powerful American, who was pro-Nazi. They had a son who is now a very prominent public figure."

"His name is Paul Slezeck. He is the Director of Homeland Security," Banyon suddenly threw out.

"How did you know?" Maya asked with a surprised and annoyed look on her face. All the women in the room suddenly had their hands on their hips, a sure sign he was in trouble for guessing the name.

"Actually, Wolf told me this morning that Slezeck is working on a plan and we needed to go after him," he sheepishly replied.

"Well, why am I doing all this work if Wolf can tell you everything?" an indignant Maya demanded as she threw up her arms in disgust.

"Actually, he can't. He can see everything, but, that covers a lot of ground. He needs a name and a reference point to start. We now have both, for the three people left on the list," he said brightly, trying to deflect their ire.

"What else has he told you that you have not passed on to us?" Previne spat out sarcastically. "You know, since you have been tied up with your new position, you don't pay any attention to any of us anymore."

Eric was moving back from the island. He could see that the Patel sisters and Loni were pissed and he didn't want any of their wraths, to come down on him.

"But I only started today," he said defensively.

"That's no excuse for ignoring your friends," Previne spat back. Loni was nodding her head in agreement.

"He made $440,000 dollars today at the office," Loni said, as if the money was tainted. "I had to drag it out of him, too." She looked at him accusingly.

"I'll bet he is keeping it all to himself, selfish lout that he is," Previne began throwing more gas on the fire.

"Yeah, he cares more about the President then he does you, Loni," Pramilla said as she whipped the flames into a firestorm. Banyon could feel the growing hostility. Anger now fuelled the women in his life. They were all mad at him. He was now consumed with stress. *What have I done to deserve this?*

"Okay, I'll talk, just stop browbeating me," he said, in surrender, and threw up his hands defensively.

"Now, we are getting somewhere," Previne said as she slammed her hand on the counter top. "Tell us what Wolf said today. What were you were involved in at the office?"

"I'm not supposed to tell anyone about today," he started. He noticed the women become rigid with their fists clinched. They were about to blow. "But I want nothing hidden between us," he lied when he continued.

"Spill the beans, Colton," Previne demanded. Her body was shaking with frustration; a furrow had developed, on her forehead. Banyon thought she looked rather alluring.

"The President's granddaughter was kidnapped by a drug cartel in Cancun. Wolf and I helped the President get her and five other girls freed. It was a very stressful day and now I have to deal with all of you chewing on my ass."

"Oh, I had no idea," Maya said as she brought her hand to her mouth.

"I saw it on the news," Loni suddenly added. "Over fourteen people died, but none of them were Americans."

The women recoiled in horror. They had been involved in many gun battles in the recent years, and, in the last one, they had lost Agent Gregory Gamble.

"That's right, so you can't tell anyone," Banyon pleaded. "There are many people involved. The Mexican President thinks Americans came to his country, to do the killing, which, of course, we did."

"My lips are sealed," Previne quickly said as she made a gesture like closing a zipper on her pouty lips.

"It gets worse. The dead cartel leader was recently talking to someone in Washington D.C. They had provided the information about the granddaughter to the cartel. The President wants me to find out who made the call. I was going to ask Wolf, a little later. Wolf told me earlier today the kidnapping was part of a bigger plan by the Effort. It was controlled by Paul Slezeck. Is that enough information?" Banyon replied sarcastically.

"Oh," Previne exclaimed.

"And for your information, I have already told Loni to use some of the money, to add desks, in her office, for each of you. We are also going to put in a state of the art communications system for you to use." Loni shook her head in agreement. Her ponytail whipped up and down.

"Yeah, he did, but it was only after I threatened to go to his office and scope out the women there," Loni announced. This raised eyebrows on all the women. The Patel women were also very jealous of any woman that looked at Banyon.

"I was going to offer the money anyway, Loni," Banyon said sincerely. "I was just trying to keep everything secret."

"I'm sorry for doubting you, Colt," Pramilla the career diplomat quickly said. "You're right; this information can never get out. It could create an international incident. I don't think America wants to go to war with Mexico."

"I don't know if Wolf can tell me the plan because it would be telling me the future, but I don't think the kidnapping was just an opportunity. I think there will be more incidents. Wolf told me that Slezeck wants the President distraught, so he could further his goals, whatever they are."

"Why don't you talk to him right now and get some answers?" Pramilla proposed.

"I have several questions for Wolf that only the President should know the answers too," Banyon replied. "Besides, he is always tricky with his responses. I need a quiet environment to talk to him," Banyon said defensively.

"In other words," Previne said, "You want us to go."

Before Banyon could respond, Maya cut in. "Well, we need to discuss the other reason we are here first."

18

For most of its history, Laredo, Texas, had been a small prosperous city, on the Mexican border. It is separated from Mexico by the, not very wide, Rio Grande River. The sister city of Nuevo Laredo, Mexico, is twice the size of the American Laredo, with around a half a million people. Ninety-five percent of the citizens of Laredo, Texas are Latino and Hispanic, with the vast majority of them having Mexican roots.

Laredo, Texas was originally a part of an independent republic known as the *Republic of the Rio Grande*, but had been folded into Mexico by force. At the end of the *Mexican-American War,* in the mid-eighteen hundreds, the land north of the Rio Grande River was ceded to the United States. It is one of the oldest border crossing points along the lengthy U.S. and Mexican border.

Today, it is a major transportation and warehousing hub for goods flowing in and out of Mexico. Roughly half of all the goods the U.S. exports to Mexico pass through the port city, and about a third of Mexico's exports are hauled over the five international bridge crossings and railroad lines. As a result, it is also a major crossing point for illegal drugs.

For nearly a decade, at least two drug cartels have fought for control of the drug trafficking trade on both sides of the border. The majority of violence is confined to Nuevo Laredo, but some does spill into the U.S. side. On any given day, gunshots in Nuevo Laredo can be heard on the American side of the border. Carjacking, kidnapping, extortion and seemingly random shootings are common place. With the constant flow of drugs and the continued number of illegal aliens slipping across the border, the Border Patrol is undermanned, out gunned, often out maneuvered, and can do little to help Mexican authorities. However, there are people who get involved. These people report the news.

KAVT is a Spanish speaking entertainment station, located in the heart of downtown Laredo. The news department consisted of two anchors, Mia Chavez and Alberto Delgado, and a crew of six other people who ran the cameras, the sound equipment, and directed the news. In order to build ratings, the two anchors, much to the protests of management, had ventured into Mexico several times, in an attempt to provide investigative reporting to their viewers. They had uncovered several names of cartel members and even a location of a cartel warehouse, in the U.S. They had been threatened, many times and ordered to drop the investigation, by phone, email and letters. But they believed, what they did was important.

The news segment started at eleven o'clock each evening during the week, just as the rest of the staff went home for the evening. The station signed off at mid-night. There usually was no one else in the building during the news broadcast.

At about the same time as Banyon, and his team, were hugging each other, the pretty anchorwoman, Mia Chavez went live and started reporting the news. Suddenly, noise of a commotion could be heard in the background. Her eyes grew wide as a man dressed in Mexican army fatigues walked brazenly onto the set. His head was covered by a black ski mask and he carried an automatic gun in his hand. He walked behind the two anchors. They were frozen with fright. He placed the gun on the back Alberto Delgado's head.

In Spanish, he began to talk. "My friends, we have warned you many times to stop reporting the news of our business. It is time we end this. Say good night Alberto," the man said loudly.

The stunned anchorman hesitated for a minute, causing the hooded man to nudge him with the gun. "Good night," Delgado whispered. The hooded man nodded in agreement, he then shot him, in the head, on screen. Mia screamed, but was made quiet as the man moved the smoking gun to her head.

"Shut up, bitch," he growled. "Don't move a muscle." Mia heard six more shots as all of the news crew were shot by other men, off camera. She was now alone in the news room with several killers.

The hooded man then thrust a sheet of paper into her hands and said, "Read it."

Mia stared at the paper, unable to understand the words because of her absolute terror. She knew she was going to die. "I can't," she muttered.

"You will live if you read it," the hooded man announced. "Otherwise, you will receive the same treatment as Delgado."

With tears streaming down her face, Mia began to read what was written on the paper in front of her. She had just finished the first two words, when the hooded man roared and slapped the back of her head.

"Say it in English, so all Americans can understand."

She tried to compose herself and wiped the tears away with her hand. She was resigned to dying, but decided she needed to act dignified and make her life count. She sat up straighter in her seat and looked at the camera, as she held the paper in front.

"Americans stop interfering in business that does not involve you. This is our business, not yours. Today your government killed several innocent Mexican citizens, on Mexican soil. This is an act of war. Those responsible must come forward and accept our justice. If this does not happen by tomorrow night, at this time, we will execute more of you. No one is safe. We are always watching."

Mia then dropped the paper and prepared to be shot in the head.

"Now sign off, Mia," the hooded man ordered.

She immediately said. "This is Mia Chavez reporting. Good night."

19

"Okay, what's the other reason that you are here?" Banyon questioned Maya suspiciously.

"Well, it has to do with what else I found in the ledger," Maya replied. "There were more than just names in it."

"So, what else is written in it?"

"There is a treasure map and we are going to find that treasure," Previne announced excitedly as she jumped up and down like a school girl.

"What kind of treasure?" Banyon asked.

Ignoring his question, Previne spoke rapidly. "But we need Loni to go with us to hunt for it."

Surprised by the comment, Loni was suddenly suspicious, herself. "Why would you want me to go with you, even if I could go?"

"Because you need to help us sail the ship," Pramilla said matter-of-factly.

"Is it a boat or a ship?" Banyon needed qualification.

"What's the difference?" Pramilla asked as she showed frustration by flapping her slender arms.

"A ship is big enough to carry a boat. A boat cannot carry a ship," Banyon replied to qualify.

"It's a boat then," Pramilla replied.

"What boat?" Loni asked as excitement started to build in her little body. She was bouncing up and down now too.

"The one that an old friend is lending us so we can sail to the spot and dive for the treasure, of course" Pramilla informed her.

"Oh, my God," Loni exclaimed. "I need to pack." She started to leave the kitchen island even before she knew where she was going. Her impulsive nature had gotten her in trouble many times before.

"But you'd better hurry, our private plane leaves in two hours," Pramilla pointed out. "I've also gotten one of my friends to lend us his corporate jet, while he is in prison. We'll be gone at least four days, pack several bathing suits."

Banyon was confused and panicked. He knew he and Loni were being railroaded and he had to put a stop to it. Holding up his hands, Banyon said. "Hold on, let's start at the beginning. Maya what did you actually find? Let's start there."

"Alright," she said. "As you know, Kammler was very detail oriented," she replied. "One of the pages in the ledger contained notes, he had written about another member of the Effort. The notes were dated July 23rd, 1939."

"That was probably just before he visited the cave in Death Valley for the last time," Pramilla noted.

"Right," Maya told her. "Anyway, the notes were about additional German plunder. It seems an Effort member, his name was Gregor Kahn, was supposed to deliver a small chest, loaded with diamonds and other precious stones, to someone in Istanbul. He would smuggle the loot into South America and put in a bank vault there. The stones were earmarked for the Effort fund for America."

"Where did they come from?" Banyon suddenly asked.

"From what I can tell," Maya said, "they came from Romanian Jews. At that time, Romania was an ally of Germany, which meant the Jews in Romania were being systemically stripped of their possessions and lives."

"But something happened," Previne butted in.

"Right again sis," Maya agreed. "Kahn traveled, by land, from a town called Bacau, in Romania, to the Ukrainian port, of Odessa," she then paused to let that sink in.

"But that was under communist control then," Banyon the historian pointed out to the women.

"He was disguised as a peasant," Maya told him. "He hired a fishing boat to take him out into the Black Sea. At sea, he transferred to a fast-attack German torpedo boat, known as a *Schnellboot*."

"The allies called them E-boats, for enemy boats," Banyon quickly pointed out. "They were mostly used in the Mediterranean Sea, but some made their way into the Black Sea during the war."

"And they were hunted down by the communists, who control the Black Sea," Maya continued. "This E-boat was no exception. Soon after Kahn transferred over, the E-boat came under attack by several communist war ships. Kahn realized he was never going to make it to Turkey, so he dumped the chest over the side of the boat, radioing Kammler that he had failed. The E-boat was sunk four miles off the coat of the Romanian city of Constanta, in about fifty feet of water."

"Maya, I'm sure the boat would have been found and looted already," Banyon suddenly felt they were going on a wild goose chase.

"That's true Colt, but the chest was dropped, several miles, before the communists sunk the boat, I have the exact coordinates. Kammler wrote them in the ledger, thinking that someday he could go back and pick up the loot. But of course, Petra made sure he didn't have a chance to collect it."

"You have the exact coordinates?" Banyon asked with growing excitement.

"Not only that, but the box is two foot square and has metal hinges. They will be easy to spot with the modern equipment on the boat."

"What was the chest made of?" Banyon inquired.

"Wood."

"Well, bad luck there," he replied. "After seventy years, the wood and probably the metal have completely disintegrated. The stones have probably washed away."

"What do you know about the Black Sea?" Maya suddenly asked him. There was scorn in her voice. "I am not an idiot."

Taken a little bit back, Banyon decided to impress her. "Well, I know at one time it once was a much smaller, fresh water, lake, with no inlet to the Mediterranean Sea. This was thousands of years ago, of course. It was formed from runoff from the great glaciers. But the seas rose, at the end of the last ice age, around 5,000 B.C. Many scientists today believe, sea-water flowed up an old riverbed from the Mediterranean Sea and began empting into the Black

Sea, making it a large inland sea. The scientists believe that it took maybe a hundred years to fill. It is a mile and a half deep in the middle." Banyon proudly stated from memory.

"But did you know that much of the Black Sea is dead?" Maya asked.

"I don't understand, what that means?" Banyon said with a perplexed look. "There is a huge fishing industry in the Black Sea."

"Let me explain," Maya the archeologist said. "The Black Sea is formed like a big bowl." She used her arms to demonstrate. "Below the surface currents, the water is basically stagnant because there is no outlet for the currents to mix the water. As a result, oxygen can't be replenished. Without oxygen, nothing lives in the water. They are considered dead zones, or *anoxic zones*."

"No algae?" Banyon asked.

"Nothing lives in the zones," Maya said, while shaking her head. "And as a result of that, anything which falls into these zones; does not deteriorate. Colt, they are finding pieces of wood thousands of years old in these areas. Much of the Black Sea has not even been explored. Until the collapse of the Soviet Union in 1989, scientists were not even allowed in many areas of the Black Sea. It's only recently that exploration has begun. So far they have found several entire villages still standing and many boats."

"So, you think it is still intact?" Banyon said as his enthusiasm grew.

"It is right on the edge of one of the anoxic zones. We should easily reach it in scuba equipment."

"Well hang on, I'm going to consult with an expert," Banyon threw out. "Wolf," he yelled out. "Does this chest still exist?"

"Yes, it most certainly does," the voice replied. "I am looking at it right now. It is half buried in sand, but they should find it, easily. Colt, please talk to me later, I have news to tell you," Wolf added.

"Well, I guess we are going on a treasure hunt," Banyon cheerfully announced to the group. They were all jumping up and down now, clapping hands and hooting.

Suddenly serious, Previne cleared her throat and spoke. "Only Loni is going, Eric is staying here with you."

"What?"

"You see, Eric can't get caught in that part of the world. He will never make it past immigration. His face is on record, so he can't go," Pramilla said.

Banyon looked to Eric. "That's true Colt. This area is off limits because of some things I did when I was a SEAL. It was secret government stuff, you understand."

"And we need four people to sail the boat," Previne informed him. "So, Loni needs to go with us on this treasure hunt. Don't worry, I know the area, she will be safe."

"It's up to her," Banyon looked right at Loni as he said it.

"What is the weather like?" Loni asked. "Just so I know what to pack."

"It's summer there, so lots of bikinis," Previne responded with a grin. "It will be a mini-vacation for just girls."

Banyon suddenly had visions of all four women, in small bikinis, prancing around the deck of a sail boat, in the hot sun. He wanted to go too.

"But it'll take me more than two hours to pack," Loni said nervously.

"Well, you better get started," Banyon joked.

"Sweetie, just pack your essentials," Previne told her. "We will land in Odessa around mid-day. We can't board the sailboat until the next morning. I believe Colt could spring for some new outfits, can't you Colt?"

"I'll buy all your outfits," Banyon announced.

"That won't cost you much," Previne replied sexily. "We plan on being nude most of the time.

20

It was well after mid-night when Banyon finally sat down in his great room and prepared to contact Wolf. He mixed himself a *stoli* and tonic, to calm his nerves. He placed a pen and paper on his knee.

The last hour had been a whirl-wind, with Loni packing, unpacking and repacking one small suitcase many times. Her clothes were strewn everywhere in the bedroom as she discarded what she decided she didn't need. Banyon chuckled to himself. *Elizabeth would have a lot of laundry to deal with in the morning*. Pramilla finally had gone in the bedroom to help her pack. Maya and Previne continued to chat about their upcoming adventure at the kitchen island. Eric had gone to watch TV. Banyon could see Eric was dejected over not being able to participate. He felt dejected too, but knew the girls wanted to do this on their own. Along the way, it was decided that Eric would stay at Banyon's house so he went back to their house and returned with a suitcase of his own. When the girls left, he told Banyon he was going to bed, leaving Banyon alone to talk to Wolf.

"Wolf, are you out there?" Banyon started.

"I am here," the spirit replied.

Not sure where to start, Banyon decided to ask Wolf about old business first. "Did you find out who was calling the drug leader in Cancun?"

"It was Werner Klotz," Wolf quickly replied.

That's interesting," Banyon said. "He is on my list of people for you to find. Who is he?" Banyon asked.

"Werner Klotz is a long-time lobbyist in Washington D.C. His offices have represented several administrations since he started the firm in the nineteen-fifties. He is a member of the Effort and a good friend of Paul Slezeck. He currently lobbies for organizations who want to ban guns in America."

"But that sounds so opposite of Nazi beliefs, doesn't it?"

"On the contrary, Colt," Wolf replied. "Remember the long term goal of the Nazis, now the Effort, is to take over America. Without guns, how will people defend themselves against this menace?"

"Now it makes sense," Banyon realized as he made some notes. "So by appearing the opposite of the Effort, he is actually helping them," Banyon speculated. "But why would he call drug dealers in Mexico?"

"It is part of a bigger plan."

"Explain the plan would you?"

"The Effort now realizes a political takeover of the government is many years away, maybe decades. So, they are concentrating on fixing what they feel are problems they can actually influence. They are Americans, after all. They want the best for their country. It's just that they go about fixing things brutally and ruthlessly."

"So, why, kidnap the President's granddaughter?"

"They want to put pressure on the President to make him so upset, he makes a mistake," Wolf replied.

"What do they want?"

"Slezeck wants the President to sign a new executive order. It would beef up Homeland Security. The new order would nearly double the size of the agency, especially the Border Patrol, and would give them powers to clean up the illegal alien issue while wiping out the drug cartels. America has the technology and the intelligence to do it."

"Wolf, I kind of agree with doing that. Why won't the President sign the order?"

"The order gives Homeland Security too much power. Under the proposed guidelines, no one would be safe from the agency. While, they will be able to fix these current problems, they will also eliminate anyone that stands in their way. Remember, collateral damage means nothing to these people."

"So, the plan is to force the President to give Homeland Security more powers, is that right?"

"Yes." The answer sent chills up Banyon's spine. His experience with the secret agency had not been good in the past. They already had the ability to take over any investigation, without passing any information back. They also had the Patriot Act, to arrest anyone they chose, and a fast attack small army with extreme powers. They controlled TSA, the Border Patrol and even the Coast guard. They were pretty powerful already.

"What else do they plan to do?"

"You know I can't tell you that Colt. But I can tell you what they have already done. It is very damaging."

"What else has happened?"

"First, Klotz has leaked to the Mexican President that Americans were responsible for the takedown in Cancun. The Mexican President is furious and is considering an act of war against the U.S. But there is more."

"So, now both Presidents are upset," Banyon noted. "What has happened since?"

"A few hours ago, a group of men, dressed like the Mexican military, broke into a TV station in Laredo, Texas and killed all the news people, on air. They also made the anchorwoman read a statement. It said, the drug cartels intend to do more violence, even kill more people, if America doesn't stop the war on drugs."

"My God," Banyon muttered. "The President will want to know who did that. Can you help?"

"I can help, but it's already too late. The damage is already done," replied Wolf. "A video disk is currently on the way to the White House. The disk was shot from a hidden camera in a drug cartel safe house in Mexico. The FBI knows about the house and has it in their records."

"What's on the disk?"

"It clearly shows the men who invaded the TV station. Just as they are celebrating and taking off their masks, several men in American SWAT uniforms break in. They executed the men. All were made to kneel and were shot in the head, just like they did to the news people. The SWAT team speaks English. It looks like pure retaliation."

"Is it?"

"No, it was all arranged through Werner Klotz, to make it look like America is as ruthless as the cartels."

"It sounds like a ping pong match across two borders," Banyon muttered to himself. "So the ultimate goal is to get the President to sign the executive order, right?"

"Slezeck has scheduled a news conference early tomorrow morning. He intends to tell American they have the ability to stop the killings, but the inept, ultra-liberal, President refuses to sign the document."

"Will it stop the killings?"

"No."

"But if I tell the President Werner Klotz is responsible, won't he stop Klotz from implementing more of the plan?"

"That is exactly what Slezeck wants you to do. He is not above sacrificing Klotz to further his agenda. When the President signs the order to take out Klotz, Slezeck will blackmail him into signing the Homeland Security document. Everybody will have blood on their hands, including the President."

"So, what should I do?"

"Tell the President he cannot know who is arranging the killings because it is a trap. Get approval for using some of the Dewey & Beatem people to take Klotz down publicly. You and Eric need to do this."

"Wait a second," Banyon said, as he backed up to something Wolf had already said. "You said Slezeck knows I will tell the President about Werner Klotz. How does he know that?' Banyon felt fear growing in his throat.

"You heard correctly," Wolf calmly answered. "Slezeck knows about you and your team. He also knows that you can help the President, but does not know that we are on to him. In fact, Klotz has contracted for a group of killers to eliminate all of you on orders from Slezeck. The killers will be arriving in Chicago tomorrow. They intend to hunt each of you down, which is why I got the girls to go out of town."

"You arranged that?"

"I gave Maya a little nudge to look more closely at the ledger. Don't worry; no one knows where they have going. They are very safe, but you and Eric are not."

Feeling more stress than ever before, Banyon asked. "So what do we do to protect ourselves?"

"Go to the office tomorrow, take Eric with you. They can't get to you there. Hire some body guards from the staff. After work, get on a plane and head to your condo in Las Vegas. It will take the hit men time to find you. Take the bodyguards with you. I will arrange for some of my other friends to watch your place until you get there."

Banyon knew Wolf could talk to other people who worked on different projects for him. Some of them had helped protect Banyon during other mysteries. "So you want me to run and hide?"

"You need time to figure out how to take down Klotz and also Slezeck. This buys you the time. We will take on the hit men on our terms."

Banyon realized that Wolf was right. He needed some time to figure out what to do about the Efforts plans. He did have one more question. "But Wolf, what about the other name on the Maya's list, Bernard Schultz?"

"He can wait," Wolf replied.

21

While Banyon prepared to sleep, knowing it was probably a fruitless effort, Werner Klotz was still at his desk, in his office, near the White House. Despite being over ninety years old, he still often worked late, especially since he didn't want anyone in his office to know about his work for the Effort.

He had just received notice from his contact that the Mexican hit team would land in Chicago and begin their killings by the mid-afternoon tomorrow. He didn't know why Slezeck wanted these people dead, but he knew there must be a reason. It also meant Klotz would have to travel to Chicago in the morning. He didn't dare send the photos and information about people he wanted killed over the internet. He needed to meet them in Chicago to give them the information.

He made arrangements to leave at ten o'clock in the morning. He would take a private jet to Chicago, hand out the information, make the payment at a car rental agency parking lot near Midway airport, and return home. As he looked at the pictures he wondered why Slezeck would want to kill all these beautiful women. *Why not just take them and use them for fun*, he thought. But he knew better than to question Slezeck.

Werner Klotz had spent the afternoon at a lovely state luncheon, at the White House, where he planted some damaging information. It would send the government into panic tomorrow morning. When he was satisfied he had caused enough damage, he returned to his office to create more mayhem.

During the evening, from his office, he had arranged for more killings. He contracted for a man to drive a car, filled with explosives, up to the main border-crossing checkpoint in Laredo. The man would approach from the Mexican side.

The plan was to have the man leave the car right under the police overhang. Another man would detonate the bomb by remote control, from across the river, in Mexico.

This would cause the border to be closed along its entire length, trade goods, people, and even drugs would be prohibited from passing through. Soon, there would be discontent, even riots on the bridges. Immense pressure would be put on the guards on both sides of the border. No one would take credit for the bombing which would add to the confusion and growing anger. The Effort's plan was working. The President would be under a huge strain.

He had more mayhem to schedule but decided he wanted to be awake to watch the drama unfold in the morning, at 9:00 A.M. Eastern Time. So, he closed his light and headed off to bed, chuckling to himself.

22

The President was woken at 6:30 A.M. It was one hour after the White House staff had received the special delivery disk, sent by private messenger. He had gone to bed, contemplating what to do about the massacre of the American news people, but now had to switch gears in an attempt to deflect the damaging video. The very reputation of the United States was on the line. He charged into his office and found the DOJ, Marlene Moore, standing there, right in front of his desk.

"Swear to me your people didn't do this, Marlene?" he ordered as he plopped into his executive chair.

"We did know about the safe house, but have never crossed the border with any force, sir," she quickly replied. "Why would someone try to pin this on us?"

"That is the same question I am asking you, goddammit."

"We have to call a news conference and deny it," she reasoned.

"I have to give the public more or we will just look like school children caught with our hands in the cookie jar," he replied.

"The Mexican President has already said as much in a news conference, late last evening. He got a copy of the video, as well. He has also put his military on high alert."

"How long ago?" the President showed sudden interest.

"He held his special report at two o'clock in the morning Mexico City time."

"Well, let's figure out a way to spin this," the President said as he pressed a button on his phone. "Get the usual crowd into my office, now," he ordered his secretary.

The secretary quickly replied. "Ah...Mr. President the Director of Homeland Security is here. He says he needs to see you urgently."

"Send him in," the President ordered. Within seconds, Paul Slezeck burst through the door, but hesitated, as he eyed the DOJ, standing in the oval office.

"What do you want?" the President asked in a gruff voice.

"This should be done in private, sir," he announced, as he stared at Marlene. "And she doesn't have the clearance, nor should she," Slezeck added.

"The DOJ stays."

"Very well," Slezeck conceded. He then continued. "It is about the executive order we discussed several days ago."

The President didn't like Slezeck, but he had been appointed by the previous administration. There was something about him that was underhanded and sleazy. The President did not feel he could trust him. "What about it?"

"I think it is time for you to sign it, sir. Our borders are under siege. Americans are dying. We can put a stop to the threat, if we had your backing." He brought out a folder with the prepared document inside, attempting to hand it to the President.

"Not now Paul. I'm in the middle of a crisis. Make an appointment for next week," the President said off handily as he dismissed the Director.

"Let's hope it is not too late by then," Slezeck pouted as he left the office.

23

Banyon got up around 7:00 A.M. He showered and got dressed in business casual clothes. He called Elizabeth, the house keeper, and told her not to come in, but promised a week's wages anyway. She was delighted. He just wanted to keep her safe, in case some bad guy decided to come to his house. He then packed a small travel bag and went to wake up Eric. He told Eric he had to go to the Law firm with him this morning. He said he would explain everything in the car, on the way. He had just finished making coffee, when Eric entered the kitchen dressed in ripped blue jeans and a wrinkled shirt.

"Eric, we are going to a Law firm, for god sakes. Now, go back and change into better clothes and shave. Don't forget to bring your bag either," Banyon reprimanded him, just like he had done with his own sons, so many times.

"But I want to wear these clothes," Eric protested.

"Not today. Now hurry," Banyon ordered.

While Eric went and changed, Banyon tried to collect his thoughts. He tried to figure out what he would tell Eric about the office staff at the Law firm. Eric would be stuck there all day as Banyon put his own plan in motion. Eric returned in less than ten minutes dressed in respectable clothes, he said nothing as they started out for the office.

Once they were in the car, Banyon explained about the Effort's plan, telling him all he knew about the hit squad. "So, we are going to have to protect each other for a few days. When we get to the office, I'll get both of us guns."

"And you're sure the girls are safe?" Eric asked.

"They are safe, Wolf will watch over them, as well." Banyon told him.

"I'm kind of glad to be away from them for a few days, but I want them back," Eric suddenly said.

"Why do you say that?" Banyon cautiously asked.

"I told you," Eric replied. "They have a different concept of open marriage. They like to share, especially me. I just need a little time to recover," he remarked. "Loni has no idea what she is in for," he added.

"What does that mean?" Banyon said with a little panic in his voice.

"Well, you know, they are going to be prancing around, on a private yacht, naked in the soothing, hot sun, sleeping in only two bunk beds, on the rolling sea. I know you have seen them naked Colt. Sex oozes from their bodies. Loni is also beautiful and sexy. The Patel sisters will find her hard to resist."

"There are only two bunk beds on the boat?" Banyon repeated in shock.

"Two small bunk beds," Eric responded.

Banyon suddenly had a vision of oiled up, naked bodies, withering in the sunshine, and teasing each other. *What will Loni do?* He wondered, she was always impulsive and she certainly loved sex. *Was it too farfetched for her to get involved?* he wondered.

"I'd just like to watch," Eric noted.

Banyon thought he would too, but didn't say it. He decided to change the subject. "Eric, the employees of the Law firm are a bit unusual, so be prepared."

"How so?"

"None of them are who they appear to be. They each have more than one talent. In fact, I'm going to have you interview several of them to find us some bodyguards. We are going to take them to Las Vegas with us for protection. How does that sound?"

"I just hope they all aren't muscle bound and dumb."

24

At precisely 8:00 A.M., central time, a car bomb exploded at the largest of the Laredo checkpoints. Thirty people were immediately killed, with several hundred injured. Cars and trucks were thrown everywhere. The main office of the Border Patrol was completely flattened and six Border Patrol officers simply disappeared. The remaining officers was so shocked, no one knew what to do. Finally, the remaining agents on duty closed all the remaining gates, moving vehicles to block where the gates had been destroyed. A call for help and a recall to all off-duty agents quickly ensued.

The bridge looked like it had been hit with a nuclear bomb, it appeared very unstable, causing thousands of pedestrians and drivers to begin running from the site, shouting and screaming as they fled. It was complete chaos. Emergency services vehicles couldn't get near the bomb area, but the news helicopters found the scene in minutes. Werner Klotz roared with laughter, as the station he was watching, broke in, with the news flash.

He had just been watching the President of the United States reassuring the American public that the events of yesterday were unrelated and about to be solved. *Timing is everything*, he chuckled to himself. This disaster made the President look like an idiot; just as Werner had planned it.

Shortly, a limousine pulled up to his door and he left for the private airport feeling like he was the master of the world.

Part Three

Coping

25

As Banyon and Eric entered the reception area at Dewey & Beatem, Banyon immediately knew something had changed. Mandy was not running back and forth in the large reception area. Instead, she was standing behind the counter and she looked very different to him. As he ambled to the desk he realized she was still dressed in light blue, but her attire was not a speedo swim suit.

"Good morning Colt," she sweetly greeted him. "And who is this handsome young man with you," she added as she pointed her slim arm and now painted finger nails at Eric. She gave him her broadest smile, but didn't show her braces.

"Good morning Mandy," Banyon replied sincerely. "This is Eric. He is a good friend of mine and will be visiting with me for the entire day. I hope the firm doesn't have any rules against that?" he asked.

"Not for you Colt, you are an Alpha. You can do whatever you like, to all of us," she replied in a sexy voice as she spread her arms wide. *She is tempting me,* Banyon thought.

"Thanks for reminding me," he laughed, as he remembered his first day in the office. It was only yesterday.

"Okay, I hope I get to spend some time with both of you today?" Mandy pleaded in a more confident voice then yesterday.

"I don't know, we will be very busy," Banyon answered her as he signed in to the log book allowing Eric to visit.

"Colt, what do you think of my new image?" Mandy asked as she raised her arms and slowly rotated on the platform where she stood. Eric was nearly panting and moved closer to the counter. She wiggled her taunt body as she turned.

Banyon was concerned over her change in image and he thought he knew why. She had been pretty worked up yesterday and he had rejected her. When he left the office, Mandy and Heather were headed for the showers. Heather had clearly given Mandy some training and instructions.

She was dressed in a tiny mini-skirt. The tank-top was just like Heather had worn yesterday. She had on very high, stiletto-heeled, shoes. Large oval hoops hung from her ears. She looked very sexy and could easily pass for the ripe old age of seventeen.

"Eric, don't go near her, she is a world class pickpocket. She is also lightning fast at everything." Banyon quickly turned to Eric and told him.

"Nice," was all Eric said.

"And close your mouth," Banyon added.

"Heather has been giving me some more lessons. She is a quite a genius. She is very good at making me feel better," Mandy said, as she batted her now long lashes at Banyon. "She is not as frustrating as you are."

"How fast are you?" Eric blurted out.

"Well, Eric, I can't tell you, but I will gladly show you," she offered. Banyon could see she was preparing to leap over the counter like she had yesterday.

"Not now Mandy," Banyon said as an order. "There are a couple of situations we have to deal with right now."

"Maybe later then?" she replied as her posture slumped. She placed a dagger like stare at him, just like someone else he knew.

"We are headed up to my office right now. Please call Bart and tell him I need to see him immediately."

"Yes, sir, Mr. Ogre." She pouted, but winked at Eric. Banyon missed her flirt as he was already headed for the door to the offices. Eric winked back and followed.

In the hallway, Eric asked Banyon a question. "You seem to know her a little too intimately for working here only one day?"

"She was the contract employee from yesterday. We spend most of the day together. I believe she is still a virgin," he added to get him off track.

Soon, they were in Banyon's office and he inserted his Bluetooth. He quickly understood that something had happened; there was too much chatter in the phone line. He picked up the remote to the TV on the far wall and pressed it. The screen filled with pictures of the devastation from the bomb in Laredo. Eric took a seat on the modern couch; he was glued to the reporting. Banyon quickly whispered. "Wolf, what's happened?"

"Our friends have exploded a car bomb at the largest checkpoint on the Mexico and U.S. border. Many people died."

"You're sure they are responsible?"

"Werner Klotz made the contract on Slezeck's orders," Wolf replied. "Colt, you need to stop these people quickly. They are planning even more devastating disasters."

"I'm putting together my plan as we speak." Banyon then sat down and fired up his computer.

The screen had just come online, when Bart blew into the office. Today, he looked like an old college professor with a tweet jacket, complete with patches on the sleeves and a frizz of hair that was totally unkempt. He looked at Eric for a few seconds and then proceeded to the front of Banyon's desk.

"A client, I hope," he opened as he thumbed towards Eric.

"He is one of my team," Banyon replied.

"The President is looking for you," Bart quickly said. "The White House has already called, I have been told to offer you any and all of our services," Bart rubbed his hands together thinking of the huge billings he would soon receive.

"Well, we are certainly going to need some." Banyon told the managing partner. "First, I'm going to need two guns. One for me and one for Eric over there," Banyon started without preamble.

Bart stepped forward and shook his hands at the desk. There was a puff of smoked and two .45 magnums appeared on the desk. A second puff of smoke followed and a box of ammunition joined the guns.

"Will these do?"

Unimpressed by the trick, Banyon continued. "Next, I need two of your best surveillance people. They will need to record and get audio of a meeting. It needs to be done clandestinely, there can be no screw-ups. They will have a second, more dangerous mission when they finish, it needs to be done this morning."

"A surveillance team will be in your office within the hour," he calmly replied.

"I'm also going to need two bodyguards. They will need to travel. They will be gone with me and Eric for several days. Their assignment will be dangerous. They will need to be armed for protection."

"I have several to choose from," he answered.

"Eric will do the interviews, in this office, this morning," Banyon noted.

"I will set them up at half hour intervals, starting in at eight-thirty."

"I also need Timmy to do some hacking and eavesdropping. It may not be strictly legal as well," Banyon said as he looked him straight in the eye.

Bart pressed his Bluetooth and spoke quickly. "Timmy, get your scrawny ass to Colt's office. You have five minutes before I check the showers."

Banyon gave him a questioning look, "What?"

"Heather has already had her first appointment today. Timmy likes to go and watch her shower. She constantly flirts with him and then slams the door." He said as an explanation and then shrugged.

Banyon felt a little sorry for Timmy, he was clearly overmatched. "Finally, I have an assignment for you Bart. But I warn you, it could be very dangerous."

"What do I have to do?"

"I want you to impersonate someone."

"Tell me who. I can be ready by eleven o'clock."

"You'll need to be ready by nine o'clock. And be ready to travel locally."

"I'll be here by nine," Bart agreed. "So, who am I impersonating?"

Then Banyon told him.

26

Meanwhile, Paul Slezeck returned to his office and began setting the next stage of his plan in motion. He couldn't use Werner Klotz for this part, because Klotz was going to be the victim. He opened the folder he had carried into the President's office and began extracting pictures of Marlene Moore and Werner Klotz together. Slezeck had several people take the photos over several months. They, of course, knew each other as he was a lobbyist and she was part of the administration. Several photos showed her, along with Klotz, whispering into each other's ear at parties and socials. The most damaging photos were of her and Klotz, sitting on a bench, in a park. The series of photos showed her passing a folder to him.

It was actually a list of restaurants from her home state that Klotz had requested, but it looked like sensitive material in the photos. Slezeck then attached a phone list of the calls between them. Most of the calls were from Klotz, as Slezeck had requested little bits of information from her through him. Klotz had no idea that Slezeck was using him to create his own demise. But to anyone studying the material, it looked like he and Marlene were planning something.

When he had gone to the Presidents' office earlier in the day, he realized the President would not sign the executive order. He wasn't under enough stress yet. But Slezeck thought he would be ready when he found out that the person behind the disasters was Klotz and he was working with Marlene Moore. Having Marlene in the room was unexpected bad luck. Slezeck had expected the President to sign the receipt, for the pictures, in front of him. Now he had to set the trap in a different way.

Slezeck deluded himself into thinking Marlene Moore was his most powerful enemy. The FBI, she controlled, had a hand in the takedown of several Homeland Security people. They were all Effort members. He wanted to take revenge. He also wanted to send the FBI into chaos. He could then step in to rescue the agency. He wanted the FBI to be another agency under his control. He felt he could force the President to make the decision.

He had turned the corner, mentally; he believed that it was Homeland Security versus the world. He believed the employees of Homeland Security were his private army and he could fight anybody for control of America. He had lost his sanity, but that didn't mean he wasn't dangerous.

He included the damaging evidence for Wornor Klotz, as well, putting everything in a top secret, President's eyes only envelope. He added one more thing.

He had personally written a letter to the President about his "findings". He pointed out that he could not discuss his findings with him at the morning meeting, since Marlene was in the room. He added that Homeland Security could handle the takedown of Klotz and Marlene Moore, if the President desired. He also wrote he would come by at 2:00 P.M. to discuss the plan, and requested a signature, at the bottom of the memo, to confirm receipt of the documents. He suggested the President return the signed receipt, to his assistant, who would personally delivery the packet. He would wait for the receipt.

It was, however, a ruse. The paper had been specially treated with a chemical compound which had been invented, in a clandestine lab, of Homeland Security. The compound hid two addition sentences written, just above where the President would place his signature. The two sentences were:

Although I find it repugnant to terminate the lives of Americans, we at Homeland Security serve the President. Your signature will activate the process of eliminating Werner Klotz and Marlene Moore.

The President would not see the sentences, but five minutes after he activated the chemical compound, by signing the receipt with his pen, the words would appear on the paper. The compound would then dissipate into the air, without a trace. The letter would be an executive termination order from the President of the United States. It would be in Slezeck's hands, minutes later, thus giving him the leverage he needed.

Slezeck knew no forensics science had yet been invented to detect any trace of the compound. To anyone examining the paper, it would appear to be genuine. The document would give him what he needed.

Slezeck would immediately have Marlene and Werner terminated. He had people watching them already. He knew where they were at all times. He would then attend the afternoon meeting with the President. By that time, the last of Klotz's disasters would be completed and one of the President's biggest supporters would be dead. His stress level would be high enough for the President to be manipulated, especially when Slezeck showed him the signed termination letter.

It would be pure blackmail, to be sure, but Slezeck would get the President to sign the Homeland Security executive order in exchange for his destroying the letter. Nothing could stop Slezeck then.

Slezeck dreamed Homeland Security would become the true protector of the American people, as it was designed to be. Slezeck would close the borders, send forays into Mexico, and other countries, and cut off the head of many cartel snakes. Illegal immigrants would be rounded up and the road to the original plan of the Third Reich would be paved. So what if there was a little collateral damage. *With strength came some suffering*, he thought. In addition, he would never destroy the executive order signed by the President. He believed he might need it again someday.

He then thought about Colton Banyon. Slezeck knew Banyon had been instrument in the demise of many of his colleagues at the Effort. He didn't know how, but Banyon always seemed to have information about them. Slezeck had decided, some time ago, Banyon too, must go. The chaos Slezeck was creating was a perfect vehicle.

He had Werner Klotz hire a six-man hit team from Mexico. They would land in Chicago and eliminate Banyon's entire team today, hopefully, before his meeting with the

President. Banyon himself was under surveillance. Slezeck knew he was currently at the Law Firm of Dewey & Beatem.

Slezeck called in one of his best assistants. The young man appeared before his desk within minutes.

"Take this ultra-secret package to the President, immediately," Slezeck ordered.

"Yes, sir," the eager man said.

"And stand at his desk until he signs the receipt in the envelope. Bring it back to me immediately. Do you understand?"

"Yes, sir," the man replied.

"You can't leave the office until he signs the receipt. When he does sign it, immediately put it in this additional envelope and seal it. Bring it back to me as quickly as possible," Slezeck demanded.

"Doesn't that break protocol?" the assistant pointed out. It was not the way things were done at the White House.

"Let's put it this way," Slezeck leered. "Either get him to sign it, or don't bother to come back here."

27

Bart had just left the office when Timmy came jogging in. He didn't even look at Eric and proceeded to the front of Banyon's desk. "You called, oh great one," he then bowed with his arms extended out.

"Your zipper is open," Banyon noted dryly.

"Oops," Timmy quickly replied, zipping up his pants. His face was now the color of a fire engine.

"You know," Banyon said philosophically, as he shook his head. "If you ignored her, you would have a better chance. Right now, she is tormenting you and loving it. Take away her fun, let's see what happens."

"Those are righteous words," Timmy admitted as he bounced from one foot to the other. "I'll try."

"Well, right now you are going to be very busy. I need you to do some hacking. I need it done quickly. It may not be strictly legal, as well."

"My fingers are ready," he answered as he pretended to be working a keyboard. "Who is the chosen one?"

"His name is Werner Klotz. I need you to dig up all you can about him, especially any contacts with Paul Slezeck. In addition, I want you to tap his phones, and to steal all his emails from the last six months."

"Those are some heavy dudes," Timmy said.

"I also need you to cut off communications between them. Any calls, to each other, needs to be routed to you and sent to a dead voicemail box. No emails or messages can go through either."

"Piece of cake," Timmy replied.

"I need it done in less than two hours, too."

"Heavy," Timmy muttered as he scratched is day old beard.

"Can you do it?"

"I'm not supposed to ask, man, but why these guys? It might help if I know what to look for. There will be a lot of data."

Banyon thought for a second and decided the Timmy would be more useful if he knew what to look for while sifting through the data. "Do you know about the crap going on with Mexico right now?"

"Kind of scary, huh, dude?"

"Well, these two are responsible. We are going to take them down, but we need to connect them together. You will be looking for proof of their conspiracy. We also need to know why they are doing it. I have a good idea, but I can't prove it yet. That will be your job. Can you handle it?"

"You're talking to the best hacker in the world; of course I can do it. I'll be back in two hours with some information." Timmy stopped moving and asked a question sheepishly. "How much are you paying me?"

"Don't know yet. But it will be more than enough to get you some new clothes," Banyon hinted. He was sure Timmy had noticed Mandy's new attire.

"Awesome," Timmy quickly said and pumped his skinny arm like a quarterback that had just thrown a touchdown. "Maybe she will notice me then?" he exclaimed. He turned on his heels and jogged out the door.

As Timmy left the office, Eric laughed and suddenly yelled out. "I'll bet he is your hacker, right?"

"How did you know?" Banyon responded.

"No social graces," he replied and chuckled. "He also dresses worse than me." Eric then got up and closed the office door, then returned to his couch. He resumed watching the big screen and the recuse efforts, from the explosion, in Laredo.

Banyon knew there was something he had to do, but was interrupted, by a knock at the door. Before Banyon could tell the knocker to enter, Eric bounded off the couch and opened it. He stepped back in horror.

Sister Teresa smoothly glided into the room, looking very angel-like. Her hands were steeped in prayer, her dimples showed on her smiling face. She turned to Eric and said softly, "Hello, I'm Sister Teresa." She then bowed slightly.

Banyon could see that Eric was in complete panic. He suddenly crossed himself and looked at the floor without moving. Banyon knew, like himself, Eric had been raised a Catholic. Growing up, Catholic children were required to take religious lessons. The nuns usually ran the classes. They were generally very tough on children who didn't know their lessons, or were disruptive. Banyon recalled one of the nuns carrying a wire hanger up her sleeve. If he didn't give the correct answers, she would whack him on the hands with it. Banyon lived in fear of the nuns, and apparently so did Eric. Sister Teresa looked at him expectantly, but remained as calm as a windless pond.

"I'm Eric Grey," Eric finally responded like he was in a lineup at a police station. He didn't raise his head.

"Please to meet you," the nun cheerfully countered as she held out her slender hand for him to shake. Eric reluctantly took it, shook it once, and then dropped it like a hot potato. It was clear to Banyon he was very uncomfortable around Sister Teresa.

"Don't worry, Eric, this is just one of her personas, she is not a real nun," Banyon yelled across the room to him.

"I am so," Sister Teresa replied indignantly. "I comfort people," she added as proof of her calling to a higher order.

"What are you doing here?" Banyon asked her.

"I am half of your surveillance team. The other half will be here in about ten minutes," she told him.

"You're a nun that does surveillance on people?" Eric questioned in disbelief.

"You would be surprised what I can hide under my habit," she remarked. "And no one pays attention to a nun. Most people are afraid, like Eric here," she nodded her head towards him as she spoke. "I am very good at watching people, Colt. I'm the best the firm has to offer," she added as she posed with her hands on her hips.

"Okay, I believe in you," Banyon held up his hands in defeat. "We'll start as soon as the other expert arrives. Until then, take a seat and wait."

She floated over to the couches and demurely took a seat on the edge of the couch. She sat across from Eric. She began talking to him in soothing tones. She looked like she was hearing confession from him. Banyon chuckled to himself. Eric had no idea what Sister Teresa was capable of doing.

Just then, his eye caught movement out on the overhang balcony. There was a flash of light blue and a lot of leg suddenly leaping over the railing. She once again struggled with the big door, but within seconds Mandy was standing very close, right next to him, with her back turned towards Eric.

"I heard you need a bodyguard Colt," she cooed breathlessly as she crossed her small arms confidently. "I'm your guy."

This surprised Banyon. He also felt this was all wrong, at so many levels. He struggled for something to say. "Well, I'm not the one doing the interviews for the job. Eric over there will hire the bodyguards. Also, Mandy, this might get very dangerous. Some people may be killed," he reasoned.

"I won't let anyone hurt you," she replied sincerely.

"And you need an appointment with him, anyway." He said to deflect her ambition.

As he glanced over to Eric, he noticed Sister Teresa was now standing over him and he had leaned back on the couch. He had a grin on his face and he wasn't watching the news. He was watching her hips pumping back and forth and her habit rising, just like she had done yesterday to Banyon.

When he turned back to Mandy, he noticed the determined, pouty look on her face. He also noticed her finger tips were touching her very short, light-blue, mini-skirt. She had already raised the hem two inches and showed no sign of stopping.

"But I have the first appointment," she whined and continued. "But it looks like Eric is a little busy now. So I'm talking to you instead."

"You're a bodyguard?" Banyon gasped, not believing her.

"Look, Colt," a suddenly furious Mandy uttered. "I am more physically fit then anyone here at the firm," she sputtered. "I'm second in firearms rating, in the firm, too. I'm faster and have greater reflexes then anyone alive. Yet I still constantly need to prove my worth to everyone. I thought you were different. I want the job," she demanded and stomped her small foot.

Holding his ground, but with more sympathy than a minute ago, Banyon said, "Well you are still going to need to convenience Eric." He thumbed towards the back of the office.

They both turned to look at him and saw Sister Teresa grinding her hips in front of Eric.

Eric was now grinning ear to ear. It looked like Eric wasn't afraid of nuns anymore.

Turning to look Banyon straight in the eye, Mandy said confidently. "It will be a piece of cake for me to convince him, don't you think?"

Not knowing what to say, Banyon turned to Eric and yelled out, "Your first appointment is here."

"I'll be just a minute," Eric replied in a husky voice.

Mandy batted her eyes at the cowering Banyon. "Well, I guess we will have a little more time before the interview. Perhaps we can get to know each other a little more," she breathed and raised her skirt and inch higher. *Why does she keep tempting me?* Banyon thought. *She is almost one third my age.*

28

The President cancelled all his scheduled appointments for the morning. He locked himself in the oval office, trying to make sense of everything that was happening. To him, it almost looked like someone was trying to discredit him and his administration. He wondered if it was some Arab terrorists, a Mexican cartel, the Chinese, the Mexican government, or was it people in his own country, like the Effort. Only one person could answer that and so far today, he hadn't called. *Where was Colton Banyon*, he wondered.

The buzzer on his phone notified him his secretary was calling him. "I know you don't want to be disturbed, but Kevin Davis is here from the Homeland Security office," the President's secretary spoke into the phone.

"I'm busy, I don't have time for anyone, including anyone from Homeland Security," the President replied gruffly into the phone.

"Sir, he says it is very urgent," his secretary insisted. "He has a 'President's eyes only' package with him. I think you should see him."

After a few seconds, the President acquiesced. "Very well, send him in, but tell him I only have a minute."

"Yes, sir,"

The President was sitting at his desk, with his head down, pretending to be reading some news clippings when Kevin walked through the door to the oval office. He closed the door after him and strolled up to the desk. "Good morning sir," he said.

The President actually liked Kevin Davis very much. He had known him since he was a little boy. He came from a good family. His father was a General over at the Pentagon and Kevin, like his father, was a proud graduate of West Point. The Davis family had a long history of service to their country, going back to the Civil War. He had gone into government work after he had fulfilled his obligation to the army. He was working his way through the bureaucracy of Homeland Security, intending to someday, become a leader of one of the divisions of the giant organization. The President trusted him. It was the only reason he agreed to see him now.

"What's so urgent?" the President asked as he looked up over his glasses.

"I have a 'Presidents eyes only' envelope from the Director," Kevin answered, without hesitation.

"But he was here only an hour ago? What's in the envelope?" The President felt the Director of Homeland Security was sometimes a little overbearing and an alarmist.

"I don't know, sir. I was just handed the package a few minutes ago and was ordered to deliver it to you. Director Slezeck also made me promise, to obtain your signature, on the receipt," Kevin said hopefully.

"Well, let's see what's so important," the President said with little humor as he stood up and made a hand gesture for Kevin to pass it over. He opened the package and looked inside without letting Kevin see the contents. He saw the personal letter enclosed inside and pulled it out dropping the package on his desk. As he read the letter, Kevin could see the change in emotions, on the Commander and Chief's face. At first, he saw absolute shock; then he saw growing anger. The President quickly composed himself.

"Kevin, you may go now," he said quietly as he continued to stare at the letter.

"But sir, Director Slezeck told me to come back with your signature, or not to come back at all," Kevin said with alarm.

After a few seconds the President answered. "Yes, yes, I understand why he would want the receipt," the now distracted President agreed. One of his top supporters was now the front running candidate for all the chaos that was happening, to him, and his country. "The Director of Homeland Security would want his ass covered on this," the President continued.

"Thank you for understanding, sir," Kevin said with relief.

The President picked up his pen and started to sign his name when suddenly, his private cell phone rang. He quickly grabbed it as he continued to write.

"Hello," he said evenly into the phone. Immediately his expression changed, He dropped the pen like it was on fire. He glanced at Kevin with a look of confusion and then stared at the letter receipt.

"Hold on a second," the President said into the phone. He covered the mouthpiece. To Kevin he growled, "Swear to me, you know nothing about what is in the package Mr. Davis."

Now nervous, Kevin quickly replied. "Sir, I swear on my family's name. I never saw or was explained anything about what is in the package," he replied with a cracking of his voice. "I was just told to get the receipt, or else."

The President quickly pressed a button under his desk and two secret service men suddenly appeared. "Have Mr. Davis wait outside until I call for him. He is not to have contact with anyone in the meantime."

29

Colton Banyon was the person on the other end of the President's phone. He had suddenly remembered he had to call the President this morning. But first he had to get rid of the aggressive Mandy.

"Why don't you go over there and cut in on Sister Teresa." Banyon pointed to Eric.

"Cut in?" Mandy asked.

"Yeah, tell her it is your turn. After all, it is your appointment time. She already has her assignment."

"I think I just might do that," she announced as she steadied her gaze on the unsuspecting Eric.

"You'd better hurry," he pushed her verbally.

"See you later, Colt," she said cheerfully and waved.

"Later," he mumbled to thin air as Mandy was gone and already standing behind Sister Teresa.

She tapped the nun on her shoulder and smiled. "Mind if I cut in, sis. This is my appointment time."

Sister Teresa was gracious as always. "Of course you can, my dear. I have comforted him enough. You'll find that he is a fast learner." She said it as she winked at Eric. She quickly dropped her habit, smoothed it out, and went to sit on the couch across from them. A smile never left her face.

Mandy stood before Eric with her hip cocked. She said nothing for a full minute as she made sure that Eric had time to scan her body.

"Hi," he said through glassy eyes.

"This morning you asked me how fast I was. Well, I'm here to show you," she said in a sexy determined voice. She hiked up her mini-skirt, leaped onto his lap and went to work. She wrapped her arms around his head and pulled him close to her face. The whole process had taken less than a second. "Are we comfy?" she asked the much larger Eric.

"You're fast. Everything is just peachy."

"Let's not talk about the color of my underwear," she purred. "I have great credentials too. What to see?"

Before he could answer, she continued. "Now, let's talk about that bodyguard job, shall we."

Banyon watched the whole show and wondered if Eric would be influenced by her tactics. He then wondered about all the women at the firm. *Is there something in the water? Are these women as sexually aggressive as they appear, or do I just see them that way and they were just trying to please me?* He decided he had to think about it later. Right now he had to call the President.

Banyon bent down to retrieve his cell phone from his bag and whispered. "Wolf, is there anything new for me to report?'

"You have to stop him," Wolf replied with some anxiety in his voice.

"Stop who?" a confused Banyon whispered still bent over.

"The President, that's who. He is about to put his signature on a document that would be unprecedented in the history of the nation. You must call him and stop him from signing the receipt, Colt."

"What are you talking about?'

"There is no time to explain. The man is at his desk now and once he leaves with the signed receipt, the President will be compromised," Wolf urged him. "The receipt is a trick to get the President to sign a termination order for one of his own people, only he can't see the writing on the paper yet, it's invisible. It is part of the plan by the Effort. Call him and stop him before it is too late," Wolf ordered the still confused Banyon

"But...?"

"Godamnit Colt, get your head out of your ass. Stop thinking about all these women and get your mind on the people that are dying while you are playing. Nero had nothing on you, buddy. It is all part of the Slezeck plan. Explain all that to the President." Banyon hit the call button on the phone when he heard Slezeck.

When the connection was made, the President said, "Hello".

Banyon quickly screamed into the phone. "Mr. President, don't sign the receipt in front of you. It is a trick set up by Paul Slezeck. If you give me a few seconds, I can explain everything and can outline my plan to stop all that is happening. This is all a conspiracy set up by Paul Slezeck and also Werner Klotz," Banyon babbled into the phone.

The President said nothing for a few seconds. "Hold on a second," the President finally ordered and then covered the phone.

30

Meanwhile, it was early in the morning in Mexico City, the capital of the United Mexico States, the official name of Mexico. The President of Mexico was fuming with Latino machismo. He had been up all night because of the killings, caused by unknown persons, and now had to deal with the bombing in Laredo. But that was not why he was mad.

His honor had been challenged and whenever that happened he would go on a rampage, things happened quickly. The challenge came from a communique he had just received from the Mexican Ambassador in Washington D.C. The communique had been listed as top secret, for the President only.

The memo was filled with innuendo and speculation, but was enough to trigger the famous temper of Mexico's leader. His Ambassador claimed he had received an inside tip from an anti-gun lobbyist named Werner Klotz. Klotz claimed the President of the United States was about to sign an executive order allowing the dreaded secret agency Homeland Security to venture into Mexico and eliminate the drug cartels, without gaining permission from the Mexican authorities.

Klotz intimated that this was a response to the current mismanagement by the Mexican government of the current crisis. Klotz claimed he had been at a state function the night before, where he overheard the U. S. President. The President told someone the Mexican President didn't want to clean up the cartels because Mexico was making too much money from the drug trade and the facilitation of illegal immigrants into the United States.

The Ambassador claimed the signing of the executive order would take place within a day. The final sentence of the communique was pure speculation, but it infuriated the already angry Mexican President. The Ambassador wrote that Klotz suggested the United States President was actually responsible for all the disasters. They were staged to gain support for the executive order he was about to sign.

"Who does that *'Gringo'* think he is? How dare he challenge the President of the United Mexican States?" The Mexican President roared, as he slammed his fist on the desk. His top General sitting across from him flinched. He knew bad things would be coming. The Presidents top aide was also in the room, he had the same premonition.

"We must be very careful," the General warned. "This information sounds like it was made up to me."

"The General has a point," the aide agreed.

"I have been wondering about all that has been happening," the President of Mexico proclaimed, as he stared at the ceiling. "Every disaster has been a little too convenient, don't you think?"

"But many people have died, sir," the aide pointed out. "That's not very convenient for anyone."

"They have all been Latinos," roared the President. "Even the American news team that died was all Latinos. Don't you think it is a little suspicious?"

"It could just be a coincidence," the aide continued.

"No, I don't believe it is a coincidence. We must respond to this," The President of Mexico insisted as he ripped the Cuban cigar out of his mouth and threw it onto the carpet. It was a sure sign that he was about to take action.

"But sir, the United States is three times our size. It has the most advanced technology available. How can we possible respond?" The General was rightfully concerned about a military response.

"But we can protect our own borders from invasion, can't we?" The President confirmed the General's worst nightmare. "We can also harass the American tourists."

"But sir, the tourist trade with the United States is the largest contributor to our economy. Cancun and Cozumel are two of the most visited places by American tourists in the world," the aide protested. "If we disrupt the tourist trade, it could mean financial bankruptcy for the country.

"I don't give a shit about that right now," the Mexican Leader roared once again and slammed both fists on the desk. "We must respond to the challenge. It is my honor that is challenged, not yours."

"But we have no plan," the aide noted.

"Well, here is the plan," the leader said confidently, as he leaned back in his large leather executive chair. "First, I want you to mobilize all the troops you can muster," the President pointed to the General.

"Yes, sir," the already defeated General said. He was suddenly wondering if he could take an early retirement.

"Position them all along the border. I want a show of force," he growled.

"That sounds reasonable," the General agreed.

But the President of Mexico was not done. "I want the military and the police to search any white-looking Americans they encounter for contraband. This includes any coming over the border. We want to make them feel very uncomfortable. They will speak for us. Their complaints to their government will weaken the resolve of the U.S. President."

"Yes, Mr. President," the General replied, not believing his President. He also knew many in uniform, the military, especially the police departments, were corrupt and would look for ways to profit from the situation. This would create an even more hostile environment. Many women would be strip-searched.

"I want all communications from our government to the United States government to cease immediately. There is to be no phone calls, no emails, no text messages and no letters. I want the United States to experience a complete blackout with our government. Is that clear?" he demanded.

"Won't that just create more hostilities?" the aide suggested.

"Let's see who blinks first," the fiery leader proclaimed.

Not sure about the tactic, the aide replied with resignation. "I'm not sure cutting communications is a good idea."

It fell on deaf ears. "Next, I want an immediate tax levied on all American tourists. Before they can enter the country, they must pay an additional one hundred dollars, for the privilege of gracing our shores," he said as he looked right at his aide with a determined face. "We will collect the levy at the border."

"Sir, I don't know if that is legal?" The aide was now consumed with the probability that his country was going to be financially ruined.

"This is a time of crisis. I am instituting the legal powers vested in me in time of crisis," the Mexican leader dismissed the subject with a wave of his hand.

"Yes, sir," the aide said.

"When the Mexican people learn how the brutes to the North are manipulating us, they will agree," he added.

"But how will they find out?"

"I want you to schedule a news conference for three o'clock this afternoon," The leader smoothly replied.

"To say what?"

"I will tell them the truth about our relationship with the United States, of course," the now smiling President answered. "When I am done speaking, world opinion will be on our side and many will support us, they will provide aid."

31

"But will your plan work?" The President of The United States asked skeptically. He had many resources available to him, but didn't know who he could trust. So, he decided to go with Banyon's plan. He had been successful in the past.

"Yes, sir, I'm confident it will work," Banyon replied. He had filled the President in on Slezeck, Klotz, the Efforts plan, and his own plan to defeat them. The President asked several questions, Banyon responded truthfully.

While they were talking, the President sheepishly asked if Marlene Moore was part of the conspiracy. Banyon said, "Let me put you on hold for a second."

"Wolf," he whispered. "Is Marlene Moore part of the conspiracy?"

"Marlene Moore is madly in love with the President. She would do anything to protect him," Wolf answered quickly. "So, no, she is not part of any conspiracy against him, or the country."

Banyon took the President off hold and responded. "Marlene is not part of them. She is no threat to you. You can trust her, sir," Banyon told the leader of the free world. The President was relieved because he knew Marlene was more than a friend. She had pictures to prove it. They had been lovers on occasion, in the past after his first divorce. She could easily bring him down, if she desired. It brought a smile to his lips.

"But why can't I just have them arrested right now?" The President was anxious to begin unraveling the damage caused by the Effort's plan.

"As of right now, we don't have any evidence, sir. But my plan includes getting what we need to destroy these assholes," Banyon responded.

"But what about the additional two disasters Klotz has planned? Can you find out what they are?"

"Sir, I can't get information on the future. I can only report what has already happened," Banyon patiently replied.

"How many more people could die," the President moaned.

"Hopefully, I can find a way to stop the disasters before they happen. But sir, there is no guarantee. You should prepare for more bad things to happen."

Before the President could reply, the door to his office swung open, his secretary walked silently in. She approached his desk dropping a single piece of paper on the top. She then turned on her heel and left the oval office.

"Wait one minute," the President said into the phone as he picked up the urgent message and read it. It was a flash report from the DOD, Department of Defense. It was written in simple English and said the DOD had detected massive troop movements in Mexico. The troops were pouring into all the border towns. It further speculated that it could be a prelude to an invasion. "Oh my God," the President muttered.

"I think I know what the next disaster is," he informed Banyon. "The Mexican army is massing on the border," he relayed into the phone.

"Yes, I just heard that from my source," Banyon replied. While the President was reading the flash report, Banyon had asked Wolf for an update. "Also the Mexican President has scheduled a news conference for three o'clock, Central Time. That's four o'clock your time, sir," Banyon added.

"What is he going to say?"

"Only he knows so far," Banyon told him.

"Do they intend to invade?" The President quickly asked with a little panic in his voice. "I know they have many supporters along the border, on the U.S. side. How will we know who is on our side?"

"No, sir, but they want to show America they should not be taken lightly. They are however, going to create many problems," Banyon told the President.

"What do you mean?"

"The army has orders to search every American they encounter, even those that have just crossed the border. Mr. President, some people will resist. The army then has orders to subdue them by any means required and take them into custody."

"But most of the people that cross the border are Latino looking. How will they know the difference?"

"The army has been instructed to only detain white-looking people. You know what that means."

"Yeah, several pretty girls will disappear and many men will be beaten or killed," he answered with anger. He knew the Mexican army was as corrupt as the police force.

"They have also initiated a new tourist tax effective immediately."

"What?"

Banyon explained it to him. "Any American entering Mexico, from now on, will be charged and additional one hundred dollars in taxes, at the border. They will have to pay or not be allowed in the country."

"That will throw the State Department into complete chaos. I'll be getting phone calls from everyone that has made a campaign contribution and has ties with Mexico," The President lamented.

"Not to mention what it will do to the import and export business with Mexico," Banyon stated. He knew Mexico was one of Americas largest trading partners, any disruption in trade, would send both economies into ruin.

"Colt, we need to solve this mystery quickly. It has to be done before the Mexican President makes his speech this afternoon," The President ordered.

"We are trying," Banyon said a little too defensively.

Suddenly, Banyon heard, "Wait one minute," again as the President put him on hold.

While Banyon waited, he took a second to look around his computer monitor to see how Eric was doing. Mandy was just standing up and fixing her mini-skirt. Sister Teresa was clapping and Eric looked very satisfied. Mandy headed to the open balcony door. As she passed Banyon she wore a broad smile.

"See you later Mandy," he said.

"Not if I see you first," she coyly replied as she zipped out the door and climbed over the rail. She then leaped and was gone.

Banyon turned back to Eric, just in time to see someone else, come through the door. Sister Teresa quickly stood up and joined the man as they both glided towards Banyon's desk. Eric was once again crossing himself. Before he could greet him, the President came back onto the line.

"Colt, are you still there?" He heard the President say into the phone.

"I'm here, sir."

"I have to go," the president started. People from the DOD, the Pentagon and the NSA are camped outside my door. They want to discuss the Mexico crisis.

"I understand, sir," Banyon politely replied.

"You're sure about this invasion thing?"

"They have no intentions of invading," Banyon reiterated to the President.

"Good. Call me when you have something more concrete, and it had better be soon," the President ordered.

"I will," Banyon promised. "But you need to do something to make this all work," he said.

"What's that?"

Banyon explained what had to be done. "Can you do that?"

"I'll do it right now, before my meeting," the President replied.

"Thank you, Mr. President," Banyon sincerely said.

"How long do I have to put these guys off?"

"We'll have something in a few hours," Banyon replied.

"I don't know how long I can hold off this pack of war-mongering wolves," the President said. "They always want to make a preemptive strike whenever there is a crisis," he said with disgust.

The President hung up the phone before Banyon could say anything in return.

32

Banyon set his phone on the desk and stared at the man. He was portly, around sixty years old, bald and held a bible in his hands. He was a priest. Banyon suddenly had some big concerns about his surveillance team.

"Hello, I'm Father Grey," the man said and held out his hand. The hand was large and callused.

"He's not a real priest," Sister Teresa quickly noted. "He is actually Jim, from accounting," she added.

"Sister Teresa and I have worked together many times before," the priest nodded towards the nun.

Banyon stood up and shook his hand. "Okay, but the assignment could be dangerous, are you able to protect yourselves."

Father Grey opened his bible. Inside was a semi-automatic hand gun. He opened his suit coat and Banyon saw a set of three knives, hanging from Velcro tabs, inside the coat. Father Grey flicked his wrist and a derringer appeared in his hand. "I'm also an ex-professional boxer," he added for emphasis. "Do you have any questions now, Mr. Banyon?" The priest took a pious pose. Sister Teresa had her hands clasped in prayer mode. They looked like they were about to conduct a service.

"Want to see my weapons?" Sister Teresa suddenly blurted, with a flurry she began pulling up her habit. She had reached thigh level before Banyon stopped her.

"Okay, you two will do," he announced, with his hands in the stop position. "You will be working with a third person today. What I want you to do, is video and record every-thing that transpires."

"Who's the vic?" Father Grey asked.

"Walter Klotz."

"You mean the asshole anti-gun lobbyist from Washington?" Father Grey asked with distain.

"The same," Banyon answered him. "He is coming to Chicago this morning. He will be meeting with six Mexican hit men in the Ajax car rental parking lot, at Midway airport. They are part of a bigger plan. They are here to attempt to murder me and my friends."

Suddenly, nervous and shocked, Sister Teresa asked Banyon, "You want us to eliminate them? We are not equipped to take down that many targets."

"No, stay far away from the Mexicans, Eric and I will take care of them. I want you to take pictures of their faces and the license plate of the car that they are driving though. I need to know where they are, at all times. Then we will take them down when no one else can get hurt."

"That's all?" Father Grey grumbled.

"No, it will be after they leave the lot that your real work will begin," Banyon informed them.

"So, who is Klotz meeting with then?" The nun asked.

"I'm guessing he will be meeting with me," a voice said from behind the religious duo.

Banyon once again stood up and the surveillance team turned around. "Meet Paul Slezeck, Director of Homeland Security," Banyon announced.

"It's really, me, Bart," the man said.

"Very good likeness, I'm sure you will fool Klotz, especially because he wouldn't be expecting you," Banyon complimented Bart. "You're a little shorter than he is though," Banyon brought up his hand to his chin in thought.

"Pleasure to meet all of you," Bart said in the exact voice of Slezeck.

"Got it," Banyon blurted. "We will have you seated in a rental car. It will hide your height. You can also place cameras in the car."

"Brilliant," Slezeck said dramatically.

Banyon handed each of them a sheet of paper he had just written before they had entered his office. "Here is the location and the timing for the sting. "Klotz will have a watcher from Homeland Security following him, so you will have to take him out. No need to kill him, he is just an employee of Homeland."

"We will get there early and be ready," the man who looked like Slezeck said.

"As soon as you are done, call me, and give me any information that will help stop these clowns. Then get back here ASAP. Up load all the videos on the way in."

"What about Klotz, should we eliminate him, before we return?" Sister Teresa suddenly asked.

"No, his usefulness will end as soon as he activates the hit men. Slezeck plans to have him killed using Homeland Security black ops people later this afternoon, back in Washington. We intend to catch them in the act. It is all part of the evidence we need to corral the real Slezeck."

"But what do I say to him?" Bart asked.

"Say this," Banyon outlined his plan for the conversion.

33

The surveillance team left with their plan solidly worked out. They had just cleared the door, when Banyon glanced at his Movado watch and noted it was just 9:30 A.M., in the morning. He asked Wolf if anything was new and found that nothing had happened since his last update.

He grabbed his phone and had just pushed the button to connect him to the President, when, as expected, Heather strutted into his office like she owned it. She assumed a sexy pose and looked at Banyon with smoldering eyes. He quickly pointed to Eric, while indicating he was on the phone. She then pointed her slender toned arm at Eric, asking if he was to interview her. Banyon nodded his head in agreement. Eric quickly pointed to himself joyfully. Banyon immediately realized Eric knew her previous profession. He was sure Eric had seen her before, with fewer clothes adoring her body.

Today, she was dressed like a ninja. She had on black stretch pants, a black long-sleeve turtle-neck sweater, and black running shoes. She wore no jewelry and no makeup. Not that Eric noticed anyway. Her hair was pulled back severely in a ponytail. With three strides of her long legs, she reached the now standing Eric. They shook hands firmly and she took a seat across from him, sitting more like a man then a sex goddess. Eric started asking her questions.

"Hello," Banyon suddenly heard from his phone. He leaned back in his chair so he wouldn't be distracted.

"Mr. President, this is Colton Banyon," he spoke into the phone.

"What have you got to report?" The President tersely asked.

"The surveillance team and Bart, dressed as Slezeck, are heading for the rendezvous with Werner Klotz," Banyon filled him in on the plan.

"Finally, some action," The President declared.

"How did you do on your end?" Banyon asked.

"Pretty well, I think," the President replied. "I sent Kevin Davis back to Slezeck without the signed receipt. I told him to tell Slezeck I will sign the order, when we meet later today, at the White House."

"Well, I'm pretty sure he will show for your meeting, at two o'clock," Banyon said to the President.

"Colt, I now see the additional sentences on the receipt. I have it right here in front of me. I had already signed my first name, when you called, so the chemicals were activated. I can't believe Slezeck attempted to blackmail me. Thanks, you saved me from probable impeachment. Slezeck has got to go."

"I'm glad I was able to stop you in time," Banyon said humbly.

"Yes, it could have been worse," the President added, thinking about the implications of a blackmail attempt, on a President.

"Did you find a way to get him to leave his office?" Banyon's plan required that Slezeck not have an alibi for the next four hours.

"Yes, I did," the President laughed. It was the first time today. "I sent a verbal message back with Kevin as we discussed. The message told Slezeck he needed to confront Marlene privately and get her to admit to something before I could publically announce she was part of a conspiracy. I also indicated the sooner the better and he needed to confront her before our meeting this afternoon."

"Good," Banyon replied. "That will put enough pressure on him to react."

"Then I called Marlene and filled her in. He has no idea what a women scorned is like. But he is about to find out. "

"Where are they meeting?"

"Marlene sent him a message that she had some information to share with Homeland Security about the bombing earlier today. She requested he meet her privately, without bodyguards, in downtown Baltimore, on her yacht. It's about a three hour round trip to the location."

"He has someone following her you know. Are you sure she can handle Slezeck?"

"I sent three Secret Service men over to help. They are going to arrest the follower and tie him up with legalese, so he misses the meeting. They are also going to record their conversation. He thinks he has a green light to trap her, when actually; she has a green light to trap him. Very Machiavellian of you Mr. Banyon."

"Thank you, sir. I'll take that as a compliment."

"Let's hope the rest of your plan goes as well," the President said.

"How did your meeting with the warmongers go?" Banyon asked.

"We put the retaliation meeting off until the Mexican President gives his speech later this afternoon. But The State Department is issuing a warning for all U.S. citizens to avoid Mexico, until further notice. They are also tracking down any Americans in Mexico and directing them to our embassy, or out of the country. In addition, we are calling in everybody from the Border Patrol. We are also sneaking special ops personal to the major crossing points, just in case."

"It's the best you could have done under the circumstances," Banyon remarked.

Hopefully, I'll be able to give the Mexican President some answers before then and this crisis will be over. But I have to tell you Colt, the timing is very critical."

"Don't I know it," Banyon agreed.

"What is your next step?" the President suddenly asked.

"If everybody does their job, we should have the information on the next disaster and the confession of Klotz by one o'clock, your time. Your meeting with Slezeck is at two o'clock and you should be able to call the Mexican President before three o'clock. This should all be over by four o'clock," Banyon gave him the timeline.

"And what about the hit team after you?" The President inquired. "I could send you some SEALs to take them out for you."

Gerald J. Kubicki & Kristopher Kubicki

"There are too many people around here. Some will surely get hurt. I'm going to lead them around by their noses. We'll take them down when no one else is around."

"Let me know if you need anything," the President sincerely said.

"Thank you, sir," Banyon replied for the umpteenth time today, the connection was broken.

Banyon took a big breath, sighed and leaned back in his chair. The one thing he hadn't been able to figure out was what and where would be Werner Klotz's final disaster. He hoped Bart could pull it from him, but Klotz was no fool and might not reveal what he had planned, even to his comrade.

Banyon was just about to talk to Wolf and beg for a tip when he sensed movement in the back of his office. He looked around his monitor, once again, and saw Heather stand up. Eric likewise stood and they shook hands. She turned and headed for the door, waving at Banyon as she left.

Banyon spread his arms asking Eric, what happened. Eric shrugged and said, "She has another appointment."

At that second, a man came through the door. He looked like a reincarnation of James Cagney. He wore a dark suit and very shiny shoes. "I'm here for the what-you-call-it interview," he announced in Brooklynese. Eric quickly called him over; Banyon tried to not listen, but within seconds heard the man say, "forget-about-it."

Suddenly, Timmy came dancing through the door. "I didn't do it. I didn't do it," he sang as he rock 'n rolled his way up to Banyon.

"Didn't do what?" Banyon asked the geek.

"Man, it was so cool. I took your advice and didn't even look."

"What are you talking about Timmy?"

"Heather, the witch-bitch, of course," Timmy replied like Banyon should know. "I didn't even look at her as she passed me in the hallway just now. I taught her good, man. I got her goat this time. It feels good too."

"Are you sure?"

"Yeah man. I didn't even notice her skin-tight black outfit, with only the black tong underneath. I'm going to make her pay for how she has treated me."

Banyon moaned softly. *Poor Timmy*, he thought. "Timmy, why are you here?"

"Oh, yea…I found something I think will help."

Quickly sitting up at attention, Banyon asked, "What?"

"Well, you know how you asked me to sift through that asshole Klotz's stuff?" He paused.

"What did you find?" Banyon asked anxiously.

"I found an invoice for twelve machine guns, man."

"Guns?"

"Yeah, I thought it was a little strange that an anti-gun activist would be buying guns."

"And?" Banyon jumped in.

"The guns were delivered last week to a house in San Diego California. I got the address and crossed checked it, with several government databases. The house belongs to a black, San Diego drug gang."

"There is more, I hope," Banyon thought Timmy was on to something.

"There is. I checked his phone records and found he made several calls to the San Diego area, just before the delivery. So, I decided to access the NAS phone banks. They routinely record most phone calls, you know, and then run them through some software, looking for key words that terrorists might use."

"Okay," Banyon said as he hoped Timmy would finally get to the point.

"I found the actual phone conversations," Timmy exclaimed. "I am the world's best hacker," he proclaimed as he spread his arms in self-adoration.

Suddenly excited, Banyon asked, "Can you give me the gist of the conversations? Why did he send guns to black gangbangers?"

"They are planning something that will happen at eleven o'clock pacific time. That is one o'clock, our time, and two o'clock eastern time.

"So, what are they planning?"

"That I don't know for sure," Timmy admitted. "But it will involve lots of lead," Timmy said as he pointed his hands like a machine gun and made believe he was peppering the room with bullets.

Realizing he now could ask Wolf about the gang-bangers plan, Banyon said, "Good job, Timmy. Now I want you to go back and do the same thing for Paul Slezeck. Particularly, I want you to tie down a conspiracy between Slezeck and Klotz. Can you do that?"

"I'm on it," he replied and danced out the door.

Banyon glanced at Eric and noticed that the Cagney lookalike was pretending to strangle someone. Eric didn't look amused.

"Wolf, are you there?" Banyon whispered behind his monitor.

"I'm here," the spirit replied.

"What are the black gangbangers up to?"

"I have just finished the search myself. Timmy is very good," he said. "Their plan is to spread themselves along the highway I-5 just before the border station. Since, the border is now very backed up; there will be hundreds of cars waiting for their turn to cross over. They will all be Latinos. The gangbangers intend to strafe as many cars as possible, in one minute, and then disappear. Colt, hundreds will die."

"But why would they do that?" Banyon asked.

"They will then make an anonymous phone call to a local radio station and proclaim they are loyal Americans, who are sick and tired of wetbacks steeling their jobs."

"My God, this could start a war," Banyon said. "Is there time to stop them?"

"They plan to be at the house for one more hour," Wolf told Banyon.

"I need to call the President," Banyon said as he reached for his phone. "Then I need to call Bart as well."

34

Harry Gold burst into his hotel room in the Mexican tourist town of Acapulco, Mexico. His wife was already inside, frantically packing their clothes. They had received a phone call from the U.S. State Department twenty minutes ago. The message was simple and clear, get out of Mexico now.

They had traveled to the famous beach resort town three days ago, for a one week vacation, from the land locked city of Rapid City, South Dakota. Their vacation had been perfect right up until they had gotten the phone call.

"They're gone," he screamed at his wife. She had sent him down to the pool area to collect their two daughters. They were both in their late teens and wanted to get some early morning sun. Harry suspected what they really wanted to do was flirt with the several charming and handsome pool boys, but he let them go out in their small bikinis anyway.

"What do you mean by gone?" she screamed back as she turned to look at him.

"One of the pool boys told me several policemen came into the pool area and announced that every white American needed to be searched. They had on bikinis for god sakes," he lamented.

"Oh, God, no, not my girls" wailed his wife Mable as she put her hand to her mouth in horror.

But Harry wasn't done. "I found the place where they were doing the searches and an older man and wife told me they saw two handcuffed girls forced into a police cruiser. The police on the spot denied there were any other policemen stationed at the hotel."

"Harry, someone has kidnapped our beautiful daughters," Mable cried out. "What should we do?" Mable collapsed onto the bed and started sobbing loudly.

"I'm going to call the American embassy right now," he replied, as the fear of losing his daughters, gripped his heart.

35

"Are you sure this is the last of the planned disasters?" The President questioned Banyon.

"Yes, sir," Banyon replied.

"That address for the house is less than ten miles from the SEAL base," The former Californian told Banyon. "Maybe, we got some luck for a change."

"We only have an hour to stop them, otherwise, we will have to seek them out along the highway," Banyon said.

"Okay, no matter what, these boys need to be stopped. I'll have boots at the site in one half hour. I'll head for the situation room right now to get things going. I want you hooked up to the situation room in twenty-five minutes."

"I'll be there," Banyon replied. The line went dead

Banyon quickly pressed his Bluetooth. "Timmy, I need you to hookup me up with the White House situation room, just like you did yesterday. I need it done in exactly twenty-five minutes."

"Got you covered, dude," Timmy answered.

Banyon then hit the speed dial on his phone for Bart. He answered in three rings. "Yes, Colt," he professionally said.

"Bart, the final disaster is going down today. Several gangbangers in California are going to strafe cars on the freeway. Then call a radio station and say they are fed up with losing their jobs to Mexicans."

"So, I can use it to incriminate Klotz?" Bart asked.

"He arranged it and even bought the machine guns, we have the proof," Banyon responded.

"Well, let's see what else we can get him to admit to," Bart offered. "He's due here within an hour, we will be ready. I'll tell the others."

"Good luck," Banyon told him and hung up.

When Banyon looked around his monitor this time, James Cagney had been replaced by a Hispanic man in a gardening outfit. When Eric casually turned his head towards him, he noticed Banyon was slicing his hand across his own throat. Eric gave a slight nod of his head in acknowledgement. He wrapped up the interview in just a few minutes and the disappointed gardener left. Eric then walked over to Banyon's desk.

"How is it going?" Banyon asked.

"We definitely have some good choices so far, but I have two more interviews yet before I have to make any decisions. One is coming in five minutes."

"Well, brace yourself Eric. We are about to get some company," Banyon said with a little humor in his voice.

"How do you know that?" Eric asked.

"Because we just landed another mission from the President, that means we have to hire a contract employee," Banyon replied. "The internal communications gossip network here is instantaneous."

Within seconds, Heather came running through the office door and Mandy zipped in from the balcony, pulling down her skirt. They both shouted at the same time. "I'm your contract employee for this mission."

"Sorry girls," Banyon told them as several more people crowded into his office, heading for his desk. "This mission is a top secret takedown, not worth much in terms of money. Besides, I have to appoint the person who uncovered the data that led us to the takedown. It is only fair."

Banyon quickly pressed his Bluetooth and said. "Timmy, I need you in my office in exactly thirty minutes. You are the contract employee for this mission, even though you blabbed it to everyone in the organization."

"You are righteous man," Timmy responded. "I'll be there."

Banyon then addressed the rest of the people in his office. "I want you all to make money, believe me. If you can bring me things to find and solve, I will always cut you in. You will be the contract employee for the mystery. Is that clear to everybody?"

Reluctantly, they all nodded in agreement. "But how will we know when it is our time?" A man that looked like a linebacker for a football team asked the question. He had no neck.

Banyon thought for a second and then turned to Mandy. "She," he pointed, "will keep a log. Any of you that want to participate must have her put your name on the list, we will go in rotation. Mandy will always be able to tell you when your chance is coming up." He then winked at Mandy.

"First come, first serve," she quickly said, winked back at Banyon and headed for the balcony, hiking up her skirt to leap over the railing. The mass of people in Banyon's office suddenly dissipated, as they all rushed out the door to get their name on the list.

"This is not like any office I have ever seen," offered Eric. "It would be fun to work here."

"You have to know the law and also have a special talent, Eric. What's yours?"

"I know you," Eric replied with a grin.

"Touché," Banyon responded.

"We should be ready to go to Las Vegas before the lunchtime deadline. Will Bart be back in time?" Eric asked.

"So far, we are still on plan," Banyon replied. "But make sure our bodyguards know we will be traveling very soon."

"Yeah, and I want these bodyguards to blend in and not draw too much attention to themselves. No flashy clothes or carrying anything that people could remember."

"They need to hide in plain sight," Banyon agreed. He was about to say more when Eric's next appointment came through the door.

He was an African-American that stood about 7 feet tall.

36

While Banyon waited for his screen to boot up he found himself thinking of Loni. His first thought was that she could never be allowed in the office. One look at Mandy and she would immediately see the similarities and become uncontrollably jealous. And, if she ever saw Heather, well, all hell would break loose. He decided he needed to coach Eric on what to say around her. He also decided he missed her. She had been gone just twelve hours and was probably still in flight to Odessa, but he wanted to talk to her. She always gave him good advice and comforted him, like no other woman could. He needed some advice now. While, so far, his work for the President had been fun and rewarding, Banyon wondered if he could keep up the pace, or even if he wanted to. *Did I make a mistake by agreeing to work for the President?* He thought.

He was not ashamed about the constant sexual titilation the women at work provided, in fact, he thought it enhanced his relationship with Loni. But how long could he live two lives, one at work and one at home? Loni was everything to him. "*Nothing compares to you,*" he said to himself and realized his thought was actually a lyric of a popular nineties tune.

His reverie was broken as the tall black man got up and left. He was immediately replaced by a roly-poly man in a chef's hat and garb. He had a large handlebar mustache. Banyon could see several tattoos peeking out from his sleeves and neck. Banyon was pretty sure Eric would not hire him.

Banyon realized he was feeling slightly uncomfortable in his chair. He glanced at his watch and was relieved to find he had enough time to find a bathroom and make it back before he was connected to the situation room. He got up, for the first time that day and headed out the door.

Part Four

Solutions

37

Banyon returned to the office in five minutes. Eric was sitting on the couch alone and deep in thought. He was wrestling with his choices for their bodyguards, Banyon figured. He decided to wait until Eric approached him, with the decision. He already had his choices, but was a little concerned about them. He hoped that Eric concurred.

"We are starting the operation to take down the gangbangers in about three minutes," Banyon said to him. "Want to watch?"

"Absolutely," Eric replied and jumped off the couch. He followed Banyon to the back of the office and his desk.

"You can watch, but you can't be seen by the camera," Banyon told him, as he pointed to the opening, on his monitor. "The President is ticklish about who is looking in."

"I'll stand to the side," Eric quickly replied.

"No talking either," Banyon ordered.

Timmy entered the room carrying a laptop. Banyon gave him a questioning look as he slid into one of the chairs, in the front of the desk, in a slumped position. He was not his usual smiling self.

"I had to get out of my office," he said as a reason to for his early arrival.

"It's okay," Banyon replied.

"You guys watch the takedown. I'm just going to work on the Slezeck project, right here," he continued in a subdued tone.

"I think you will be more comfortable on the couch over there," Banyon pointed. He didn't want Timmy near his desk, as he might have to contact Wolf and Timmy might hear him talking.

"Whatever," Timmy replied displaying teenage attitude. He got up and moved to the couch.

Gerald J. Kubicki & Kristopher Kubicki

"Is something wrong, Timmy?" Banyon recognized he was not in his usual jovial mood.

"It's the damn witch-bitch," he yelled across the room. Banyon could see that Timmy seemed frustrated.

"What's happened now?" Banyon was sorry he had given Timmy some advice about women. He was no expert himself.

"The witch-bitch was just in my area and was talking to one of the girls there," Timmy replied angrily.

"Uh oh, what did Heather do now?"

"I heard her talking. She used me as an example of someone to not to get involved with. She said I had too many sexual hang ups and would only disappoint a women. Colt, I have been working on the girl for nearly a year. I was almost there. That witch-bitch ruined it all," Timmy lamented.

"Wait, maybe Heather said that on purpose," Banyon told him. Eric shook his head in agreement.

"Yeah, she wants to destroy me. Just like always," he said vehemently.

"Timmy, maybe you are actually getting to her. She may be pissed that you are ignoring her. Women like Heather can't stand to be ignored."

"Really," Timmy replied hopefully.

"I think you are making progress," Banyon proclaimed as he recognized he was once again giving Timmy advice.

"You think so?" Timmy said, as he perked up.

"Keep ignoring her," Eric agreed. "I've found that when you ignore them, women think they have lost their attraction, and will want to get it back. Believe me, I know. I have to deal with three beautiful women, every day."

"Right now, dudes," Timmy exclaimed. "I've got her right where I want her," he said as he clinched his fist. Banyon hoped he was right.

Suddenly, the monitor blinked and the situation room came on screen. As before, the big screen was divided into four smaller screens. The first box showed an overhead view of a house. It was fairly small and was on a postage stamp sized lot, just like all the other houses around it. The neighborhood seemed rundown and depressing. The house was surrounded by a chair link fence, with only a few scruffy bushes for cover. The view also showed a utility van across the street, with workers opening a manhole cover.

The second view was from the utility van. The picture showed fourteen heat signatures in the small house. One looked female. The other two boxes on the monitor were empty. As Banyon looked to the screens that showed who was watching the takedown, he was surprised to see only his own image, the other screens were blank.

He could hear voices on communications links and people giving orders off screen. The Presidents voiced suddenly boomed. "I want this to look like a rival gang hit them. Make sure the police see it that way," he ordered. "Make it fast and final," he continued. "This country doesn't need any trials, where an ACLU lawyer could have a chance to get these guys off. What they want to do to this country is treason. They must pay the price."

Banyon quickly whispered, "Wolf, who is the additional two people in the house?"

"They are the leader of the gang and his girlfriend. She is as dirty as the rest of them," Wolf replied. Banyon quickly relayed the message to the situation room.

"Thanks, Colt," he heard the President say.

"Are they expecting trouble?" Banyon whispered.

"Most are still asleep, but their guns are nearby."

"How many are asleep?"

"Eight," Wolf immediately replied. Banyon passed the information on to the situation room.

The two men watched the screen as a black SUV pulled up on the street behind the gang house. With surgical precision, six SEALs, dressed all in black, piled out and with guns aimed ahead. They charged across the adjoining lot, leaping over the chain link fence. They lined up on the back wall of the white stucco house.

"Team one in position," Banyon heard the leader report. The SEAL then activated his head camera and the third box on the monitor came alive.

Two more vans quickly pulled up on the front side of the house, one on each side, but far enough down the street, to not be seen, by anyone looking out the window. Six more SEALs lined up on both sides of the lot. One carried a battering ram. They slithered in single file along the side fences and crossed over to the front of the house. Four men broke away to block the windows on each side of the house. When all entrances and exits were covered, the second team leader spoke.

"Team two in position," he said and activated his camera. A third and four camera view came from the men by the side windows. At the same time four more SUVs pulled up in the front and two on the street behind the house. Agents with DEA and FBI in windbreakers now lined the streets.

Banyon could feel a bead of sweat travel down his back. He wondered how the SEALs could put their lives in jeopardy, in the line of duty, every day. He always respected men like them, but today he was even more thankful someone could do this work. He glanced at Eric, who now stood tall and proud. Eric had been one of them.

"On my mark," one of the leaders spoke. "Three, two, one, go."

Like they had practiced many times, a SEAL broke the glass on each window in the house with their guns. Other SEALs tossed stun grenades through the holes. Everyone then hunkered down and waited for the concussion.

The blast blew out the glass in all the windows and doors. Banyon could clearly see glass flying over the heads of the cameras. The glass barely landed on the ground, when the SEALs were up and executing the break in. The battering ram broke the door right off its hinges, two SEALs leaped through the now open windows and the rear team ripped the back door open. Then the shooting started.

The agents on the street closed ranks in the yard surrounding the house. All had their guns drawn and Kevlar vests visible. They set up a killing field of firepower. No one was getting out of the house.

The roar of gunfire was then continuous. Bullets were flying everywhere in the house. The four head cameras were in constant motion and the tips of the firing machine guns could be seen, as they spewed out a fiery death to anyone that came into view. Some of the gang members managed to fire back and Banyon heard two SEALs utter, "I'm hit."

But it was soon over. All fourteen gang members were dead or dying in the small house. Banyon watched as the SEALs quickly exited the building and ran to their vehicles. One was holding his arm while blood dripped down his sleeve, and one was carried by two other SEALs. It looked like he had taken a bullet in his leg. In seconds, they loaded up and the SUVs sped off. There was no trace of them left behind.

The DEA and FBI agents swiftly moved into the house, blocking anyone from entering, until they had done their canvas. Police cars immediately began to fill the streets with unneeded ambulances arriving right behind them. Police Officers began to bring out rolls of yellow tape and block off the area. Officers started knocking on doors, in an attempt, to find anyone that might have witnessed something. Those people would be quickly taken downtown before the press arrived. Anybody that asked what happened was told it looked like a skirmish with another rival gang. The whole operation was a lesson in effectiveness.

Suddenly, Banyon heard more gun fire. It sounded like just one machine gun and then everything was quiet. A DEA agent quickly reported to the situation room that there was one perpetrator still breathing, but they had subdued him. Banyon knew what that meant.

Within minutes, several large white trucks, with dish style antennas, screeched to a stop just outside the yellow tape. News helicopters hovered overhead. Reporters and video crews exited the trucks, even as the reporters were still combing their hair. Several ducked under the yellow tape and headed to the front door, with crews trailing behind. They knew they were not allowed into the crime scene, but believed that until they were thrown out, they might get some exclusive footage.

Banyon watched as a DEA Agent stopped them at the front steps by using a stop gesture with his hands. The

President suddenly ordered someone off screen to put two of the live feeds on the front monitor and to turn up the volume. He wanted to see, to what extent, the news people were fooled.

"Can you tell us what's happen in the house?" A cute reporter asked as she pulled her long blond hair away from her photogenic face.

The DEA agent was from the Public Relations Department of the DEA. He was accustomed to dealing with reporters, which was why he was assigned the task of providing them with disinformation. "We have only arrived a few minutes ago, ourselves," he deflected the question.

"What can you tell us?" she persisted.

"We have found several dead bodies in the house. There appears to have been a shootout," he confirmed.

"Why is the DEA here?"

"We received an anonymous phone call. The house is a known center of a gang that deals drugs," he replied.

"So, is this shootout drug related?"

"I'd rather not speculate at this time," he said.

"Did a rival gang do the shooting?" another reported asked.

"At this point, your guess is as good as mine," he replied.

"How bad is the carnage?"

"It will take us several days to collect all the evidence. We'll let you know then," the agent assured them.

"How many are dead?"

"I can't tell you that right now. I'm sorry, but you are contaminating a crime scene. You must return behind the yellow tape now. I can't answer any more questions." He motioned to several police officers nearby. They herded the reporters behind the tape.

Everyone in the situation room continued to watch the monitors as the cute blond attempted to spin a recap of the news story.

She stood facing the camera, with the bullet ridden house in the background. She, once again, pushed the hair from her face before she started.

"It appears that the violence caused by drug dealers, fighting over turf, has once again erupted in this quiet suburb in San Diego. With the current problems along the Mexican border, it seems likely that a drug gang has attempted to eliminate their rival. According to a DEA spokesperson, there are many bodies and much carnage inside the drug house. It will be days before we know the full extent of the devastation. This is Katie Foss reporting live from the scene."

A banner suddenly appeared on the screen. It said "More gang violence in San Diego", a picture of the gang house loomed in the background.

"That's my girl," the President cheerfully exclaimed. "I love yellow journalism," he added. "By tonight, every other drug gang in Southern California will have taken credit for the hit." Banyon silently agreed with him.

The President's face appeared on Banyon's monitor. "That went well, Colt," he remarked.

"Yes, sir," Banyon replied.

"You know a takedown only pays $200,000 dollars, right?"

"I'm just glad I could help," Banyon answered diplomatically.

"I'll message Bart to cut you a check. You'll get it some-time today, when he is back in the office," the President continued.

"There is no hurry," Banyon replied as he noticed Timmy disagreeing.

"Now get back to work on the rest of the plan," the President ordered.

"Yes, sir," Banyon replied as the screen turned blank.

38

Paul Slezeck pulled up to the large Marina in Baltimore and parked his car. He scanned the area, looking for any watchers, but couldn't find any. The guard at the gate, who was actually one of the watchers, let him through and told him Ms. Moore expected him. He pointed down the long dock to direct him. Slezeck ambled up the walkway looking for a fifty-foot luxury yacht called the "DOJ". He knew Marlene had bought the expensive toy as a getaway. When her husband had suddenly died five years ago, she had inherited his substantial estate. It was her replacement for a husband.

Slezeck was worried about the information she would share with him. He was sure Werner had planned the operation secretly and well, but he needed to know what information she had and what she could possibly pass on to others. He wasn't too worried about her and Werner though, after all, they would be eliminated as soon as the President signed the executive order, in about four hours.

He found her boat slip. He was impressed with the gleaming white ship, with its trim, in green. A man was dressed in a white outfit, standing on the dock, by the gang plank. He greeted Slezeck and told him Marlene was waiting for him, in the lounge area, He pointed to a sliding door aboard ship.

Slezeck made his way up the entry way and slid open the door. The inside was cool, elegant, with top of the line leather furniture, and modern décor. Marlene sat on a chair in the back of the room. She was dressed in a pink top complemented by white shorts which showed off her long legs. Slezeck wondered if she had dressed that way to entice him. She looked up from the book she was reading, slid off her reading glasses, then stood, to greet him. She looked straight into his eyes with her hand out as he crossed the room, but said nothing.

Slezeck and Marlene were not friends. They were rivals, controlling the two largest intelligence agencies, in the Federal government. They had never collaborated on a case before and Slezeck was very leery of the polished DOJ. *Why now?* He wondered, as he raised his hand to shake Marlene's.

But instead of shaking his hand she continued raising her hand, suddenly slapping him hard, across his face. He was caught completely off guard, exactly like she intended.

"That's for insulting me in front of the President," she admonished him. "If you ever do that again, I'll cut your balls off." She then stared at him with loathing in her eyes.

Slezeck was now squarely on the defensive side of the ball. He struggled to gain control of his own emotions. He wanted to punch her in the face, but reasoned it might be exactly what she wanted him to do. He decided to be conciliatory instead. He needed to know what she had learned about his operation.

"I'm sorry, Marlene," he said sincerely through gritted teeth. "We have all been under tremendous stress lately. I meant no disrespect."

"Now that we have that in the open," Marlene drove home the advantage. "Let's sit down and discuss the current crisis." She indicated that he should sit down, right now. It was more of an order than a request. He perched on the edge of one of the couches. She sat across from him, crossing her bare legs.

"You said you wanted to share some information," he began. "I came here to share as well," he lied.

"Alright," she replied with a nod of her head. "I'll tell you what I have first," a suddenly all-business Marlene stated.

"Please do," Slezeck responded as he tensed up.

She took deep breath which caused her abundant chest to rise. It was quickly noticed by Slezeck. "I got a call earlier today, from my counterpart in Mexico," she said. "They have captured the man who set off the explosion in Laredo."

"What?" Slezeck questioned. The explosion had occurred only two hours ago.

"I called you immediately because there are some strange circumstances surrounding the explosion."

"Like what?"

"As they were interrogating him, he brought up the name of someone we both know," she easily lied.

"Who?" Slezeck said as a lump formed in his throat.

"Walter Klotz. Both you and I know him. The man said that Walter Klotz masterminded the disaster and paid him. What do you think of that?" Marlene then sat back and studied his face.

"I really don't know what to think," Slezeck accurately replied. "But I'll have to verify this information of course," he added.

"Well, call him yourself," Marlene responded. "Oh, wait, as of an hour ago, all communications with the Mexican government have been cut off. You'll have to verify my information later."

Not believing her, he whipped out his cell phone, hitting the speed dial. He soon got a voicemail which said, no American calls would be taken by Mexican Federal employees. Undaunted, he dialed a second number and got the same message. "It seems you are right," he agreed. He had not anticipated this in his planning.

"I'm giving you this information because Werner Klotz's activities fall under your jurisdiction of domestic terrorism. You need to arrest him," Marlene made it sound like she was doing him a favor.

"Or maybe your information is not too solid and you'd rather risk my neck, then yours," he quickly replied. "Werner Klotz is a respected lobbyist. He has powerful friends, who will come to his aid," Slezeck warned her.

"Oh don't worry about that. Klotz is our man alright," Marlene said dismissively. "The President has a guy who seems to be able to figure things out and he is always right," Marlene set the stage. "He has hard evidence, I'm told. You might have heard of him. He is the one who helped recover the Presidents granddaughter."

"Colton Banyon," Slezeck blurted out. Banyon's ability to find things was why Slezeck wanted him dead, before he could uncover the Effort plot.

"Yes, I didn't know you knew about him. It is a very 'need to know' about his abilities," Marlene offered.

Considering Colton Banyon only had a few more hours to live before the Mexican hit team silenced him forever, Slezeck admitted he knew of Banyon, but the President had never introduced him. "I have run across his name in reviewing some of Homeland Securities most recent cases," he admitted. "I need to interview him and collect the evidence, before I can arrest Klotz. Banyon works out of Chicago, right?"

Marlene smiled. Slezeck had finally given her the means to set Banyon's plan in motion. "Actually, he is headed to his home in Las Vegas, on a noon plane. Lucky guy. The President told me on his last call. He said he had something for Banyon to do there. I understand he is collecting his whole team as well. Why do you ask?"

Stunned by the news, Slezeck didn't respond to the question but said, "Marlene can we take a short break. I am in need of a restroom. It's a long drive up here." He was a puppet in her hands and said exactly what she expected.

"Of course," she sweetly replied. "It's the third door on the right," she used her finger to point the way. He quickly got up and almost ran to the bathroom. He knew Werner Klotz would be meeting with the hit men in less than a half hour. They needed to know where Banyon was going.

When he finished locking the door, Slezeck again whipped out his cell phone. He hit the number for Werner Klotz. But what he didn't know was two things. First, was that Marlene was video recording his trip to the bathroom, secondly, Timmy had blocked Klotz's number. The phone went straight to voice mail.

"Werner, this is Paul," he said in frustration to the voicemail box, when he couldn't get him on the phone. "Banyon is not in Chicago. He is headed to Las Vegas, to his home there. Make sure our Mexican friends know. Also, the President is on to you, so don't come back to your office in

Washington, head to your place in Wisconsin. You need to erase this message as soon as you get it."

Slezeck then quickly dialed his man who was following Klotz, but couldn't connect with him either. Since, the man was not only a regular Homeland Security employee, but also an Effort member, Slezeck spoke openly. "As soon as Klotz gives directions to the Mexicans, I want you to take him out." He closed his phone, composed himself, and returned smiling, to the lounge area. He was satisfied, he had averted certain disaster.

"Now, where were we?" he confidently said as he returned to his seat.

"Well," Marlene continued. "We have more evidence on Klotz," she baited Slezeck.

"There is more?" the stupefied Slezeck croaked.

"The President just called me before you got here," she paused, to watch horror form on his face. "He said Werner has been linked to a group of gangbangers in San Diego and a plot designed to machine gun cars at the Mexican border."

"What?" Slezeck was suddenly sick to his stomach. He now expected the worst.

"Luckily, they were neutralized, before they could cause any problem," she cheerfully told him.

Suddenly weary, Slezeck asked Marlene. "Do we know where Klotz is right now?"

"We haven't found him yet," she responded. "But it is only a matter of time before we run him down. Then you can arrest him."

Quickly standing, Slezeck said. "Well, I'd better get on this." He stretched out his hand and shook hers. He left the ship in a jog.

As soon as the man was halfway down the dock, Marlene picked up the phone, calling the President. When he answered she only said five words, but they explained everything.

"He is good to go."

39

About a half hour earlier, Sister Teresa along with Father Grey, were canvasing the Ajax car rental parking lot. They appeared like two clergy, wandering around the lot, looking for their car. They spied the watcher almost immediately. He had arrived earlier than Klotz, only because he had taken a commercial flight from Washington, while Klotz went by private plane. He knew where Klotz was going and when he would arrive.

The two fake clergy wandered over to where the man stood smoking a cigarette, against the back fence of the lot. He did not react as they drew near.

"Please sir," Sister Teresa said sweetly, as they approached. "We can't seem to find our car." An angelic smile covered her face, keeping him off guard.

Father Grey quickly pulled a sheet of paper from his inside pocket and offered it to the man, to give directions. But it was a deception. As the man's eyes went to the paper, Father Grey pulled a sap from his pocket, with his other hand, and smacked the watcher hard over the head. He immediately tumbled to the ground. Sister Teresa quickly produced plastic cuffs, a blind fold, and a gag, from her sleeves. They trussed up the man in seconds, then carried him to a nearby car and deposited him in the back seat, face down.

"You'd better take his wallet, phone and watch," Father Grey told Sister Teresa. "We want this to look like a mugging." She quickly gathered the materials, sticking them up her sleeves.

"We'll come back later to take back the bindings," he informed her.

"But what if he is awake?" the nun asked.

""Well, we'll just have to give him another bump," the father replied cheerfully. "We can't have him arrested because he hasn't committed a crime, as far as we can tell."

Sister Teresa then hit a button on her phone and connected with Bart. "Watcher is down," she said into the phone without greeting Bart.

Bart was parked at the other end of the large lot. He had rented a small car and sat ready for Klotz to appear. "Good, now set up your video equipment, Klotz should be here soon."

As they were getting everything ready, a phone started ringing. Sister Teresa reached up her sleeve and produced the watchers phone. It was the one ringing. As she looked at the screen, she realized the call was coming from Paul Slezeck.

40

"We leave in about an hour and half," Banyon said to Eric. "And we need the give them time to get ready. So, who are your choices?"

"Well, the plan calls for us to be low profile and not memorable. We need good shooters that don't appear to be a threat. My only concern is they will be with us for a couple of days in close quarters," Eric replied.

"So, you've reached the same conclusion as I have," Banyon stated.

"I guess so," he said.

Banyon immediately pressed his Bluetooth. "Mandy and Heather get up to my office right now."

"May God help us around these two," Eric said under his breath, knowing they would be incredible temptations and distractions.

"We need to agree, Loni and the Patel sisters can never know about this mission. It is dangerous in two ways. And either way could get us killed," Banyon remarked with little humor.

"Amen," Eric replied as he ran his hand through his hair. "I think I am more afraid of our women then the Mexicans," he said jokingly.

At just that second, Banyon's cell phone rang. It was the President. "Hello," Banyon spoke into the phone.

"We've got the goods on Slezeck," the President announced excitedly. "Marlene has sent me the spy videos. He clearly implicates himself and Klotz. She is on her way, back to the capital, with the original tapes."

"Where is Slezeck now?" Banyon asked as he noticed the two women enter his office from different entrances. They skidded to a stop in front of his desk and stood at attention. They were still dressed in the same clothes as earlier. Banyon stuck up his finger, indicating he needed a minute while talking to the President. Eric got the message and waved them over to the couch area.

Meanwhile, the President kept talking. "Marlene had one of her watchers put a bug on his car. He is headed back to his office as we speak. I'll be ready for him when he comes for his meeting," the President said with determination.

"Good," Banyon offered.

"How goes it there?"

"We are still waiting for Klotz at the parking lot," Banyon said. "It should go down at any time."

"Then, we start damage control," the politician announced.

41

Paul Slezeck was speeding down the highway which separated Baltimore and Washington D.C. He had tried to call Klotz, several more times, only getting voicemail. He had the same bad luck with his watcher. His frustration level was high. His face was beet red. He had an over whelming feeling that he was in a trap. The noose was tightening. He was also angry about how Marlene had treated him. True, she was a clever woman, but something didn't feel right about their meeting. He just couldn't put his finger on it.

He knew his phone was completely encrypted, with the most advanced technology. He was sure his calls could not be intercepted, or understood. But he failed to understand Timmy. He had broken the encrypted code earlier, when he blocked the calls to Klotz. Any calls he made were routed through an NAS listening center and everything was reported directly to the White House.

Slezeck suddenly wondered if his plan to have the President sign the executive order was in jeopardy. He was just a few hours away from success. He could not allow himself to fail to reach his goal. He had counted on the last disaster to put the President over the top. He now realized he needed another disaster.

He tried to think logically. He was in charge of the largest government agency in the world. He also had the complete backing of the Effort. He just had to figure out how to use them to get his plan back on track.

Suddenly, it hit him. Kill Banyon now. Get him before he got on a plane. A sinister smile crossed his face. He began to feel the adrenaline flow through his body. Yes, this would put the President in just the right mood to sign the document at their meeting. The only question was how to kill him?

He picked up his phone, from the seat, where he had thrown it, and dialed the number of an Effort member in Chicago.

42

Bart watched from his car as a bus pulled up to the rental agency. Several people got out, including six, tough-looking, Mexican men. He quickly pressed a button on his phone. "They're here. Make sure you get head shots of each one and send them on. I want full jackets on these guys before you get back to the office."

"Shooting them now," Father Grey reported back.

Bart watched as they moved, as a group, around the parking lot, trying to find their car. It was in the middle of the huge lot, but Bart could see them easily. They gathered around the front of the car, smoking cigarettes, and chatting, while they waited.

Within a minute, Bart spotted a taxi making its way into the front lot of the rental agency. The taxi stopped. Werner Klotz slowly pulled himself out of the back seat. Bart watched as Klotz leaned into the front window and told the cabbie, to wait. Klotz then turned and began walking to the larger lot.

He used a cane to walk, but Bart knew the cane was also a deadly weapon. The shiny black cane had a steel tipped knife on one end and the handle contained a two shot derringer. He also carried a small slim briefcase. Bart assumed it contained the pictures of Banyon and his team. He guessed, Klotz had been nearby watching for the Mexicans to make their appearance.

"Klotz has arrived," he spoke into his phone.

"We've got him," the nun replied.

Bart put the running rental car in gear and quickly caught up to Klotz, before he got near the now curious Mexican men. He opened his window halfway and called out to Klotz, in his Slezeck voice.

Gerald J. Kubicki & Kristopher Kubicki

"Werner, hold up, I need to talk to you," he said. Klotz turned towards the car, but said nothing. "Werner it's me, Paul," Bart continued.

"What are you doing here?" Klotz suddenly said in surprise as he looked towards the man impersonating Slezeck. The shiny sun and Klotz's old eyes made him squint, preventing him from recognizing an imposter.

"Stop, I need to talk to you for a second. It's important, otherwise, I would not have traveled this far to see you," Bart pressed.

"Why didn't you just call me on my cell phone, you idiot," Werner Klotz chuckled. But Bart now had his attention.

"I've been calling you since early this morning, Werner," Bart evenly said. "Either you can't hear it ring, or your phone is broken. You're the idiot," Bart shot back. This quickly put Klotz on the defensive. He had missed many calls in the past, because of his poor hearing. He quickly reached into his pocket, pulled out the cell phone and glared at his phone screen. It showed he had missed twelve calls. Timmy had salted the call signatures on his phone, when Klotz was still up in the air.

Rather than say something like I'm sorry, Werner just got mad. "So, what is so damn important that you came all the way to Chicago, to tell me, anyway?"

"It's about the target for the Mexicans, Werner," Bart said as he pointed to the group of Mexicans milling around like he often saw, at his local plant nursery parking lot.

"What about him?"

"He has left Chicago and is headed for Las Vegas, his whole team too. You need to send these guys to Las Vegas."

"But?" Klotz started.

Bart slipped a piece of paper out the window. Klotz grabbed it in shaky hands and read it carefully. The Mexicans were beginning to get suspicious. Twelve dark menacing eyes were now watching them. "It's his address in Las Vegas," Bart said.

"I'll have to get them tickets," Klotz mumbled. "This will take some time to arrange, Paul," he croaked.

"I don't care, make it happen, Werner," Bart ordered him. "When you are done, I want you to immediately head back to your office in Washington. I might have more work for you today."

"More work?" Klotz protested. "Haven't I done enough for the Effort already?" Bart could see that Klotz was tired and frazzled.

"Your plan for the gangbangers in San Diego blew up," Bart told him.

"But I bought the guns myself," Klotz protested. "I personal flew out there and met with the head guy two weeks ago, when the guns arrived. I moved money to his account, five million to be exact. What happened?"

"Somehow, another drug gang found out about the guns and a major war started. The gang members are all dead. The disaster never happened. I need another disaster, if we want the President to sign the executive order." Bart lied to Klotz.

"Damn," Klotz swore. "All that work for nothing," he roared as he threw up his arms in disgust.

"That's not all, Werner. The Mexican authorities captured the man that set off the explosives remotely in Laredo."

"What?" Klotz yelled. "I told him to run as soon as he hit the button. He and his brother cost me a bundle." Bart now had all the evidence he needed on Klotz.

"Well, make this one work or else, you'll need to start watching your back," Bart threatened. He then rolled up the window. Klotz stood in disbelief, for a few seconds and then proceeded to the group of Mexicans. Bart slowly rolled past the now angry looking predators, in his rental car, just as Klotz opened his briefcase and scattered the pictures of Banyon and his team across the hood of their rental car.

"You get all of that?" he asked his watchers.

"Every word," Father Grey replied.

"I'm headed back to the office. You guys stay with Klotz. Make sure the Mexicans get on a plane to Las Vegas and Klotz gets on his plane to Washington. I'll notify the President, he can decide if he wants to pick him up there, or continue to watch him."

Part Five

More Stress

43

Banyon hung up his cell phone. He had just finished talk-ing to Bart, who had filled him in on the Klotz situation. Bart told him he was returning to the office immediately, to put together profiles of the Mexicans.

Banyon asked if he wanted him to call the President and report in, but Bart told Banyon he already had, and the President had decided to have Klotz put under arrest, by U.S. Marshalls, as soon as he landed, back in Washington D. C. *Well, two out of three parts of the plan have already been completed and it is just eleven o'clock*, Banyon thought.

As he hung up the phone, he motioned for Heather and Mandy to return to his desk. They had been talking with Eric in the corner. They didn't know why Banyon has sum-moned them to his office, but he was sure they had a pretty good idea. They walked purposefully towards the back of the office.

He flipped through some paper on his desk to give him-self some time to think. He wondered if he was doing the right thing. While they were acting very professional right now, he had seen them act otherwise. He now turned his eyes to the two women that had returned and now stood at attention in front of his desk. He wasn't sure what he wanted to say. He knew he had to allow them to get pre-pared for the trip, but also knew he had to say a few things to them, as well.

"I want you to know we chose you two to be our body-guards," Banyon said with little excitement.

"Oh, goodie. I knew you would choose me, Colt," Mandy exclaimed. "By the way, how much are you paying us, or do we have to work by the hour?" There was no mis-taking her innuendo.

Clearing his throat, Banyon ignored her comment. "You were chosen because you give us the best chance of success, not because of your physical attributes, or of any perceived friendships."

"Where are we going?" Heather asked professionally as she nudged Mandy to shut up.

"We will be heading to Las Vegas within the hour."

Mandy started jumping up and down; Heather said nothing, she was cool as a cucumber, but did smile provocatively. Banyon wondered what was currently going through their minds. They had both reacted differently.

"I've never been to Las Vegas," Mandy gushed. "I can't wait to see it. I want to see the strip, Colt. Can I? Can I?"

"I've been there several times before. For the Porno conventions, they have them there twice a year," Heather added knowingly as she gazed at him evenly.

"Hold on," Banyon said as he held up his hand, to stop their reactions. "You need to agree to a couple of rules, before you are officially hired. If you can't comply, you can't go. It is just that simple."

"What are the rules?" Heather asked in her husky voice. "Do I need to wear leather or maybe latex?" Eric was close to nodding his head, but refrained.

Suddenly serious, Banyon said. "The first rule is; this mission will be dangerous. People will probably die. You may be required to shoot them. You need to be vigilant, at all times. We have been authorized to use deadly force." Wolf had already told Banyon the Mexican hit men were responsible for more than one hundred deaths, in the past three years. It included women and children. Banyon relayed the information.

"These scumbags need to die," Heather agreed and nodded her head. Her long hair flew everywhere.

"They'll get no mercy from me," Mandy added.

"Second rule," Banyon said as he counted on his fingers. "You can never tell anyone about what you see, or hear, during this mission. Is that clear? Especially, if you want more missions from me," Banyon threatened them.

"I can keep a secret," Heather told him.

"And that includes anyone in this office," Banyon added. "It seems to be a hotbed of gossip."

"I won't even tell myself," Mandy joked and got a stern look from Banyon.

"Third rule," Banyon continued. "You can't go with us looking like you do now. You will need to change your clothes and attitude."

"To what?" Heather asked

"Mandy, I want you dressed like my daughter and Heather, you need to dress down. Try to look less sexy. We want to go unnoticed."

"Yes, sir," both quickly replied as they bowed their heads. Mandy glanced at Heather and said, "his daughter, really?" Heather just shrugged her shoulders.

"Next, you two will be responsible for supplies and things we will need done during the trip," Banyon said.

"I can cook," Mandy quickly told him. "I'm also good at shopping. I'm not too good at cleaning though."

"I don't think he means domestic supplies, do you, Colt?" Heather said to Mandy.

Feeling a little frustrated, Banyon clarified. "I want you two to go to the armory and requisition two sets of night vision goggles for yourselves. You will also need guns and a box of ammo. Eric and I already have ours. He pointed to the desk where the guns that Bart had conjured up, lay side by side.

"How will we get them through the scanners at the airport?" Heather inquired.

"We are taking a private plane. It has been arranged. As long as we don't bring them into the cockpit, we're good," Banyon answered her.

"Wow," Mandy said. "I've never been on a private plane. Will it be just us on the plane," she quickly asked with a gleam in her eye.

Banyon now wondered if she was thinking about the mile high club. "It will be just the four of us."

"Does it have a bed...?" Mandy started, but was nudged by Heather to shut up.

"Finally, this is a mission, not a holiday," Banyon noted. "You need to act professionally. That means no lap-dances or enticements. Do I make myself clear?"

"We will act professionally," Heather responded. This time when she glanced at Mandy, she was not smiling, but was frowning.

"Good, now be back in my office by noon. We leave then," Banyon said as he waved them out the door. This time Mandy headed through the office door, but stopped by the entrance and addressed Banyon.

"Can I at least bring a bathing suit?" she asked with a plea.

"Of course," Eric quickly replied. "You too Heather," he quickly added. Banyon raised his eyebrows, but let it go.

When they finally left the office, the girls were chatting away about Las Vegas. Eric turned towards Banyon. "You handled that well, I think."

"Only time will tell," he replied.

"Now, we only have to worry about the Mexicans killing us and not our women," Eric joked.

"Let's hope so," Banyon answered.

Suddenly, Banyon's phone rang. He picked it up and answered it without looking at the screen. It was the President

"Colt, I'm in the situation room. We have another crisis to handle."

44

"What's happened now?" Banyon found himself saying again. He thought he had covered everything.

"Two American girls have been kidnapped in Acapulco, Mexico," the President replied tersely. "We need to get them back. Can you help?"

"What are their full names, from what hotel and when were they taken?" Banyon asked as he gathered a piece of paper and clicked open his pen. Eric looked over his shoulder with concern. He wondered how many of these situations Banyon would have to deal with because of the current crisis in Mexico.

The President gave him the information and then added. "I've got twelve SEALs, in the air, from Panama. They are in helicopters from the Navy base there. They're over the ocean in international waters. I can vector them into land as soon as you can tell me where the girls are located.

"I understand," Banyon answered.

"I also need you on screen in the situation room."

"Give me five minutes and I will get back to you," He told the President and hung up his phone.

"Sounds like more trouble?" Eric asked.

"Yes," Banyon said, with tension in his voice. Then he started barking orders. "Go find Mandy and have her send up the next contract employee. Also, tell her our trip, will be delayed for an hour. Tell Heather too. Here's the number for the private plane crew." Banyon drew a sheet of paper from his bag.

"Okay," Eric said.

"Have someone call the crew and update them," Banyon ordered. "And then find Bart and tell him what is going on. Also, make sure he finishes the profiles of the men we are going to lead to Las Vegas."

"Will do," Eric said as he jogged out the door.

"Timmy," Banyon yelled into his Bluetooth. "I need the situation room on my screen, now."

"Booting up as we speak," Timmy answered. Banyon saw his screen quickly come alive. There were several people on the side monitors, in the situation room, this time.

The President spoke. "Do you have the address?"

"Still working on their location," he said into the monitor. He then quickly hit the escape button and addressed Wolf.

"Wolf, where are the girls?"

"Give me a minute, too," Wolf growled. "I'm researching them now."

While he waited, he detected movement by the office door. A frail-looking woman stood there and knocked on the open door. She was dressed in a very conservative brown business suit with a skirt the covered her knees. Her hair style was from the sixties and was a mousey grey. She carried a pad of paper and a pen, close to her buxom. She appeared to be around fifty-something years old. Banyon was sure she was an administrative assistant or secretary. He waved her up to his desk.

"Who are you?" He inquired.

"My name is Beth," she replied. "I'm the contract employee for this mission," she answered proudly in a clear, but squeaky voice.

"Okay," Banyon said. "Go over to the couches and make yourself comfortable. This shouldn't take more than an hour."

"But what should I be doing?"

"That's just it, you don't have to do anything, just be here. I can turn the TV on, if you want?"

"I can do some filing or reviewing while I wait?" she said weakly as she looked around the office for something that needed organizing.

"Just go over there and be quiet," an annoyed Banyon ordered. He dismissed her with a wave of his hand. She slinked over to the farthest couch and sat primly with her legs crossed. She looked very intimidated by the office.

"Anything yet?" he whispered, but there was no answer.

"Did you say something?" he heard Beth ask hopefully, as her head rose.

"I'm talking to myself," he angrily replied and reached for the remote to turn the TV on. He didn't want her to hear his conversations. He glanced at his watch. It had already been more than five minutes. *Where the hell is Wolf,* he thought. *The President and those poor girls are relying on me and I don't have any answers yet.*

"Wolf, are you there?" he asked in a concerned voice.

"I'm here, Colt," the spirit replied as if distracted.

"Have you got the location yet?"

"Colt, I do, but there is something else you need to know."

"What?" Banyon all but screamed.

"There has been another disaster planned. You need to fix this one too, right now."

"Why, right now?"

"Because, you are the target," Wolf told the stunned Banyon.

"When and where?"

"Just outside your building I'm afraid, in about fifteen minutes," the spirit replied.

45

"Son-of-a-bitch," Banyon yelled out. "This couldn't happen at a worse time," he said in frustration to no one. He pounded the desk several times in anger.

Beth perked up and looked at Banyon hopefully, again. "Do you need my help now, dear?" she quickly asked in her squeaky voice. She started to get up from the couch, but Banyon waved her back.

"Just sit quietly. No talking" he screamed at her over his monitor.

"Oh, my," she uttered.

"I've now got a second crisis to handle I can't deal with you right now." She was taken aback by his outburst. It showed as she huffed at him showing her irritation and plopped back down on the couch.

"No need to be rude," she yelled back. She then started writing on her pad. Banyon was sure she was writing a complaint to Human Resources. He wondered how many demerits he would get.

Banyon did not answer her, but addressed Wolf, instead. "First, give me the location of the kidnapped girls. I need to get the rescue on track."

Wolf instantly replied. "If you die, I will never complete my curse. You must save yourself, for the greater good." Wolf had been known to be callously selfish. He always felt his needs overrode any others.

"I'm saving these kids first," Banyon replied with gritty determination. "What's their location, Wolf?"

"As you wish," Wolf sadly answered and gave him the address. He also added that there were five policemen currently with the girls in the house.

Banyon pressed the escape button on his computer and was immediately onscreen in the situation room. He relayed the address and then said. "Mr. President, I have another crisis to deal with as well."

"What?" the President inquired.

"Yes, sir, someone is trying to kill me, right now, and maybe blow up the Law offices at the same time. I need time to work on a solution."

He then waited for the President to respond. Banyon could hear people talking in the background, before the President answered. "You've got ten minutes before we have boots on the ground. You must be back on screen by then. I need your eyes to make this work without collateral damage," the President informed him. The President was, like Wolf, selfish when he needed something done.

"Thank you, sir," Banyon said.

"And Colt, you are authorized to use any resources you need. You have my full authority, even deadly force."

"I'll be back," Banyon promised and pressed the escape key. He then whispered to Wolf. "Tell me what you know about the threat?"

"In about fifteen minutes," Wolf started. "A blue panel van will pull up to the offices and park by the front door. A Mexican looking man will immediately run from it. When he is far enough away, he will detonate the explosives in the van by a remote control device. The charge is sufficient to blow half the building away. Several people will be killed, including you, unless you find a way to stop it. The two men that sent the Mexican are right outside already, with machine guns. They will shoot the Mexican. Then they will enter the building, looking for you. If you're still alive, they will finish the job. If you leave now, they will mow you down."

"Who has sent the Mexican? Is it the cartels?" Banyon was now scared. If it was the cartels, then they knew of him and would not stop, even if he could prevent this current threat. He knew they would never stop until they killed Banyon and anyone associated with him. This included Loni, Eric, the Patel sisters, and his three sons. He had hoped to never involve his family in any of his cases, but now they were all in jeopardy.

To his relief, Wolf corrected him. "No, it is not the cartels. As far as I can tell, they don't know you exist."

"Then who?"

"This threat comes from the Effort and originated with Paul Slezeck. He knows his gangbanger plan has been neutralized and decided he needed a disaster to happen, before he meets with the President, in a couple of hours. He contacted some Effort people in Chicago and they have put this threat together for him. They are the ones with the machine guns. I have their names for you as well, when you are ready," Wolf said.

"Why use a Mexican though?"

"Remember, Slezeck's ultimate goal is to get the President to sign the executive order. He believes security cameras will record the Latino driver and everyone will assume the cartels are responsible. He believes this will cause the President, during his grief, to sign the order when he meets with him. He doesn't care how many people he kills to achieve his goal."

"But how does he even know where I am?" Banyon asked.

"I told you, Slezeck has someone watching you. The man is in the huge parking lot for the shopping center, just outside your own parking lot. He follows you everywhere you go, but he is just a Homeland Security agent. He thinks he is shadowing a 'person of interest' for the agency.

"Can you give me any additional information?"

"You only have thirteen minutes now."

46

"Bart," Banyon screamed into his Bluetooth. "I have just uncovered a bomb threat to Dewey and Beatem. It will explode in about thirteen minutes. We need to evacuate the building right now."

"Be there in thirty seconds," Bart responded.

Beth suddenly jumped up from her couch and moved towards Banyon's desk. He expected to see fright on her face, but she appeared excited instead. "Now, will you let me help you?" she asked him.

Before he could answer, Bart ran into the room, no longer looking like Paul Slezeck. "Tell me what you know?" he demanded before he got to the desk. Banyon filled him in on the details then asked about the evacuation plan, considering there were two men with machine guns already outside the building.

"We don't evacuate, we neutralize," Bart answered more like a philosophy.

"But we only have eleven minutes left," Banyon complained. "And the President expects me back on the screen in nine minutes. There must be a plan?" Banyon was overstressed and didn't share the confidence that Bart exuded.

Bart was busy thinking and did not quickly respond. While he was considering his options, Banyon's office was filling up with people. Eric charged in first, followed by Heather and Mandy, Edger soon loped in, and several others gathered in the hallway. Despite the warning Banyon gave over his Bluetooth, no one was heading for the exits. Everyone looked apprehensive, but no one moved.

"You said the bomb will be detonated by remote control, right?" Bart suddenly asked Banyon.

"Yes," Banyon replied wondering where Bart was going. "The Mexican is supposed to hit the remote, as soon as he is out of the explosion range."

"Good," Bart uttered. "We can handle this."

"Are you kidding?" Banyon asked.

"Not at all. We have planned for this situation," Bart said with confidence. "Timmy, please get your laptop and station yourself in the lobby. As soon as you see the van, hit the jamming device."

Timmy got Colt's attention by waving his hands in the crowded room. "Colt, just so you know," Timmy said. "Once I hit the jammer, all electronics will shut down, that means you will lose your screen to the situation room, but also it will render any remote control device useless." He turned on his heel and was gone.

"Oh," Banyon croaked. "How long before I can reboot?"

"I can answer that," Beth suddenly spoke up. "It will take fifteen minutes to defuse the bomb."

Banyon looked at her with a questioning look. "How do you know?"

Bart quickly jumped in. "Beth's special talent is defusing bombs. She is the best in the world. If she says fifteen minutes to defuse it, it will be fifteen minutes. You can take that to the bank."

"Then I'd better notify the President to stall the rescue," Banyon muttered mostly to himself. He sat back down at his desk, took a deep breath and pressed the escape button on his computer. He addressed the President with everyone standing in the room. He raised his hand for silence as he talked to the leader.

"Sir, I'm going to be tied up with this bomb threat for a half hour. I won't have access to the internet. I suggest you postpone the rescue until I'm back on line."

"I see," said the President. The disappointment was evident in his voice.

"It can't be helped, sir. The lives of many people are at stake," Banyon offered.

"The choppers will be running low on fuel by then," the President quickly responded as Banyon heard someone tell him in the background.

"But can you postpone?" Banyon pressed.

"We'll make due, these men are SEALs," the President proudly said. "But you had better be back by then."

"Yes, sir," Banyon responded and pressed the escape button.

Meanwhile, Bart was issuing orders. "Beth, go get your gear. I want that bomb defused in record time. Be ready, in the lobby, to go to work."

"I will do my best. Just don't yell at me like Colt, over there does." She left the room moving faster than Banyon believed possible.

Bart continued, "Andre and Guido, draw guns from the armory and take up a position outside. When the Mexican starts running, grab him." When Banyon questioned him with a look, Bart told him, "the chef and the Brooklynese orator."

"Then what?" Banyon heard in his Bluetooth as one of them asked.

"We'll have to find a way to take down the guys with the machine guns," Bart commented as he thought. "But I don't want a firefight against machine guns, especially when there are so many people around."

"I think I have a better and safer plan," Banyon suddenly spoke.

"Well let's hear it?" Bart said.

"Bart can you impersonate me?" Banyon asked.

"I did the mold yesterday. It will take me five minutes to put on the finishing touches. Why do you ask?"

"Good," Banyon said. He threw him the keys to his Jaguar. "Give me your keys," he requested. Bart drove a Honda.

Bart gave him a questioning look. "Why, my car?"

"Here is the plan," Banyon explained. "I'm going to have Mandy and Heather distract the machine gunners long enough for you, looking like me, to reach the Jaguar. Take Andre and Guido with you. Then head for my house in Barrington. They will undoubtedly follow thinking I'm going home and then I can slip out when I'm done with the President and drive your car to the airport."

"And the Mexican?"

"Heather and Mandy can catch the Mexican." He looked at the two women who were bobbing their heads emphatically. "They will already be outside."

"Sounds good so far," Bart said.

"On the way, call the police and have them be ready to ambush the shooters. It will take about twenty minutes for you to get there. There will be plenty of time."

"Or, we can take them out ourselves," Bart said brightly.

"That's your call," Banyon told him. "The keys to the house are on the key chain, but Bart, don't wreck my home, please."

Bart chuckled. "Well, you see it's like this, I don't like people who try to blow up my office," Bart responded. "There is a measure of revenge to be gained and we won't wreck your house, either."

"It will also draw the watcher," Banyon continued. "I don't want him following us to the airport and possibly notifying anyone where we are going. He will follow you."

"The plan sounds solid to me," Bart exclaimed. "Does anybody have any objections?" he yelled into the room. When no one answered, he yelled, "Let's do it then," and started to leave the room.

"Okay," several people said.

"Oh and Colt," Bart stopped and turned to him.

"Yes."

"The cost of all this is going on your bill."

47

A few minutes later, at the offices of Dewy & Beatem, Banyon and Eric stood alone on his balcony looking out at the parking lot. There were five other balconies facing the front of the building, the men could hear people talking around them. Everybody had turned out to watch the show. Eric had a pair of binoculars trained on the two Effort men in their car.

Below, in the lobby, Banyon watched as people lined up for their part of the play. The entire front of the building was all one way glass, so the shooters had no idea of the backstage for the show. Banyon saw Timmy with his laptop; Beth now dressed in a sliver bomb suit, Guido and Andre looking mean enough to bite someone's head off, Bart now looking surprisingly like Banyon and the two girls, Heather and Mandy. Mandy looked his way and waved. Heather carried a purse with two guns secreted away, just in case. The players were ready, the audience had front row seats and the real danger of a bomb blowing up the building wasn't even a concern, assuming everyone did their part. All of the actors were wearing their Bluetooth communicators.

"Go, first act," Banyon said into his Bluetooth. Mandy and Heather quickly made their way out the front door. They were still dressed like they had been earlier, so Banyon knew the men would notice. The women walked lazily towards the mall and away from where Banyon had parked his car. They appeared to be two friends going shopping.

"Their looking at the girls," Eric said as he watched.

"Second act," Banyon spoke into his Bluetooth.

Mandy suddenly appeared to stumble and drop something on the ground. Both girls bent over from the waist while keeping their legs straight, like only very fit women could do.

"They're leaning forward in their seats," Eric reported. "They're taking in the show. We've got them hooked."

"Act three," Banyon ordered. Bart and the two other men shuffled out the door, quickly heading for the green Jaguar. They were more than halfway there before the man in the passenger side of the car saw them. He immediately started to get out of the car and raise his machine gun to fire, but Bart was already at the car and piled inside. Eric watched as his partner grabbed his coat and pulled him back inside.

"Act four is a go," Banyon announced. Bart now had the Jaguar running and sped out of the parking lot. Mandy and Heather were already hidden behind some bushes, at the corner of the lot.

"Come on, take the bait you bastard," Eric cried out like an angler hoping the fish would bite.

Suddenly, there were cheers on the other balconies as the Effort men backed up their car and took off after the Jaguar. Almost immediately, the Homeland Security agent fell into line behind them. Banyon breathed a sigh of relief, but it was short lived.

Eric followed the small caravan out of the mall area with his binoculars. Suddenly, he announced a sighting. "Blue van just turned into the parking lot."

"Act five, Timmy do your thing and jam the electronics," Banyon quickly said.

Shortly Timmy replied. "Done."

Everyone watched the van approach the Dewey & Beatem parking lot slowly, as if making sure of the address. The blue van pulled into a handicapped space right near the front door. A few people began to back up, but most stayed their ground. The driver, a small Latino, bolted from the truck, leaving the door open. He ran as fast as he could towards the mall area.

"Act six," Banyon yelled into his Bluetooth. Mandy and Heather emerged from their hiding place. The man saw them and tried to outrun them before they could cut him off. Mandy stepped out of her high heels and took off after him.

People on the balconies were cheering and screaming "Go, Mandy go", like they were watching a track meet. The Mexican never stood a chance. Mandy closed like a tiger chasing a water buffalo. When she was near, she pushed him in the back, throwing him off balance and headfirst into the hard tarmac. He skidded to a stop, using his face as the brake. Mandy was immediately on him and kneeled on his back. She yanked back his head using his hair, and everyone heard her talk through her Bluetooth.

"Going somewhere, scumbag." Mandy said into his ear. "How does it feel to be run down by a little girl?"

Heather was now alongside her with her gun drawn. She moved so the Mexican could see the gun. The remote control device was still in his left hand and he glowered at her with hatred in his eyes. The he pressed the button.

Nothing happened, but Heather rewarded his act of courage, by batting the remote away from him, with her foot. It landed a few feet away. She then kicked him square in his bloody face, and for a second, his eyes rolled back into his head.

"Act seven," Banyon spoke into his Bluetooth.

"I'm sure you know the drill, hands behind your back, asshole," Heather spat out in a very threatening voice. Mandy quickly restrained him in zip plastic cuffs and they began walking the woozy man back to the office, picking up the remote along the way. Heather raised it above her head for everyone to see.

Act eight was Beth's part. She bolted out the office door, with her bag of tools and ran around the van, to the open door. She dropped her bag and climbed into the front seat, disappearing from view. Banyon was tense and prayed the van was not booby-trapped. She was out in seconds.

"I'll have this bomb defused in less than five minutes," she calmly spoke. "They must have been in a big hurry to build this bomb, there are no safety measures. I just have to cut a couple of wires." She then collected her bag and returned inside the van. Everyone on the balconies remained silent and waited for her to signal.

Meanwhile, the two girls roughly pushed the Mexican through the front door. Once inside, two men grabbed him. Both girls looked up at the balcony where Banyon and Eric stood. This time Banyon waved with a smile on his face.

"What do you want to do with him?" one of the two guards asked.

"Bart wants to interrogate him, when he gets back. I don't think he means to be gentle with him either," Banyon told the guard.

The Mexican's head quickly snapped up. "I know my rights, man. I want a lawyer".

"Well my friend, that only applies if you are arrested by law enforcement," Banyon said from the balcony. "We are private citizens, but I assume you a lawyer will be present, in the room, with you, shortly." The guards took him away. When he started to protest, he got a punch in his midsection to shut him up.

While Banyon waited for the bomb to be defused, he realized the two women had entered the balcony. Mandy stood right next to him, Heather stood by Eric. Timmy was standing behind them with his laptop open and ready to end the jamming as soon as he got the all clear.

"Did we do good?" Mandy asked as she looked up at him.

"You guys were great," Banyon said. He then reached over and patted Mandy on her back with affection.

"Lower," she immediately responded. Then she looked at him and said "Oops, sorry", then added, "Daddy" with a tilt of her head.

"Danger makes me so hot," Heather breathed. "I need a shower. How about you Mandy," she said seductively.

"We can change into our disguises for the trip at the same time," Mandy noted with excitement.

"Okay," Banyon said oblivious to the implied sex of the conversation. "But be back in my office as soon as you can."

Heather grabbed Mandy by the hand and began to lead her off the balcony. She turned to Timmy. "Are you coming?" she purred.

A suddenly nervous Timmy replied. "No man, I'm done doing that."

Banyon turned just in time to see a look of concern cross Heathers face as she lead Mandy out the door.

At that moment Banyon sensed movement by the van and saw Beth give the thumbs up. "I've defused the bomb," she announced into her Bluetooth.

There was loud applause. The play had ended.

48

"Stop the jamming, Timmy," Banyon ordered. "And get me booted up to the situation room. There are several lives at stake."

"Be done in one minute," the geek replied, he was already at Banyon's desk, pounding on the keyboard.

While he waited for Timmy to do his magic, Banyon dialed Bart. He wanted to fill him in on their success. "Bart the bomb has been defused and the Mexican is waiting for you in the interrogation room."

"Great job Colt," Bart answered.

"How are things going on your end?"

"Your car has a lot of power," he said. "It has a real smooth ride too. I might have to get me one of these." Banyon was beginning to understand, Bart was very cool customer under pressure.

"Do you have a plan for when you reach my house?"

"I do, but I'd rather not discuss it on an open line," the lawyer said. "We'll be there in about six minutes. I'll call you when we are headed back." Bart then hung up the cell phone before Banyon could ask anymore question.

"You're in," Timmy shouted.

"Okay, you can go and watch Heather now," Banyon told him.

"No, not doing that anymore. Did you see her reaction when I told her, no, man? I'm winning," he gushed as he danced out of the room.

Banyon just shook his head as he was sure Timmy was making a beeline to the showers. He jumped to his desk and immediately saw his face on a side monitor.

"I'm back, Mr. President," he quickly said.

"That's great," The President replied from off screen. "I trust your other crisis is concluded?"

"No harm done," Banyon told him.

"You only took fifteen minutes," the President noted.

"We had a good plan and everybody did their jobs," Banyon replied.

"Okay, people, the rescue is back on." He heard the President say as he clapped his hands. Immediately there were many voices talking.

"How is this going down?" Banyon asked.

"The SEALS are going to be deployed over the water. They all have scuba gear and will swim to a rock outcropping, just three blocks from the house. We have two zodiacs following them in in ten minutes, they will do the extraction."

"Are you going to use the 'Danta Lopez' cover?"

"We didn't have time to get the men any guns or blood, to leave as evidence," the President lamented.

"Leave a note in Spanish," Banyon said. "Have it say something like 'Danta Lopez was here. You should be afraid.'"

"I like it," the President responded and gave the order to someone in the room.

"Is there anything happening we should know about," the President asked with concern.

"Let me check, be back in a minute," Banyon informed him and hit the escape button on his computer.

"Wolf, I need an update?"

"Glad to see you're okay, Colt." The spirit said cheerfully. "There are now only four men with the girls. The girls are tied to chairs in an upstairs bedroom. They have been stripped, but no harm has come to them, yet. The four men are policemen and are lounging on couches downstairs. They are waiting for a Chinese man. He intends to buy the girls and spirit them out to a ship. It is eight miles out from the beach."

"What's the name of the ship?"

"It's named 'the Charming' and is out of San Francisco," Wolf informed him.

"Who is the owner?"

"His name is John Chang. He is onboard. He is the leader of the triad in San Francisco and a well-known killer.

He is also an opium dealer, with a taste for young girls. When he is done with them, he just throws them over the side."

"Any innocents on the ship?"

"No, there is just his crew of seven. They are also his henchmen. He has sent one of his men, in a speedboat, to shore, to collect the girls. He is just leaving now."

Banyon pressed the escape button and brought the President quickly up to speed on the house and the ship. He listened as the President had several loud discussions with people on his staff. Then he was back.

"We know this guy," the President announced. "He is on one of our most wanted lists. We didn't know about his tastes in women, though. We are going to destroy him and his ship. I have vectored one of the helicopters to his coordinates. Satellite images will soon show on the top left monitor."

An image of a boat suddenly appeared. The image grew larger, as it zoomed in. Banyon could clearly see a Chinese man, standing on the transom, in a bathing suit. He suddenly looked into the sky as he shaded the sun from his eyes. Shock filled his face. Two seconds later the missile, fired by the chopper, found its mark. The entire ship disintegrated; the speedboat only a few feet away capsized. John Chang would never terrorize another woman again. The man in the water, from the speedboat, would drift towards Hawaii, two thousand miles away.

Eric, who was standing to the side of Banyon and off screen said, "Wow".

"Scratch him off our list. Say that his ship was sunk by sea pirates," Banyon heard the President tell someone.

"But there are no pirates in that part of the world," someone spoke.

"Well, there are now," replied the President.

The big monitor changed. Banyon could see three head camera shots as they emerged from the sea and hurried to take up defense positions. The fourth screen was a zoomed in satellite image of the neighborhood. "SEAL team landed," he heard from the leader. "Do you see any hostiles?"

Gerald J. Kubicki & Kristopher Kubicki

Banyon turned his head and in a whisper, asked Wolf for an update. He quickly said. "The coast is clear, all the way to the target."

"Let's move people," the SEAL leader ordered. The images on the monitor suddenly jiggled as the men sprinted down the street to the target. Not a single person was seen along the route.

"Where are the men watching the girls?" Banyon asked Wolf.

"They are still on the couches, in the front of the house, and the girls are still upstairs, alone," he answered. Banyon passed on the information just as the SEALS reached the front door.

They didn't hesitate or even slow down. The first SEAL to the door, kicked out with his leg and the door collapsed inwardly. The men rushed in and didn't ask for the policemen to surrender. They shot them with their silenced guns instead. Four SEALS immediately headed up the stairs looking for the girls. They found them in the back bedroom. Their binds were cut and blankets thrown over their naked bodies. "Can you run?" Banyon heard one of the SEALS ask one of them. She was clearly in shock.

"I don't know," she replied.

He quickly picked her up and threw her over his shoulder and started down the stairs, just in time to see the SEAL leader place a blood-soaked, hand-written, note on one of the bodies. He then took a picture.

They were out of the house and heading back to the beach in exactly four minutes. The leader called for the extraction boats as they ran carrying the two girls. They collected their gear and piled into the fast attack boats. Within minutes, they were a speck on the horizon.

"Well, finally something went easy today," the President spoke over all the celebration in the situation room. "Thanks to you Colt, these are getting easier and easier."

"Glad I could help," Banyon said. "But what did the note say and why did the SEAL take a picture?"

"It said just what you supplied," commented the President. 'Danta Lopez was here, be afraid'. But we

206

added 'I will attack like a ghost when I find corruption'. The Mexican people are overwhelmingly superstitious my advisors tell me. Many of them will think twice about committing a crime now."

"And the picture?" Banyon asked.

"It will find its way to a TV station in Mexico City. My advisers think it will make the Mexican government take notice."

"So, how is the crisis with Mexico going?" Banyon wondered out loud.

"The borders are a mess. The Mexicans are turning back many Americans and we are being very selective with who we let in America. There are reports of gun fire everywhere over the border and we still have no contact with their government. Trade is at a standstill. The Mexican army is still massing on the border. I'm afraid it's not going too well."

"Is there anything I can do to help?" Banyon offered.

"You have already helped too much. Werner Klotz will be landing soon. He is in for an unexpected greeting and I have my meeting with Slezeck in a half hour. That will give me great pleasure. Besides I know you still have the Mexican hit team after you."

"We leave shortly for the airport," Banyon replied.

"I know you want to do this yourself, so you can protect a lot of innocent people, but I've alerted the FBI. They will have a takedown team following the hit men. We already know what plane they are on and when they will arrive in Las Vegas. If you need them, I'm giving you this number." The President passed on a phone number.

"Thank you, sir," Banyon responded.

"Also, you will have your check for today's events automatically deposited at the firm less expenses, of course."

"Thank you, sir," Banyon said again.

"I've got to prepare for my upcoming meeting. Good luck Colt." The President said and the screen went blank.

"I didn't like it when he said, 'less expenses'," Banyon said to Eric.

49

The private plane containing Werner Klotz touched down at 1:10 P.M. at the small Virginia airport where it was based. A black stretch limousine waited by the hanger. There were several other people waiting for him too, but he didn't know that.

Klotz had slept the entire trip. At his age, any stress, wore him out. Dealing with the Mexican hit men was very stressful. But he had followed Slezeck's orders, to the letter, and had stood in the rental car parking lot while making arrangements, on the phone, to get them to Las Vegas.

They were a surly lot. Everything they did was menacing and aggressive. They circled around the front of the car impatiently. They spit on the ground, smoked cigarettes, spoke in staccato threatening tones to each other and watched him with shifty eyes. Klotz knew their reputation was well founded.

Once they took an assignment, they never stopped until their victims were tortured, mutilated and dead. Anybody, who got in the way, was killed, without mercy. He was glad he was not their target. Several of the men kept picking up and staring at the pictures of Loni and the Patel sisters. They rubbed their crotches while wise-cracking in Spanish to the other men. Klotz was sure the women faced a gruesome future.

It took him almost an hour of phone time to complete his tasks. The hardest part was getting them enough weapons. Klotz had to call in a favor from an old friend in Las Vegas. His old friend immediately charged him double the normal price for the guns.

Once he had arranged everything, he collected the pictures and handed them to their leader. He said his name was Carlos. Klotz then ushered them back to the rental van that returned to the terminals and their flight to Las Vegas.

When done, he entered the waiting taxi, heading back to his private plane. He was feeling exhausted, but satisfied he had completed his part of Slezeck's plan.

Klotz awoke when the plane made a rough touch-down. At first, he wasn't sure where he was, but as the plane taxied to the hanger, he regained his memory. He decided he would head back to his office, just as Slezeck suggested and watch some TV. He wanted to catch up on the chaos, he had personally inflicted, on the world. He was proud to be a catalyst for the Effort. He personally had brought the U.S. and Mexico to the brink of war. He had no doubt who would win.

As he looked out the window to see if his limousine was ready for him, he noticed there were three men in suits standing by the car. He knew the Federal government usu-ally deployed three agents when they made an arrest. At first, he wondered who they were after. It didn't click in his brain. Suddenly, the shock of realization hit him. He then wondered if Slezeck had betrayed him, not that it mattered much. One way or the other, his life was over. Klotz felt he would never survive an arrest, trial, and any jail time. He was just too old to endure the lengthy process.

When the plane stopped at the hanger, the pilot opened the door, dropping down the small stairway, Klotz was already resigned to his future. The old man appeared in the doorway with his cane and started slowly down the steps as the U.S. Marshalls strolled up to the plane. He made no sign of fear and even smiled at the agents.

When he reached solid ground he stopped and stared at the young men. A grimace appeared on his lips. Suddenly, he grabbed his cane with his other hand and pulled out the derringer while pressing the button for the concealed knife in the cane. He brandished both weapons at the surprised agents.

"You won't take me alive," he croaked.

"Put the weapons down Mr. Klotz," the agent on the right ordered. "You are under arrest for treason."

With a scowl on his face, Klotz pointed the derringer at the man that had challenged him and fired. He was too far away for the small gun to be effective. The bullet flew harmlessly past the man, but the three agents were well trained to respond to deadly force with deadly force of their own.

Before Klotz could aim for a second shot, all three agents put slugs into his body. Werner Klotz died on the tarmac, before an ambulance arrived. He had caused the death of many people during the crisis and now he caused his own demise.

A Homeland Security watcher was stunned by the event. He had been waiting in a car just outside the fence. It had a good view of the shooting. He realized Klotz effectively committed suicide. The watcher called in the details to his superior and eventually the information reached Slezeck, in his office. He looked at the note and chuckled. *Now they can't connect me to Werner Klotz and I didn't even have to kill him myself,* he thought.

50

At the same time that Werner Klotz died on the tarmac, Bart pressed the overhead button in Banyon's Jaguar that opened his garage door. Once inside, he quickly hit the close button. He and his men headed into the house. The car containing the Effort shooters pulled up, right in front, on the street. Banyon's Homeland Security watcher drove past intending to turn around up the street. By the time he came back, the shooters had already left their car. They were headed for the front door with their machine guns, hidden in their coats. They didn't notice the agent as he pulled into the driveway of the house next door about an acre away. Their attention was fixed on the entrance of the house.

They were three steps from the porch when Andre and Guido appeared on either side of the house with guns aimed at the shooters. The shooters reacted just as Bart had expected they would. Each turned to the man on their side; they began to raise their machine guns to fire. Bart, who was watching from the peephole, flung open the front door. He took one step onto the porch, professionally putting a bullet into the man on the right, then one into the man on the left. They were both dead before they hit the ground.

The Homeland Security watcher spilled his coffee when he saw Colton Banyon shoot the two men. He knew there was a reason his boss wanted Colton Banyon followed. Now he knew why. Colton Banyon was a cold blooded killer. He hit 911 and reported the shooting immediately. He identified the shooter as Colton Banyon. He then got out of his car, drawing his gun, but before he was able to take a step, the garage door opened. The Jaguar sped away from the house, leaving the two dead men on the lawn.

The Homeland Security watcher realized it would be impossible to catch up to the powerful car and ran to see what he could do for the men Colton Banyon shot.

The dispatcher and the local Barrington police were very efficient. Two patrol cars screamed into the neighborhood in a matter of minutes. The officers left their still running cars while they approached the watcher with guns drawn. He quickly gave up his gun and raised his hands in surrender. He was cuffed and seated in one of the patrol cars while the rest of the police went to check the bodies. They then started to tape off the crime scene.

The watcher wasn't worried, it was all SOP. But what he didn't know was Colton Banyon was on a special list. As soon as the dispatcher heard Banyon's name, she notified the Chicago branch of the FBI.

A detective soon cruised up to the crime scene. He went to view the bodies. He then walked over to police car, where the watcher was anxiously waiting. He opened the door to the car, helped the man out, but didn't uncuff him. He already had his name and his Homeland Security badge number, so he went right to the important questions.

"What were you doing in the neighborhood?" the twenty-year veteran asked.

"Following Colton Banyon," the man easily replied.

"Really, from where?" The surprised officer asked.

"From his office in Schaumburg."

"Where is Mister Banyon then?" the detective asked.

"He took off after he killed those two men over there," the watcher informed the detective, with a motion of his head.

"How do you know these men?"

"I followed them from Schaumburg too."

"They were following Mr. Banyon too?" the detective reiterated.

"In a different car," he replied weakly.

"Why were you following Banyon?"

"That's classified," the watcher smugly said.

"Were you supposed to protect him or inform on him?"

"That's also classified."

"Well, you know what I think. My experience is that when three people are following one guy, and they approach him with machine guns, they are not there to protect him."

"But...:" The detective interrupted him by using his hand as a stop sign.

The detective eyed him suspiciously and continued. "I think you and your buddies attempted to go after this Colton Banyon guy and he killed them. You panicked because you were frightened and called the police. Now, I want some straight answers. So start talking," the detective yelled.

"But I'm a Homeland Security agent, for God sakes?"

The detective held up two black billfolds. "Apparently, so were they." He showed him the two badges taken from the dead men.

Suddenly, the detectives cell phone rang and he walked away to answer it. The Homeland Security watcher stood, by the car, in shock. What was going on? He wondered. The detective returned in a few minutes.

"I just found out that Colton Banyon is currently at the Law offices of Dewey & Beatem in Schaumburg. He has been there for all day. They have about fifty witnesses. In fact, he stopped a car bombing, at that premises, less than a half hour ago. He could not have been here. So, what is your new story?"

"I don't understand. I saw him shoot those men," the watcher protested.

"Yeah, well, the FBI will be here any minute. Maybe they can get better answers from you."

"The FBI, but I'm Homeland Security," the watcher protested again.

"So you say," the detective replied.

"Get me a phone," the watcher ordered. "I can clear this up in a minute."

"No phone calls until you have been booked," the detective replied.

51

The trip had been delayed for another half hour, but Banyon was finally on the road to the airport and eventually to his house, in Las Vegas. He had spent the extra time in the office, talking to the FBI and the bomb squad. It gave him the cover he needed, to deflect the accusation of killing the two men at his house. Bart had called him from his car and instructed him on what to do and say.

Bart had also returned the keys to the Jaguar, when he returned to the office. The exhausted Banyon had ordered Eric to drive. Heather sat next to him in the front seat and Mandy sat in the back seat with Banyon. The girls were very different now.

When he had returned to his office, after talking to the police and FBI, he found the two women standing in the room, ready to go. They had their small suitcases by their sides. Heather was now dressed like a business woman. She had blond hair, in a bun, grey eyes, and big glasses that covered half her face. The tan business suit had a skirt that ended below her knees. Her legs were covered in pantyhose and she worn shoes with just a slight lift. She looked trim and proper. She was still very attractive, but not in a porno star way.

Mandy looked fourteen years old again, with a short pleated private-girls school skirt, bare legs and a white blouse. She wore cheap jewelry along with track shoes and little ruffled white, socks. Somehow, she had fashioned her hair into two short pigtails. They bounced whenever she moved her head. Her attitude was fourteen years old as well. She slapped the gum she chewed and exuded the petulance of a teenager to everyone around her. In short, she was getting on their nerves.

"Where have you been, Daddy?" she demanded. "I'm hungry," she complained as she pounded out a text on her I-phone without looking up.

Feeling famished himself, Banyon offered. "Okay, we'll stop at a fast-food hamburger joint and get some food, to go. Sound good?" Both Eric and Heather readily agreed and shook their heads.

"Eww, yuck," Mandy replied as she turned up her nose. "Can't you think of something better to eat?"

"Shut up, Mandy," Heather said with irritation. "I know you like meat. Stop being contrary, right now." That got her a flick of eyebrows from Mandy, suddenly they all laughed at her innuendo.

"Let's go then," Banyon suggested.

They ate their hamburgers in the car as Eric drove. Mandy devoured two burgers and a chocolate milkshake. She was now fidgeting, in the seat, next to Banyon. He had pulled down the seat divider to keep her from getting too close. She pulled her legs up on the seat and then dropped them back on the floor, hitting the seat in front. Heather once again admonished her actions.

"If you kick my seat one more time, I'm going to come back there," she uttered in a low growl.

"You can't make me," Mandy replied sarcastically.

"Mandy," Banyon quickly said. "You don't have to display your teenage attitude when we are alone. So, please stop."

"Thank you, Daddy, I mean Colt," she sweetly said. She then crossed her legs like a woman, making sure that Banyon noticed she wore a short skirt.

Banyon had just started thinking it could be a long trip when his phone rang. He retrieved it from his pocket and saw that it was Loni.

"This call is from Loni, so you all better be quiet," he threatened. He then answered the phone.

"Colt," Loni purred into the phone. "How are you? Do you miss me?" He could hear the sounds of an ocean in the background.

"Of course," he answered.

"You're probably bored to tears without me around," she laughed into the phone. She seemed very relaxed.

He knew better than to say he had been too busy to even think about her. "When are you coming home?" he asked instead.

"We just got the sailboat this morning. We are about an hour away from the dive sight. We will anchor for the night as it is already late. We'll dive for the treasure tomorrow morning. I should be back in two days."

"Are you having any fun?"

"You won't believe how nice this trip has been. The Patel sisters have been very friendly and the weather is gorgeous," she gushed.

"So, you are enjoying your trip then?"

"Colt, the Patel's are so much fun and they are teaching me many things," she giggled.

"Like what?"

"Oh, I'll show you when I get home," she said sexily. The last time the Patel's taught her something, Banyon wound up with a strip-tease pole in his bedroom, so, he was a little concerned.

"How was your shopping spree in Odessa?" He asked as he wondered how much she had charged to his credit card.

"Well, we bought a few things, but didn't buy any bathing suits," She baited him.

"Oh?"

"Colt, I'm naked," she announced. We all agreed to sail naked. It is so cool, so much freedom. So much fun," she exclaimed. "And Colt, guess what?"

"What?" He asked with a frown on his face.

"There are only two small bunk beds on the entire boat to sleep on. I'm going to bunk with Previne tonight," she giggled. "Tomorrow night, I'll bunk with Pramilla. We are so decadent aren't we?"

Banyon now had images of all the women running around the deck naked and playing a game of musical chairs with bunk beds.

"Watch out for sunburn. There are parts of you that don't usually see the sun," he said. Eric was peering at Banyon from the rear view mirror when he heard Banyon's reply.

"Oh, don't worry. We put lotion on each other, everywhere. Rubbed it in good too," she explained.

"Glad to hear that," he said with additional images floating in his brain.

"Well, just wanted to make sure you are alright," Loni announced. "I've got to run. Previne needs me to help clean up something on the deck. I'll have to get down on all fours to do that."

"I'll tell Eric you guys are having a good time. No need for Pramilla to call," he quickly added.

"Okay, Colt, bye for now," Loni said into the phone. "I love you."

"I love you too," Banyon repeated. The connected was broken.

"So, what is the story?" Eric asked from the front seat.

"Well, they are all naked and oiled up, with only two bunk beds, and beautiful weather," Banyon summarized.

"Sounds like every day, to me," Eric quipped. Heather and Mandy were immediately jealous.

52

They finally reached the small private airport in Rockford, Illinois. Eric parked the car in the small parking lot. Banyon glanced at his watch. He realized it was only five minutes before the President's meeting with Paul Slezeck. He thought it was a pretty good idea to get some updates from Wolf. He picked up his trusty satchel and opened the door.

"Mandy, get my luggage and put it on the plane, please." He asked over his shoulder. She looked at him like she wanted to kill him.

"I'm not your slave," she said in a bitchy voice.

"Never mind, I'll get it," Heather said to appease Mandy. She didn't want to hear anymore childish outbursts.

"You stay away from him…I mean his luggage," Mandy retorted. She quickly went around the car, pulling the bag from the trunk.

Ignoring both of them, Banyon continued. "You guys go ahead, tell the pilot we are ready to go. I have to make a phone call." He then put his cell phone to his ear, like he was talking, but addressed Wolf instead.

"Wolf, are you there?"

"You're going to have your hands full with those two," the spirit laughed. Banyon could tell he was in a good mood.

"Any updates on the hit men?"

"They now plan to come after you tomorrow afternoon. By the time they land and collect their guns it will be evening; they haven't eaten anything all day, and have been traveling since early this morning. Carlos, the leader is sending one man to see if you are home. He will stay all night."

"How is my security?"

"I have two of my friends watching your place. They are fully armed and I will know if anything changes. You know them by the way."

Gerald J. Kubicki & Kristopher Kubicki

"Who are they?"

"They are Petra's two grandson's, from Death Valley." About a year ago, Banyon had met the boys while solving the mystery of an old German war plane found in Death Valley. The boys had helped crack the case. "There are also two FBI men watching your place, the President ordered it."

"Yeah, I remember the boys. I also expected the President to attempt to protect his asset. What about the park?"

"It will be empty tomorrow night, as far as I can tell. It is a splendid place to take them down."

"Are there any problems on the horizon for Loni and the Patel girls?" Banyon really did miss Loni and wanted her back, in one piece.

"Don't worry. I won't let anything happen to any of them, Colt. Besides, they are very good at defending themselves, even if they are naked." Wolf's last statement made Banyon wonder what it must be like to see anything or anybody anytime you wanted.

"Anything else new?"

"Werner Klotz is dead. When the U.S. Marshalls showed up to greet his plane, he tried to fight them. I am very pleased about that. There is one less Nazi in the world."

"What about the crisis with Mexico? Any change there?" Banyon suddenly asked. It seemed so far away from him.

"Nothing new that I can tell you, but by the time you reach Las Vegas, I'll have some good news, I imagine."

"Finally, what about Paul Slezeck, the President is slated to meet with him in about five minutes?"

"He isn't going to the meeting. He has figured out it is a trap. He is on the run. He expects to slip up into Canada and then catch a plane for Brazil. He has Effort friends there who will help him."

"The President needs to know this. Where is Slezeck right now?"

"He has hiding in a Catholic Church right near the Capitol Building. The Catholic Church is named St. Joseph's. He is waiting for some Effort people to deliver him documents

222

to get out of the country. He is sitting in a pew and is unarmed. He never wanted to get his own hands dirty."

"How long will it be before the documents arrive?" Banyon quickly asked.

"He believes it will take two hours more before he can leave. You know, Colt, the Catholic Church has a long history of protecting Nazis, going back to World War II. Some of the most brutal Nazis were spirited out of Europe by the Vatican. The escape routes were called 'ratlines'. Some of the most infamous Nazis got out that way, including Klaus Barbie and even Joseph Mengele.

"I'm quite familiar with the history of the Church and the Nazis," Banyon replied with disgust.

"I'm still hunting some of them," Wolf added even through Banyon had not asked a question.

"Why, that church?"

"St. Joseph's has two Effort sympathizers on their payroll."

"I'd better tell the President," he said, knowing Wolf couldn't answer. Banyon quickly dialed the cell phone.

"I thought you were headed for Las Vegas," the President answered without greeting. He also sounded like he was in a good mood. Banyon knew it wouldn't last for long once, he filled him in on Slezeck. So he did.

"I wanted to confront him in person," the President lamented.

"You still can," Banyon told him.

"I can't send government people into a church to arrest someone. The press would crucify me," he said.

"Yes, but maybe we can trick him into coming out," Banyon replied.

53

In his office in Mexico City, the President of the United Mexican States was very busy reading communiques and reports. He was also watching the crisis, with the United States, unfold on TV. There was a lot to keep up with. He suddenly reared up his head and stared at the TV screen, on the far wall. The news station was displaying a picture, of the killing, of some, known to be corrupt, policemen in Acapulco. The camera zoomed in on a bloody hand written message on one of the policemen's chest. The President heard the name "Danta Lopez".

"Turn that up would you," he said to his aide. The man grabbed a remote from a table and did what the President requested.

"This guy Danta Lopez gets around," the aide noted.

"Yes, yes, he does," The leader acknowledged as he rubbed his day old beard. He was beginning to see the ghost-like warrior in a different light. *Maybe he isn't so bad*, the President thought. Lopez appeared to be a maniac killer, but only murdered people who needed to die, it seemed.

After the news had moved on he returned to his reports. They were bad. Since he had pulled his military away from their normal assignments, the drug cartels felt free to go on a rampage. There were open gun battles between rivals in almost every major city. Many people were dying, even though, most were gang members. Americans were exiting Mexico in droves while complaining about the brutal treatment they had received, especially the unnecessary searches. The reports included claims of sexual abuse and beatings.

Most of the Mexicans who wanted to enter the U.S. were turned back, without apology. Trade was at a complete standstill, no money was being made. Prominent and influential Mexicans were beseeching the government with more special requests then they could possible handle. So far, no foreign government had offered help, or any aid, to Mexico. The President of Mexico was in very hot water and it was rising. He needed to find a way to fix things with the U.S. His machismo had brought him to the brink of political disaster, for himself and his country.

"Sir," his aide interrupted his thoughts. "You are scheduled to give a news conference that will be broadcasted to the entire country in two hours. Have you written your copy for me to review, yet?"

"Maybe we should cancel," he wondered out loud. He didn't have anything positive to tell his people.

"That would be political suicide for you," the aide replied. "There would be riots in the streets and calls for your resignation, or even impeachment. You have to say something," the aide pleaded.

"Yes, I suppose you are right," the dejected leader replied.

"Maybe you should repeal some of your previous directives, say they were enacted without your authority. That way you would look like a fixer rather than a problem maker," the aide suggested.

Suddenly, feeling a little better, the President announced. "Your right, cancel the personal search order. Also cancel the new tax levy on American tourists," he ordered.

"And what about communications with the U.S. government?" the aide asked apprehensively.

"Yes, yes, of course," he replied, while deep in thought. "We will blame all of it on the drug cartels. Send out a rumor that I have uncovered corruption in the government and have put an end to it. I'll confirm it in my speech."

"We'll need to supply names," the aide said. "Who do you have in mind?"

"Hah, I could pick just about anyone," the leader said.

"We must be more specific. I can put a spin to almost anybody," the aide told him as his excitement grew. Finally, they were getting somewhere.

"Make sure it is someone who is already dead," the President pointed to the man across from him.

"I'll take care of it. I'll leak the news to the press and our friends in America immediately," the aide said. He got up to leave before the big man changed his mind again.

"I'll say the information came from an unexpected source," the President added, his wheels were now turning, he now had a strategy.

"Who?"

"I'll tell them Danta Lopez told me."

"Why use him? He has killed many of our people in the last few days," the aide protested.

"But he has only killed men that should die. You don't understand. You're too young," he confidently replied. "You would have to be my age, to understand."

"What are you talking about?"

"Do you know who the greatest Mexican hero of all-time is?" the politician asked his aide as he stood up and walked around the desk.

"No."

"His name was Don Diego de la Vega," the President announced.

"Never heard of him," the aide said.

"He is also known as 'Zorro the fox'."

"But," the aide stuttered. "He is a comic book character."

"Danta Lopez is our new Zorro. He stands against tyrannical, corrupt officials, drug dealers, and is never seen. He will be the new hero of Mexico. It might actually even help to quell some of the violence in our midst."

"It will only work if you have some way to summon him," the aide added as he thought about the scam.

"We'll work that out later, right now we have a crisis to avert" the President then dismissed his aide.

54

The church was very quiet. Occasionally, Paul Slezeck could hear someone enter, taking a pew; he eyed them suspiciously. He sat near the back of the large church. There were only about ten people praying in the pews. Several others milled around the candle area, lighting candles for loved ones that had died. It was a very serene and comforting, but Slezeck was still very nervous. He constantly texted his contact on his secure encrypted phone, pleading with them to hurry up.

A shadow passed over him and he looked up. Standing next to the pew, was an elderly nun and a Priest. They smiled at him.

"You have been here for several hours, my son," the priest said solemnly. "You must have much torment in your heart. Care to take confession and unburden your sins?"

"Err...not right now," Slezeck replied.

"In any case," the nun spoke sternly. "We do not allow cell phone usage in the sanctuary. Please close your phone, or I will be forced to take it."

"Yes, sister," Slezeck said and shoved his phone into his pocket.

"We are going to the rectory and have a bowl of soup. You must be hungry after all this time, care to join us?" the priest offered.

"No, I can't, I need to stay inside the church." Slezeck knew that as long as he didn't leave the church he was safe.

"The soup is free," the nun told him. "The soup is right through that doorway," the nun pointed to a side exit. "God can hear you in there as well as in the church."

"No thank you."

"The soup is very good and I promise to not deliver any lectures," the priest laughed. The nun reached for his arm, he found himself lifted to his feet. He didn't want to make a scene and he was hungry, so he went along.

"There that's better," the nun said sweetly as she gripped his arm tightly. "You'll be feeling like yourself in no time flat," she promised as she patted his arm.

The priest began to babble in an attempt to keep Slezeck's attention. "You know we will be conducting an afternoon mass in about an hour. Today my sermon will be about the evils of racism."

Before he could form an answer, they had passed through the rectory entryway. Half pulling and half pushing him, they continued down a long corridor, stopping in front of a closed door.

"The soup kitchen is in here," the nun pointed out. She turned the knob and threw open the door. She then pushed him through the opening. Slezeck quickly scanned the room. He noticed there was only one man inside that he could see. He was eating soup from a paper bowl. It was the President of the United States.

"Oh," the President said, acting surprised. "Come on in, the soup is very good." Slezeck turned to get out of the room, but two burly Secret Service men grabbed him by the collar and he was thrown against the wall. They expertly frisked him, took his phone. They then propelled him towards where the President sat.

"You two may go now, and thank you," the President told the nun and the priest who stood in the doorway. They were not real clergy, they were imposters sent from the Washington office of Dewey & Beatem by Colton Banyon.

"What, but....," Slezeck said in confusion.

"I don't like it when someone stands me up, Paul. You missed your two o'clock appointment with me." He paused for emphasis. "Now sit down and eat your soup," the President ordered.

"I had something else to do. I'm very busy, you know" Slezeck said defensively as he plopped into the plastic chair.

"Yes, we have all been a little busy today. Oh well, I needed a little lunch anyway, and some time out of the office," the leader said cheerfully.

"The soup is good," Slezeck said as he downed a spoonful.

"Why don't we make this a business luncheon?" The President suggested in a very calm tone.

"Okay," Slezeck said as he started to feel a little more comfortable. He looked at the President over his bowl.

"Then we should get started, I'm kind of pressed for time."

The President brought up a folder and opened it. Slezeck could read upside down and realized the document, on the top, was the executive order he submitted for the President's signature. His heart skipped a beat. *Maybe the President is so overwhelmed with the mess I created he is going to finally sign it,* he thought.

"The first thing I am going to do is give you the document you have fought so hard to get signed."

Slezeck was thrilled. *It worked, my plan worked*, he thought. "Thank you sir," he uttered as he watched the President scribble on the paper, but the President was left handed, his hand obscured what he wrote. He then sailed it across the formica-topped table, it slipped off on to the floor. Slezeck scrambled after it like it was a large bonus check. He finally corralled it and brought it up to his eyes to verify the signature. What he saw made his eyes bug out. The document had written on it only one word, the word was "nuts".

Paul Slezeck instantly knew the President was on to him. The Presidents uncle, Brigadier General Anthony C. McAuliffe had used that exact word as a response to a Nazi German surrender ultimatum, during the "Battle of the Bulge", during World War II. He was vastly out-numbered and completely surrounded in the small French town, of Bastogne. But he refused to surrender. It delayed the advance of the Nazis troops thus allowing the Allies to bring in reinforcements and win the largest battle of the war. Slezeck understood the President had decided to fight.

When the concerned Slezeck looked up, he spied another piece of paper on the table. It was the original receipt Slezeck had expected the President to sign, with the extra sentences, that he wanted to use to blackmail the President. The incriminating sentences were visible, but there was not signature. The President had scrolled across the page, "Never going to happen on my watch." Slezeck knew he was doomed.

"This third document is for you to sign, Paul," the President said with a measure of annoyance. It was his resignation letter from the Directorship of Homeland Security. It was the last straw for Paul Slezeck. Homeland Security had been his personal organization. He ran it as he saw fit. No one was going to take it away from him.

"You can't make me sign that," he bellowed. "You have no evidence to back it up," he roared.

The President calmly picked up a remote from the chair next to him, and pressed the on button. The wall mounded flat-screen came instantly to life. Slezeck immediately recognized himself standing in a bathroom and making calls to Werner Klotz while implicating himself in a conspiracy. He was speechless.

"Werner Klotz is dead, Paul. He died when I sent men to arrest him, but we had the goods on him too." He pressed a forward button and the screen changed. The view was from the inside of a car and a side view of Slezeck was clear. He was talking to Werner Klotz, at the car rental place in Chicago.

"That's not me," Slezeck protested. "I wasn't there."

"Can you prove your whereabouts this morning between nine-thirty and twelve-thirty," the President asked.

"Of course, I was with Marlene Moore. She will tell you," he nervously replied.

"Get her in here," the President ordered abruptly to the Secret Service men.

The door flew open; Marlene strutted in making a bee-line for Paul Slezeck. She once again smacked him hard across the face. He cowered under the blow. "How dare you try to involve me in you silly little conspiracy, you bastard," she riled at him.

"But I was on your boat, in Baltimore, this morning," Slezeck cried.

"My boat is in the Bahamas being refurnished," Marlene said. "And I can prove it." She produced her cell phone and called up several pictures of the boat. It was in dry dock. One picture showed a clear shot of the boat name, "DOJ", only it wasn't white, it was light blue. A man sat reading a paper with today's date, in the foreground.

"Now what do you have to say," the President asked showing irritation.

"She is a lair," Slezeck screamed.

"And you, my friend, are a conspirator and a traitor to your country. Sign the damn form and things will go better for you," the President roared as he stood and hammered his finger on the table top. "And by the way, your last two disasters were stopped before anyone was hurt," the President added. "It is over for you, Slezeck."

Slezeck thought about the Presidents demand for a few seconds. He then signed the form with a flourish. "I was getting tired of that job anyway," he said like a petulant child. He pushed the paper back to the now standing President.

"You are being taking into custody right now, may God have mercy on your soul," the President said.

"But…" Slezeck said with a sinister look on his face and his finger pointed in the air. "Now that you have mentioned God, I am in a church of God. You can't arrest me while I am in here. No court in the land will allow it," he chuckled in an evil way.

"Damn," the President pretended to be mad. "Alright, Paul I'm not going to arrest you," he said with resignation in his voice.

"Good, now we understand each other," Slezeck said as he felt he had regained the upper hand.

"I'm going to have my nominee for your old job, arrest you. Marlene, would you mind doing the honors?"

He was stunned with the President's choice. "But she can't arrest me either," he roared with laughter. "I'm in a Church."

"But Paul," Marlene corrected him. "When you came to the rectory, you left the church voluntarily. Don't you remember? There was a short hallway that you came down." She put her hands on her shapely hips as she waited for him to answer.

"Doesn't matter," He replied like a know it all. "It is still part of the church and you can't force me to leave if I don't want to."

"Actually," she said drawing the words out. "It's not." She let that sink in for a moment. "You see the church and the rectory are two separate buildings, connected by a short hallway. When you passed through the hallway, you left the sanctuary of the Church. I should know this. After all, I am the head of the United States Justice department."

"Cuff him boys," the President waved over the two Secret Service men. "You'd better read him is rights," the President added.

"You probably don't even know how to Mirandize me properly," Slezeck sneered at her from his seat.

"Oh, I forgot to tell you," Marlene said sweetly. "We are charging you under your favorite weapon. It's called the 'Patriot Act'."

"How silly of me to forget," the President said with a smile as he winked at the acting Director of Homeland Security.

"Paul Slezeck we are charging you with conspiracy, domestic terrorism, murder, attempted murder, and probably a few more things, which we will add later," Marlene said with a wave of her hand. Then she continued, "Under the Patriot act, you do not have the right of a trail. You do not have the right for legal representation. You are not allowed to contact anyone on your behalf and we can imprison you in indefinitely, which in your case, will be the rest of your slimy life. You are going to be incarcerated, in solitary confinement, in Leavenworth, for the duration of our investigation. I suggest you don't attempt to mix with any of the prisoners there. You will live longer, if you don't."

"Take him directly to the plane," the President ordered the Secret Service men.

When they had left the room, Marlene looked at the President with admiration. "That was a hell of a plan, sir."

"Thank you acting Director," he humbly replied. "But this was Colton Banyon's plan.

Part Six

Las Vegas

55

They were finally up in the air. Colton Banyon stared out the window, farmland passed below. He was deep in thought, putting the finishing touches on his Las Vegas plan. He knew it was dangerous, but he had to eliminate the hit men before his beloved Loni returned home, otherwise they would live in fear, forever.

The Pilot called to him and broke his train of thought. "You have a message from the President of the United States," he said. He was impressed that Banyon even knew him, let alone get a message from him.

Banyon lifted his weary body and went to the open cabin door. "What does it say?" he asked.

"The President wants you to know that the arrest was made," the captain replied. "He also wants you to know communications with Mexico have returned. He says good hunting in Las Vegas."

"Thank you," Banyon replied and returned to his seat near the front of the plane. It was an executive style plane, with two lounge chairs near the front flanked by small serving tables. There was a table and three more lounge chairs in the back. As he returned to his seat, he noticed Eric and Heather were facing each other on the swiveling lounge chairs. They were deep in an animated discussion. Heather was waving her arms in the air, Eric was smiling. It appeared Heather could be fun even just talking.

Mandy was sitting up front in the lounge chair, near to him. She looked tiny in the large leather chair. She had her legs drawn up in a yoga position. She stared at him with a look of mischief on her cute face.

As soon as he sat down the stress of the busy day began to fade. He began to feel sleepy. He attempted to close his eyes and get some sleep. It had been a taxing morning. In the four hours he had spent at the Law offices, he had helped take down a black gang, set up a plan that trapped and killed two murderous Effort people, helped rescue two young girls in Mexico, brought down Werner Klotz, helped incriminate Paul Slezeck, stopped a bomb threat, and was now headed to Las Vegas to eliminate a despicable hit team. He had also made some money, but had no idea what the net income would be. He was pretty pleased with his morning. A smile was firmly planted on his lips as he slowly drifted off to sleep. But it didn't last long.

"Are you smiling at me?" a small voice filled his ears. It was accompanied by a nudge on his thigh. It was soon followed by another nudge. He finally opened his eyes. He looked down at his thigh and saw a small bare foot, with painted toes, pushing on his leg. They were connected to an also bare leg. As he continued looking up the leg, he could not help but notice Mandy. She was now slouched in the lounge chair, staring at him in defiance. Her eyes were filled with smoldering lust.

"Mandy you have to stop doing that," he said wearily. He closed his eyes and plopped his head back on the chair.

"But you looked, didn't you," she replied knowingly.

"You don't have to throw yourself at me all the time," he said with annoyance, his eyes remained closed. "You know, I like you, and trust you, but there are too many complications between us.

"Like what?" she demanded.

Sitting up, he turned to her. "First of all, let's face it I'm three times your age. I'm also in a committed relationship and I don't think you are aware of the possible consequences of some of your actions," he replied logically. "You're just too young."

"Well, let me tell you something Mr. Colton, I know everything, Banyon," she sarcastically spit back at him. "I am more experienced than you think. I do what I do because I want to. I have known a lot of men, but have never had a positive experience with any man, that is, until I met you."

"What?" Banyon exclaimed. He was stunned by her remark.

"Yeah, asshole." She insulted him as her anger rose. "You don't get it. Your world is always perfect, mine is not."

"What do you mean?" he replied as he wondered where she was going. He could see she was angry. Her face was red and her tiny fists were balled up.

Suddenly, she exploded. "You see, I know I'm cute, sexy, flexibly athletic, tiny, and look like I'm a teenager. This has cursed me with nothing but problems in dealing with men," she railed. "No man has attempted to have a real relationship with me. No man has ever treated me like you have. In just the few days that I have known you, my life has changed. You have made me feel like I can eventually have a good relationship with a man. It's your fault."

"I didn't know," Banyon sputtered realizing that once again a woman had put him on the defensive.

She ranted on. "In the past, anytime, I have let a man get near to me, it always turned out the same. They all have had pedophile issues and wanted to use me like a piece of meat. I have been used and abused, like a toy. Do you have any idea how much that disgusts me? Do you?" She was now nearly shouting and her body shook with emotion. Both Heather and Eric were now looking at Banyon.

"I don't know what to say," Banyon stammered as he tried to quiet her down. Heather and Eric were watching.

Mandy wasn't close to being done yet. "Until you came into my life, I was headed down a dangerous path," she announced. "I was a bad girl and getting worse. But when you acted like it didn't matter what I looked like, or acted like, I realized our relationship could be different. I have always been afraid to be myself around men. You flirted with me, but you refused to take advantage of me, even when I offered myself to you. You are the first man to treat me like a person, not just a teenage-looking piece of meat."

Banyon now realized she was pouring out her heart to him. "But you are a person," he interrupted with emphasis.

She waved her hand and continued. "You also gave me an opportunity to make more money than I have made in my entire life. And that was during the first day that you met me," she exclaimed loudly. Both Heather and Eric leaned forward in their seats when she said that.

"Not so loud," Banyon asked her as he glanced to the back of the plane.

"You then put me in charge of your contract employee list. No one has ever given me any responsibilities. And now you have given me a chance to prove I really am a capable person. Your trust in me has opened my eyes. Don't you see? You have changed my life."

"Mandy, I didn't know," he answered sincerely.

"So, I can, and will I throw myself at you, all I want," she smacked her little fists on the chair arms with determination. "I know any long-term relationship is forbidden. I'm happy, but jealous, you have someone. I know we can't be lovers, but I sure as hell can make your days more exciting and build my own confidence at the same time. You can do anything you want to me and I will love it."

Banyon now realized why he liked her. She was a real person with needs and desires, faults, and was loyal to him. She also had a lot of spunk. She was much more complicated than he had originally thought, but she wasn't afraid to acknowledge she was different. He also admitted to himself that she reminded him of Loni and certainly provided a stimulation he enjoyed. His dark side was that he loved women, it was his weakness and he saw Mandy as a woman, not a child.

When she was done ranting, he knew he needed to say something. "I think I understand you a little better now," he said quietly.

"So, where do we go from here?" she coyly asked as she moved to the edge of her seat.

"Perhaps you should let me tell you a story," he said sympathetically. "It's the story of who I am, what I have to deal with, and why I treat you like I do."

There was a big smile on her face.

56

Carlos Mendez strutted down the tunnel from the plane at McCarran airport in Las Vegas. He had been there many times before, but his name was different then. He had several identities; his real name was Juan Ruiz. He put on his dark aviator sunglasses as he walked down the gangway. He needed to scan the boarding area to make sure there wasn't a trap. No one needed to see his constantly shifting eyes.

He immediately noticed the smell of the desert. It made him feel at home. He had grown up in the desert, except it had been in Mexico. He reflected on his thirty years of life as he led his five other men towards the trams and the terminal. His home desert was the vast Sonoran desert that covered Northern Mexico and stretched into Arizona and parts of California. He grew up in the small city of Nogales, Mexico. It was right in the middle, of the arid desert and on the American border. Nogales was a successful tourist town with a highway running straight down central Arizona, directly to Nogales.

His first thoughts in life were that he was poor, but the Americans, who came over the border to his home town, were not. He wanted to be like them. As a teenager, he shied away from drug gangs. He was smart enough to see it was a dead end. He understood, once you joined a drug gang, your faith was sealed. It was only a matter of time before you died. His parents ran an open-air produce stand, near downtown, so he had never starved. But he wanted more out of life. While working with his parents, he encountered many Americans and always asked them how they became so rich. Most replied it was because of a good education. Juan decided he needed a good education.

His family had relatives in the growing city of Tucson, Arizona, in America, just up the highway. So, one day he told his parents he was going there, to get an education. He slipped over the border when he was eighteen and went to live with the relatives. One year later, he was accepted at the thriving college known as the University of Arizona. He had discovered there were many ways to manipulate the liberal American education system and he took full advantage, even though he was an illegal immigrant.

At the university, he excelled at learning, but also found the rich America students attending the school, were easy prey for someone as street-smart as he was. He was soon organizing poker games, smuggled in drugs, and providing entertainment, for his new friends. Unfortunately, he also became hooked on gambling. He saw it as a way to get rich, quick. It was easier then studying for exams.

On his first trip to Las Vegas, he had actually made money, which ensured he would come back. Soon, he was making the eight hour car trip every month. His studies faltered, his business also suffered from the lack of attention. In the second semester of his junior year, he was asked to leave the university. Juan was devastated. But like many young men, he felt he could make his mark in Las Vegas. He went there.

He was able to blend into the large, illegal immigrant community in Las Vegas. He quickly realized he could be successful if he provided his people with entertainment. So, he began running illegal cock fights, buying the roosters from several unsuspecting local farmers. Cock fighting was banned in The United States, but not in Mexico, where the majority of illegal immigrants grew up. To them, it was like going to a rock concert. Juan even provided bands and singers, just like in Mexico. He held weekly cock fights, on farms, outside the city. He began making money, and squandering it, all on gambling.

At one cock fight, a man approached Juan and complained that another man had reneged on a bet. He wanted Juan to teach him a lesson. He offered him a thousand dollars as payment. Juan took the money. He cornered the accused man behind a barn. A fight ensued, soon knives came out. In the end, Juan killed the man. Within minutes, he was offered another contract to kill someone else. He suddenly realized he could make as much money as he wanted by becoming a contract killer, it was easy money. He liked that. He completed several contracts in Las Vegas and his reputation spread back into Mexico.

One day he received a phone call which changed his life. The call originated from a small city in Mexico. The caller offered Juan fifty-thousand, U.S. dollars, to eliminate one of the caller's own men. The man had become too popular. The boss wanted him and his family to die. Juan quickly agreed and the reputation of *"Matador"*, or killer, was established.

Over the next seven years, he killed more than one hundred people and became rich along the way. He eventually hired a crew of five men to help. Being inherently lazy, he did the planning and they did the killing. They were the men with him today. The contract to kill the six people he was currently chasing was a huge one worth over six million dollars, to him.

He saw the sign that would take them to the shuttle bus for the large car rental complex, a mile from the airport, but he ignored it.

Instead, he strolled out the door to the taxi line. He had already decided he could afford to hire extra help for this mission. He also wanted to spend a little time gambling. There was more than enough money to go around and he still had many contacts in the illegal community in Las Vegas. So, he decided to take advantage of his old friends. The killer known as Carlos liked to do things his way.

When he and his men piled into a van big enough for them, the frightened cab driver asked where they were going. When Juan told him, the man said he wouldn't go there and asked them to leave his van.

57

The President of the United States stood at the podium in the main conference room of the Homeland Security building. Marlene Moore was stationed just to his right. Everyone in the audience was a top level manager in the organization. It included representatives from TSA, The Coast Guard, The Border Patrol, ICE, the Immigration and Customs Enforcement division, and every other division of the sprawling organization. There was a constant buzz in the room as the managers discussed what the President had to say to them. No word had leaked out to anyone in the audience.

When he was ready the President began. "My, friends," The President said as he attempted to be non-formal. "Today, I am here to announce that Paul Slezeck, for personal reasons, has resigned as the Director of Homeland Security." He held up the signed resignation paper. "Paul has decided to retire after more than thirty years of continued government service. He has already left for parts unknown by me." He paused to let that sink in.

"We wish him well in whatever endeavor his chooses," The President lied, with a straight face.

"But," he continued with his finger pointed upward. "The business of government must go on. We must always be vigilant. Your organization needs a competent leader. Therefore, I am nominating Marlene Moore to take his position, effective immediately. You will now report to her, as of today. I expect her confirmation from Congress in the very near future." The stunned audience began a polite applause, many managers were shocked, especially the Effort people in the room. It was actually a step down from a cabinet position.

"This announcement will be made to the general public, in a news conference, scheduled for one half hour from now," he said as he glanced at his watch. "I will make the announcement from the front steps of this building and Marlene is required to be there. But until that time, she is here to answer any questions you have. Homeland Security is our largest and most critical agency. You," the President pointed towards the audience, "are charged with protecting the people of this great country. Marlene is here to help you. Good Luck, my friends." There were more applause. He held up his hands to quiet the group.

"And now let me introduce you to the new head of Homeland Security, Marlene Moore," the President said dramatically.

He then waved to the crowd and headed off the podium to prepare for his news conference.

58

By ignoring the rental car sign, Carlos was not changing his strategy; he was actually following the same strategy he always did whenever he was on assignment. Once he made a deal for a contract killing, he cut off any communications and any contact with the employer. He was always afraid the employer might be compromised, or would change their mind. Normally, he had his own transportation and weapons when he worked in Mexico, so it was never a problem, but in the United States, he needed both. Fortunately, when the hit was changed to Las Vegas, he knew where to go to fill his needs.

Once he agreed to a contract, the fate of the victim was inevitable. He never stopped until he completed the contract. His successful kills brought him honor and fueled his reputation. He needed to continue to build both. To Carlos, killing people was a business and he and his team were the best in the business. He had never failed. He had no intention of failing on this contract.

It took him nearly a half an hour to find a cabbie who would take him to his destination, the "Naked City". Unlike other major cities, Las Vegas didn't have huge ghettos, but there were several parts of town which were considered bad areas. The Naked City was one of them. It was located just west of the towering Stratosphere hotel and casino, on the north end of the Strip. The name, the Naked City, actually came from part of the past allure of Las Vegas. In the fifties and sixties, it was where the showgirls lived. On any given day, tourists would drive through the area, to view the showgirls, lounging by pools. Many sunbathed topless or even naked.

But in the last twenty years, the show girls moved out, and the cars that traveled through the area now were in search of drugs. The Naked City was not found on any map, it was a nickname, given by the local Las Vegans, decades ago. Cabbies never went there in the dark and most wouldn't go there, even in the day time.

The Hispanic cabbie agreed to take Carlos and his men near the small war-zone for an extra fifty dollars. His men piled into the cab. The cabbie asked Carlos if he had ever been to the area before and was not surprised when Carlos told him he used to live there.

"The area is under change, my friend," the cabbie cheerfully announced.

"How's that?" Carlos inquired.

"The land is prime real estate now. They are putting up high-rise condominiums all over the place. The Naked City is shrinking. If you want drugs, I can take you to a better place," the enterprising cabbie told him.

"I'm not going to buy drugs, I'm going to see some old friends," Carlos amiably replied, knowing the cabbie understood he meant criminals. The cabbie was silent for the rest of the trip.

He dropped them off at the corner of Sahara and Industrial Boulevard. He sped away as fast as he could. Carlos took a few seconds to get oriented and then he began striding towards Tam Avenue, the heart of the mini-ghetto. He did not notice the non-descript sedan that pulled to the curb a block away.

The FBI team tasked with following Carlos, had to adjust on the fly. They had not expected to be in the Naked City. The two, young, white men in the sedan felt exposed and decided they needed to be very careful. They were sure several eyes were watching them already. The four man FBI team was completely prepared for the plane carrying Carlos. They fully expected him to go to the car rental counter, but were taken by surprise when he changed plans. However, they were able to tail him, because it took so long to find a cabbie for the Naked City.

When they realized Carlos was headed for a Hispanic part of town, they radioed in for a couple of Latino watchers. Five minutes after they had parked, they were informed that a new team was on sight and were already watching

Carlos. The young white FBI men were truly relieved and left the area as fast as they could.

Carlos strolled down the street as if he didn't have a care in the world. He suddenly turned into the yard of a dilapidated ranch house and went straight to the front door. As soon as he rang the doorbell, it opened. A large Hispanic man filled the doorway. He had scars all over his face, tattoos decorated his forearms. His eyes were glassy from recent drug use. He gave the visitors a menacing stare.

"Leave before I kill you," he said instead of asking for a name.

"I am not easy to kill, Miguel," Carlos replied laughing. The big man quickly recognized his former employer. He stood back and let them inside.

"What brings you to my humble business office, Juan?" Miguel asked.

"Today I am Carlos Mendez," Carlos corrected him. "I am in need of some of your services."

"Well, in that case, let's have a little tequila and talk about it," Miguel said as he waved them towards two battered couches. "Maria, bring the bottle," he yelled at an unseen woman in the back of the house.

Maria entered the living room in nothing but a bikini bottom and carrying a tray, with a bottle of tequila and seven glasses. Carlos wondered how she knew to bring so many glasses, but lost his train of thought as she was followed by three other women all dressed the same as she was. They were above average looking and one was Asian.

"They were sunbathing in the back," Miguel explained. He reached out and grabbed her pulling her onto his lap. "They all work for me. Their shift, on the street, doesn't start until eight o'clock this evening, in case you are interested." Maria gave the men a forced smile.

"We need to talk in private," Carlos replied, even though his sexual desire was now growing. "Maybe after we talk," he added.

"Very well, get lost," he sternly said to the girls.

When they were alone, Carlos told him what he needed. "I want to hire ten of your best shooters. I also need guns for my men. We will need transportation for everyone. I will pay you top dollar, my friend," Carlo smiled.

"This must be a large contract," Miguel said as he tried to calculate how much to charge his old friend.

"We need to take out six people. They will be at a condominium in someplace called Summerlin. There may be several people around, so we need to prepare to kill several others. I don't want anybody to be able to identify us."

"Understood," Miguel nodded. "When will this take place?"

"I want to watch the location tonight, to set the best plan, and need two of your people to do that. We go in tomorrow," Carlos answered. "We would do it ourselves, but we have been traveling all day and need food and rest, before we make the hit."

"I see," nodded Miguel. "Where are you staying tonight?"

"That's no problem. We'll walk up to the Stratosphere and stay there tonight," Carlos replied.

"Ah, you want to do a little gambling perhaps," Miguel answered knowingly. "But we had better drive you there."

"Why?"

"This neighborhood is too dangerous to walk, even for you my friend," Miguel said.

"Okay."

Miguel studied his old friend for a few seconds then said. "My price will be four hundred thousand dollars," he replied seriously. "I won't even change you for the transportation. I'll have a couple of my boys steal some cars tomorrow morning.

"I will have to go to the bank, but I will have half of the money for you tonight," Carlos negotiated. "I'll pay you the rest after the job is over."

"You'll pay me the rest tomorrow before the hit," Miguel demanded.

"As you wish," Carlos agreed. "Now how about bringing back your girls for a little entertainment?"

59

In the sky, heading to Las Vegas, Mandy was having the time of her life. She purred like a kitten as she sat and talked with Banyon. He told her about his life and how he had gotten to be a "finder", without revealing his secret. Mandy decided to say something, but was cut off.

At that moment, the pilot announced, "We are twenty minutes from landing. You need to fasten your seat belts."

"We will be landing in a couple of minutes," Banyon announced for them all to hear. "The hit men are very good and we need to start acting professionally right now. You two are here to protect us, starting doing that, immediately."

Both women said, "yes, sir."

Shortly, the plane landed and rolled up to a hanger. Banyon noticed a tall blonde woman in a black pants suit, waiting by a black, Cadillac, Escalade. When he exited the plane, she walked over to him, holding out her hand.

"Hello," she said. "My name is Rebecca Smith. I'm with the FBI. I was told to deliver this envelope to you and to offer you this FBI vehicle to use during your visit."

Banyon shook her hand, grabbed the envelope, and opened it. It contained the pictures of all the hit men. The pictures had taken at the car rental parking lot, in Chicago. It also had all the information the FBI could obtain on each of the members. Bart had promised to have the information available when they landed in Las Vegas. He scanned it quickly and handed it to Eric. "Give it to the girls, when you are done."

"Will do," he responded as he began to look through the materials.

"Now, what do I need to know about this SUV?" Banyon asked Rebecca.

Smiling, she replied. "It is armored, has tires that can't be shot out and is faster than anything in its class. There are a variety of guns and grenades in the back trunk, as well. It is a rolling fortress."

"Thanks, we will take you up on the vehicle," he announced. She dropped the keys into his waiting hand.

"In addition, we have the hit team under surveillance. They are currently in the Naked City, if you know where that is?"

"I do," replied Banyon.

"We also have a team of ten FBI agents in SWAT gear, which will be stationed near your house tonight," she added.

"The hit team won't attack tonight," Banyon told her. "It will be tomorrow. But they will have people watching tonight."

"How do you know this?" Rebecca asked in surprise.

"It's how they operate," he said to deflect the question.

"If you need anything, you call me," Rebecca handed him a card. "I am available 24/7. We would really like to take these guys down."

"My life depends on it," Banyon retorted. Rebecca turned on her heel and strutted off the tarmac. Banyon turned back to the plane and saw Mandy hefting his bag to the Escalade. Heather and Eric were right behind. She was acting very professional. *Thank God, finally,* he thought.

"Want me to drive?" Eric asked.

"Yes, take Tropicana west," Banyon said.

"Why?" Eric asked.

"We need to make a stop on the way to the house." He then told the girls to select guns from the FBI stock and to leave their guns in the suitcases, for now.

Heather sat in the front. Mandy and Banyon spread out in the middle seat. Banyon noticed the girls were on high alert.

"You watch left and I'll watch right," Heather yelled over the seat. Mandy suddenly didn't seem to care about Banyon.

He was busy reading the file Rebecca had given him when he heard Mandy whisper in a frustrated voice. "Colt, I really wanted to become a member of the mile high club today."

He ignored her and kept on reading as Eric traveled up Tropicana. Suddenly, he snapped his head up, "Eric pull in here."

Eric turned into the parking lot and asked, "Are you sure?"

"Yes I am," Banyon replied to the shocked passengers in the SUV. They had pulled into the parking lot of a large supermarket-looking store. The marque said 'Adult Entertainment Palace'. It was an adult video store.

60

As they entered the front door, Banyon stopped them and said, "I know what I need here, don't get lost. We will only be a few minutes." Both girls glanced at each other with a questioning look, but said nothing. They both then shrugged.

"I've never been in an adult video store," Mandy suddenly announced just a clerk approached them.

"No children allowed. She has to be eighteen to enter," he said formally and stood with his hands on his hips.

"Oh, poop," Mandy whined. "Do something Daddy. We need some new toys."

"Stop fooling around and show him your identification," Banyon scolded. Mandy smiled showing her braces, but handed him her license. He scanned it and returned it to her with a suspicious look on his face.

"The identification looks like a fake to me," he said.

"What do you want me to do, show you my boobs," Mandy pouted.

"She is twenty-two. I can vouch for her," Heather said quickly.

The man looked at Heather for a second, then, something like a smile crossed his face. "As much as I would like to see her boobs, it's against store policy. We'll let it go today. You can enter the store." he said.

"Can we look around now, Daddy?" Mandy said innocently. Under her breath, she said to Banyon, "he must be gay. Everyman wants to look at my boobs. Well, everyman except you."

Banyon ignored her remark. "Well, go and look around, but keep an eye open for trouble," Banyon said as he scanned the large interior. He and Loni had been to the store before. It had a large clothing section. Loni loved to dress up in sexy outfits for him. He had bought her several sexy outfits, less than a year ago, from this same store. They had walked the entire store; he knew where to look for his items.

There were about thirty people milling about the store, most were couples, who seemed to be completely entertained. The store was clean, well merchandised, with several choices of every conceivable sexual enticement possible. Heather grabbed Mandy by the hand and immediately went to the leather section. Eric began perusing the various lotions and oils section. Banyon headed to the back of the store for the items he needed.

He found the section and selected six boxes from the display. They were bulky boxes; he could not carry all of them. The sales clerk quickly appeared and offered to help him carry the items to the counter.

"You must be going for a big party," the clerk said with a slight lisp. He grabbed three of the boxes and swung his hips as they proceeded to the counter.

"I have a special use for them," Banyon said to deflect the clerks thoughts.

"You'll need some lubricant," the clerk advised over his shoulder. "The best one is in aisle twelve."

"I'm good," Banyon patiently replied.

"You need any condemns? I see you have women with you," the clerk knowingly offered.

"No," Banyon answered.

"Perhaps, you would like some restraints. Those are my favorites." The clerk said with enthusiasm as they passed a display.

"Just these," Banyon wearily replied. They reached the counter and the clerk began to ring up the purchases, without additional comment. Heather, Mandy, and Eric soon joined him there to see what he was buying.

"Oh My God, Heather," Mandy suddenly exclaimed a little too loudly.

"What?" Heather asked.

"It's you." She pointed to one of the boxes on the counter. Banyon quickly turned the front of the box towards him so he could see it better, and stared in disbelief. The box contained a plastic blowup doll that looked exactly like Heather.

Heather's face flushed, but she quickly recovered. "Well, at least, I'll get some royalties on the sale," she quipped.

"Actually," the clerk said. "I recognized her when you came in. We have a whole section of her videos in aisle eleven. Just look for Jean Anna," he said as he leveled his gaze on the now embarrassed Heather. Eric was gone in a flash.

"I'm sorry, I didn't know," Banyon sincerely told the young woman.

"It's alright Colt. It's part of my past."

"Well, now you can compare the doll to the real woman and find out which is better," the clerk dryly joked. Banyon turned to him with malice in his eyes, he quickly through up his hands defensively.

"What do you need these for?" Mandy asked. "You have us."

He pulled both women away from the prying ears of the too attentive clerk. "These blowup dolls will be bait for the take down. From a distance, they will look real. It will bring the hit men into the trap," he explained. "We will sit them at a table so it will look like we are having some food."

"I like it," Heather said professionally. "That way there will be less chance of us getting hurt."

"But you forgot one thing, Colt," Mandy told him as she read the box.

"What's that?"

"These dolls don't come with any clothes. It would be a little unrealistic for six people to be nude for an outside dinner in the desert."

"Your right, Mandy," Banyon said as he scratched his head. "Tell you what. They have a dress up section over there," he pointed. "Why don't you girls go and pick out four female outfits and two male outfits. Get ones which appear to be right, for the occasion.

"Wow," Mandy exclaimed. "This will actually be more fun than buying shoes." She grabbed Heather by the arm and dragged her to the clothing area. Banyon thought, *that's exactly what Loni would have said.*

"You are all kinds of kinky," the clerk said. "Want to take me with you? Your group looks like fun." Banyon ignored the clerk.

"I need to make a phone call," Banyon announced as he realized that he was alone with the clerk. It gave him the perfect opportunity to check in with Wolf. He walked out of the store, pretending to call someone on the phone.

"Wolf, is there anything new to report?"

"Yes," the spirit immediately answered. "The hit team has gotten a lot bigger. Carlos has hired ten local Latinos to help with the hit. They are sending two men to watch your home tonight and plan to come after you by noon, tomorrow. You need to make additional arrangements right away."

"Thanks Wolf," Banyon said and dialed the number Rebecca had given him at the airport.

She answered on the first ring. "Wow that was fast. I didn't think I would hear from you until tomorrow."

He explained the new information, ignoring her question of how he knew about the additional men. After a few seconds, she said they would move up their plan and go to the site earlier in the day tomorrow. She told him, she would have thirty SWAT men ready and would have the park closed tonight, so no tourist would be present tomorrow. Banyon agreed and hung up the phone. He then went back inside to collect his people and his purchases.

Heather and Mandy were standing at the counter, smiling broadly. "When I was picking out the men's stuff, all I could think of was the song about the YMCA," Mandy quickly said, as she showed him what she bought.

"I guess the dolls will look normal from a distance," Banyon said as he rubbed his chin.

"And for the female outfits, I chose a school girl's outfit, a nursing outfit, a stewardess pants suit and a maids dress, without the frills," Heather added.

She has the same taste as I do, Banyon thought.

"Where's Eric?" Banyon asked as he looked around the store.

"I'll go find him," Heather said with a little irritation.

"You'll find him in booth number twenty, in the peep-show area," the clerk said sweetly. "He is watching one of your movies Jean Anna. I can see him on one of my monitors." Heather quickly headed off to the back room with an irritated look on her face and her fists clinched.

Banyon paid for the purchases. It cost him over eight hundred dollars. He and Mandy hefted the bags to the SUV. After a few minutes of waiting, a perturbed Banyon sent Mandy to find the now lost Heather and Eric.

Ten minutes later, frustrated Banyon pushed open the door of booth twenty.

61

The President of the United States hung up the phone. A smile spread over his handsome face. He quickly called his secretary and told her to send in his visitors. They had been invited to the oval office, to watch the news conference. It was scheduled to start in twenty minutes. The President of Mexico would be speaking from Mexico City. The visitors were his inner circle; the people he trusted the most. Marlene Moore was now part of the group. When they were all seated, he addressed them.

"I just got off the phone with the President of The United States of Mexico," he announced as he planted himself on the corner of his desk. The President wanted his people to see he was calm and in complete control.

"What did he have to say?" Marlene Moore asked.

"Actually, he apologized. He told me this crisis has all been fostered by the drug cartels and was masterminded by a government official in Mexico."

"Really," Marlene commented.

"Yes," the President agreed. "The man recently died during the riots there."

"How convenient is that?" Marlene snorted.

"So, you didn't have to tell him about Slezeck or Klotz?" The representative from the Pentagon asked.

"No, it will be our dirty little secret," the President replied.

"What about all the sanctions he implemented this morning?" The Secretary of the Treasury asked.

"He has rescinded them all, effective immediately. He said he would make the announcement at the news conference."

"And what did he say about removing the troops at the border?" The Pentagon representative asked.

"He said, if we start backing our people off immediately, he will order his men away from the border.

"Good. What do you want to do?" The man from the Pentagon asked.

"Make it an order from me, General." The man got up and immediately left the room to make arrangements.

"Should we notify the media?" The National Security Adviser asked. "It would make for good press for you, Mr. President.

"No, but leak it to a couple of Congressmen. It will be on national television within ten minutes, with each of them taking credit," The President chuckled. "Make sure it is leaked to those who have been criticizing my handling of the crisis."

"Why?" The National Security Advisor was confused.

"Because the Mexican President is going to announce at his news conference, he and I were the ones who worked out the crisis, no one else. The Congressmen will have to explain that."

"You are devious, Mr. President," Marlene shouted with joy.

"I know."

"But how is he going to explain all the revenge killings?" The man from the treasury asked.

The President now came off the desk; he stood as if giving a speech. "As you know, many Mexican people believe in superstitions and powers which are unexplained. They often believe in things they can't see."

"So?" The Treasury man said.

"He is going to use that, in his speech."

"Why?"

"To explain the killings and also any future retribution."

"How?" They all asked at once.

"It seems the Mexican President has found a hero. His name is Danta Lopez." The President paused to let that sink in.

"Do you mean the cartel leader?" Marlene inquired.

"Yes. He told me he is going to position Danta Lopez as the new 'Zorro', a man, who is a ghost, but fights corruption in his country."

"You're kidding," The National Security Advisor laughed.

"Not only that," the President pointed out. "But he has asked me if I could help develop communications with him. It seems that he has some more work for the new *Zorro* and no way to get in contact with him."

"That's brilliant," the National Advisor quickly said.

62

"Wolf, do you have any updates for me?" Banyon asked the spirit as he strolled along the outside of his second story patio pretending to be on his cell phone. It was a little after eight o'clock at night. They had just finished eating steaks Banyon had in the freezer. He glanced through the glass sliding doors and noticed Eric was doing the dishes. Both Mandy and Heather had refused to do domestic work, so it left either Banyon or Eric. Fortunately, Eric offered. The girls were not visible in the house.

"No need to worry about anything tonight," the spirit replied. "The Kammler boys have gone home as the FBI is now watching your home. They are also watching the two watchers, sent by the hit men."

"Where is Carlos?"

"He is at the Stratosphere Casino and will be there all night," Wolf informed him.

"But isn't that telling me the future. I thought you couldn't tell me that?" Banyon quickly replied.

"He is losing big money and he never leaves the black-jack table until he runs out, or gets the money back. He is also drinking heavily. You are safe."

"Do you have anything else to report?"

"Carlos has a bank account in America. He used it late this afternoon to get money for the men he has hired. I can give you the bank and account number. You should tell the FBI, they can freeze his assets tomorrow morning."

"Give it to me in the morning; it's too late to do anything about it tonight. Talk to you in the morning." He closed his phone and headed for the inside. He was two steps from the door when his cell phone rang. It was Loni.

"Hi Loni," he said into the phone, happy to hear her voice.

"Colt, where are you?" Loni sounded a little frustrated.

"I'm out," he simply replied.

"I tried the house phone several times, you are not there."

"That's because I'm out," he patiently replied.

"Pramilla can't find Eric, either," she added.

"That's because he is out with me and not at home," he carefully said. "How did your dive go?" He quickly asked to get her off track.

"Oh God," she gushed. "It was so great. Colt, we found the box. It only took us four hours."

"And?"

"It is loaded with diamonds and other gems. We're rich," she exclaimed. "Previne says there are several antiques which can be identified, but most of the treasure will belong to us. We will even get a finder's fee on those items."

"Got any idea on how much it is worth?"

"Previne says the total value will be somewhere between two to two and a half million dollars. Aren't you excited?"

"That's terrific," Banyon sincerely replied. "When are you coming home?"

"It's too late to sail back tonight, but we will head home tomorrow morning, early. Pramilla said we will probably land around one in the morning, Chicago time. Will you be home then?"

"Of course," Banyon quickly said. "I can't wait to see you and show you how much I missed you," he said.

"I can't wait either. I have so much to tell you about my adventures."

"How about show and tell," he said seductively.

"I've learned a few new things on this trip," she replied, also in an equally seductive voice.

"Oh?"

Suddenly serious, Loni asked. "Colt, is it cheating on your mate if you slept with someone else in the same bed?" Banyon already knew Loni and Previne where bunk mates last night.

"Well, I guess it would depend on..." But Loni cut him off.

"Then I've cheated on you. I never meant that to happen," she said with a sob.

Banyon knew that he had to say something or Loni would become a completely uncontrollable. "I know you love me," Banyon said. "And I truly love you, Loni. That's what counts, don't you see?"

"So, you aren't mad at me? You aren't going to throw me out of the house?" She asked in sheepish little girl voice.

"I don't know if I would think the same way if there was another man involved," Banyon pointed out. "But no, I'm not even the least bit angry with you. Just get your pretty little butt home, so that I can show you how I feel."

"Oh Colt, you always know the right thing to say," she purred.

"My guess is, this experience, will only add to our desire for each other," he smoothly said.

"I'm glad you feel that way, because I have to sleep with Pramilla tonight," she admitted with a giggle.

"I hope you both make each other very happy," he offered.

"You know, they sometimes share Eric," Loni blurted out.

"He has mentioned it."

"Previne thinks the three of us should try it."

They talked for another ten minutes. Banyon had the feeling the Patel's were trying a little too hard with Loni, but didn't say anything. He decided to have a talk with Previne, in the near future. He wanted all his friends close to him, but not necessarily in the same bed. He was sure it would lead to complications, the same kind of complications as dealing with the ever-aggressive Mandy and Heather. They eventually hung up, without Banyon mentioning anything about all that had happened during the day. He returned to the inside of the house wondering what his definition of cheating really was.

63

"We need to have a strategy session about our plan for tomorrow," Banyon announced. Only Eric was in the room. He was sitting on the couch, reading a magazine.

"He's back," Eric yelled out without looking up.

Banyon heard a door open in the house and suddenly he had a look of shock on his face as the women paraded into the room. Heather was dressed in a nurse's outfit. Mandy had on the maid's dress they had purchased in the afternoon. They both stopped by the couch and posed for him.

"We couldn't resist trying out the clothes," Heather admitted with a giggle. "Do you like?"

Banyon was beside himself with anger. This mission wasn't working. These women wouldn't stop tempting him and they were heading into imminent danger tomorrow. They could die and all these girls wanted to do was entice-ment him. He blew his stack and ordered them to sit on the couch.

"Right now, I have to know if you girls want to continue. I can send you both back tonight, if I have to. Don't you realize that all your flirting is putting us in danger? You're not paying attention to the work, I can't have that. You're both fired as of this minute," he screamed at them as they cow-ered on the couch.

Heather sat stoically saying nothing, but a pout formed on her face. Mandy dropped to the floor, on her knees and starting crying. "Colt, please don't do this. We'll be good, I promise. I care too much about you to let anything happen, to you. You have trusted me before, please trust me now."

Banyon realized his outburst had a lot to do with his con-versation with Loni. His own head was spinning with carnal thoughts; his resistance was getting very weak. He wanted to punish Mandy for tempting him, but knew it was really sexual desire and how much of that was actually Mandy's fault. His current state of sexual frustration was clouding his judgment. He was on the verge of making mistakes of his own.

"What do you have to say, Heather?" Banyon asked roughly, to give him time to think things through.

"You hired us to do a job. It was to protect you. So far there has not been any threat. I don't see what your problem is with us, except maybe, you are sexually dissatisfied or frustrated. We can take care of that, anytime you want." She spoke clinically like a doctor and her words hit home.

Banyon now looked to Eric for support. He shrugged and said. "I'm good. I think both of these women would put their lives on the line for us, if needed. When I was a SEAL, we depended on that to survive. I trust them."

Banyon said nothing for several seconds as he contemplated what he had heard. *Well at least I have made my point*; he thought. He reached out for Mandy's hand to pull her off the floor. She quickly grabbed it and he pulled her into his arms. He gave her a big hug. She, all but squealed with delight. "Now sit down and pay attention to the plan," he said.

"Yes, sir," all three people on the couch responded sincerely.

"We need to blow up the dolls and then dress them before we leave in the morning," Banyon said first. He immediately regretted saying it.

"Can I do the Heather doll?" Eric wise cracked.

"I don't mind blowing up a few male dolls," Heather retorted with a smile and batted her eyes at him.

"Can I have one too," Mandy added.

Banyon realized they were all joking to relieve some of the tension he had built. He said nothing, he let it go. "We will leave here at ten o'clock in the morning. We will need to divert the attention of the Mexican watchers outside, while we load the SUV."

"I believe I can handle that," Heather said.

"We need to make sure they follow us. It will take us over an hour to get to the takedown location. It has to look like we aren't coming back to the house anytime soon. The watchers will call the hit team as they follow," Banyon told them, "that's the plan."

"Do we have back up? There are six of them, right?" Heather asked.

"Well, actually, things have changed. The hit men leader Carlos has hired another ten locals to help. There will be sixteen shooters after us."

"That's a lot," Mandy said in a nervous voice.

"Don't worry. The FBI will follow the shooters, into the park. There will be thirty SWAT team members. They will help box the hit men in."

"So, what is the rest of the plan?" Heather asked.

"We will get to the location first, set the dolls up at a picnic table, the hit men will close in, and we will eliminate them. It is that simple. The FBI men will prevent them from getting away, but we don't want any prisoners. The entire hit squad needs to die in the park," Banyon said with force. "Otherwise, we all will have to live looking over our shoulder forever. Their reputation is they never fail."

"Remind me how many people they have killed, so I will feel better about shooting them?" Mandy inquired.

"They have killed over one hundred innocent people. They are indiscriminate killers. They leave a lot of collateral damage. They need to die."

"What about other people in the park?" Heather asked.

"The FBI will close the park tonight. No one will be able to enter. There won't be anybody at the overnight facilities either. Tomorrow, only we and the killers will be allowed into the park. No chance of any civilians getting hurt."

"So what is the name of this park where we going tomorrow?" Mandy asked.

"It's called the 'Valley of Fire'."

The meeting went on for another twenty minutes. Banyon assured them, they would have the high ground and ample cover. It was why he had chosen the park, he told them. He spent ten minutes describing the park and why it was the best location. Soon, there were no more questions. Banyon then made his last announcement of the evening.

"We are going to sleep in shifts of four hours, just in case something changes," he told them. Eric and I will sleep first. We will relieve you two girls, at one o'clock. Are there any questions?" When no one answered, he told them he was going to bed. It was only nine o'clock in Las Vegas, but their bodies were still on central time.

It took him only ten minutes to prepare for bed. It included a quick shower to cleanse the dirt of the day away. He laid out his clothes for the morning, climbed into bed nude, just like he did at home, and turned out the light. He was actually happy to be by himself. He soon drifted off to sleep. That lasted all of five minutes.

He heard the bedroom door quietly open and close, but pretended to be asleep. He waited for the aggressive assault from Mandy, but it never came. He expected her to start at any minute, but it never happened. He was sure she was in the room and strained to hear a zipper opening or cloth scrapping against skin, but heard nothing. After a few minutes, he was sure something was wrong. He reached over and turned on the light. Mandy was nowhere to be seen.

"Mandy, are you in here?" he spoke softly.

Suddenly, her head peeked over the end of the bed. "I'm here," she said in a nervous voice.

"Why are you in here?" he asked as his temperature began to rise. "You and Heather are supposed to be out in the living room, protecting me."

"Er...Eric is out there with Heather. He decided to change the teams. I had no place else to go," she said. "I tried to be quiet and not wake you."

"So, you're sitting on the floor, in my bedroom?"

"I won't make any noise. You go back to sleep, Colt. I'm okay," she said sincerely.

"Well, at least get off the floor and sit in the chair over there," Banyon gestured with his arm.

"No, I'm fine here really. Don't worry about me," she answered.

"Get up off the floor now, Mandy," he ordered. When she stood up he saw she was nude except for a pair of small cotton panties.

"Why are you undressed?" Banyon roared and flapped his hands.

With her head hung low she said. "Colt, it is not what you think. Heather told me to take off the maids dress so they could dress the dolls. All my other clothes are in my travel bag right here at the foot of the bed. I tried to be quiet when I came into the room. I was waiting for you to start snoring again to open the zipper and get some clothes out."

After processing the information, Banyon asked. "Then you will sleep?"

"Just let me put on a tee shirt and I'll curl up on the chair, okay?" She pleaded.

Banyon thought about it for a few seconds and then replied. "Okay, you can sleep on the bed. I want you fresh in the morning."

"You mean it?" she exclaimed, as she pulled a shirt over her head.

"Yes, but you sleep on top of the covers," he demanded. "And no talking either," he added.

"Deal," she said and her tiny body jumped onto the bed, crawling up to him. She plopped her head down next to him and laid there quietly on her side. She didn't dare move a muscle. Banyon decided to stay awake a little longer to make sure she complied. Soon, he realized she was shivering.

"Are you cold?" He asked softly.

"Just a little," she replied in her little girl voice. "But don't worry, I won't wake you up or anything." Banyon now felt sorry he had treated her so poorly.

"Why don't you get under the covers long enough to get warm," he said.

"Really?" she asked, but was already halfway under the covers before he finished his offer. Next the tee shirt went flying.

"I thought you were cold?" Banyon said.

"But now I have you to keep me warm."

Part Seven

Valley of Fire

64

Colton Banyon awoke the next morning as the sun peeked over the windowsill and reached his eyes. He had fallen asleep on his back and was still on his back when he opened his eyes. He quickly realized Mandy was snuggled tight against him, with her arm across his chest. He turned to look at her, her eyes fluttered open.

"Morning," she muttered sweetly. She then rolled over and sprang from the bed before he could say anything. "I'm showering first," she announced as she headed for the bathroom.

They had gotten up when the alarm went off at one o'clock in the morning and threw on some clothes, then went to relieve Eric and Heather. During their stint on guard duty, they had talked and played cards. Mandy, of course wanted to play strip poker, but Banyon reminded her they were in protection mode, she reluctantly backed down. At a little after four o'clock in the morning, Eric returned to the living room and relieved them. He said Heather would be along shortly, so Banyon and Mandy returned to the bedroom, for additional sleep. This time she didn't wait to be invited into the bed.

He threw on shorts and a shirt and then went to the living room. He found Eric asleep on the couch. Heather was nowhere to be seen. Suddenly, he heard a noise on the patio. He turned and saw Heather in just a black, thong, bikini bottom, doing yoga and stretching. She didn't have on her blond wig and looked completely different then yesterday. He marveled at her flexibility, strength, and her sexiness.

"She has been doing that for over an hour," Eric said sleepily. "I don't know where she gets her energy."

"Let's hope she keeps it up," Banyon quipped and headed into the kitchen, where he got out some frozen orange juice and started to make juice for everyone.

"Oh, she can keep it up alright," Eric replied.

Suddenly, changing the subject, Banyon asked Eric a question. "Did you speak to Pramilla last night?"

"Yeah, wow, they found the treasure. I'm kind of jealous of those pretty little girls. I mean running off to the Black Sea, running around naked, sailing and bunking together. You do know about that don't you?"

"Loni told me," he confessed.

"Can you imagine? They are having a great time and doing whatever they want," he complained.

"And you're not having a good time?" Banyon asked, with his eyebrows raised.

"Touché," Eric replied. "But I do miss them."

"Me too," Banyon answered.

The patio door opened and Heather stepped through without the slightest hint of modesty or embarrassment. "Colt," she called out as she stood facing him. "I'll be ready in ten minutes to distract the watchers. I just need to take a shower." She then strutted out of the room knowing both men had their mouths open.

"We can't mention these women, or that we were in Las Vegas, to Loni or the Patel sisters," Eric said. "They won't understand."

"I quite agree," Banyon said as he laughed. "Let's tell them we got mixed up with some girls we met at a bar. It would be easier to believe then what actually is happening," Banyon said.

"Too true," Eric agreed.

The bedroom door now opened and Mandy sprinted out dressed in white jeans and a dark blue, loose-fitting, top. "You can use the bathroom now," she announced as Banyon looked her over.

"Mandy do you have a lighter top. You know something which is white or maybe a sand color?" Eric asked.

"Why do you ask?"

"We are going into the desert. A dark blue top will standout too much. We need to be as invisible as possible," Banyon told her.

She turned on her heel, without giving him an argument, but huffed and stomped back into the bedroom like a teenager being told her dress was too short.

"I'd better tell Heather before she makes a scene too," Eric said as he left the couch and went toward the second bathroom.

Banyon followed Mandy into the bedroom. "You know, I shouldn't have let you sleep in the same bed. I feel really guilty about it now."

"Don't feel guilty, Colt," she said as she bent over and kept looking in her small suitcase. "You're still a virgin with me."

"You understand it has to stay that way, don't you?" Banyon asked.

She quickly stood up and stared at him. Suddenly, she went and hugged him. There were tears in her eyes. "Just as long as you treat me like a person, I'm okay."

"Good, now put on a top quickly. We need to get started," he replied. Without additional comment, he left the room. He knew his words hurt her, but didn't know what else to say to her.

When he returned, Heather was back in the kitchen, still dressed in her thong bikini bottom, but now she had a tiny top on. She had combed her long hair and added black high-heels. Dark sunglasses hid her eyes. He was pretty sure she would distract the watchers and told her so.

Then Banyon went to a nearby cabinet and took out a pair of binoculars. He put them on the counter. He next called Rebecca and informed her they were going to distract the watchers so they could load the SUV.

He had parked the SUV in the driveway the night before, it was facing out. He had done it on purpose. There were four one-car garages, in a row, in the middle, of his building and his was the first one. He had a key for his neighbor's garage, the next one over, and could access it from the inside hallway. The garage would be part of the distraction.

Mandy soon entered the kitchen. "Take these binoculars and watch out the front window," he told her. "When the watchers turn to follow Heather, let us know." He then handed out earpieces to everyone for communications.

"Yes, sir," she said and saluted.

"Heather, the watchers are on the right hand side and about half-way down the street," Banyon told her.

"I've already been out and did reconnaissance earlier this morning," she replied. "No one noticed me. I'm going to head to the mail box. It is across the street from their car. I'll make sure their eyes are on me."

Banyon was shocked that she had been outside, but was pleased she had a plan. "Sounds good to me, any questions?" There were none, so Banyon and Eric gathered up the now dressed dolls and headed out the door leading to the garage hallway. Heather followed, tapping her high heels on the tiled floor.

In a few minutes, the sting started. "Are you ready, Mandy?" Banyon spoke into his earpiece.

"Ready," she replied. Heather pressed the door opener to his neighbor's garage door and it rolled up, allowing her to strut out onto the driveway. She paused and stretched luxuriously to get their attention.

"They see her," Mandy whispered into the earpiece.

Heather casually strolled toward the mailbox looking like she didn't have a care in the world. The watchers stayed riveted on her. "How am I doing," she whispered.

"They're hooked," Mandy said.

When she got to the mailbox, she dropped the mailbox key as if by accident. She pretended to have trouble picking up the key and dropped it several more times.

"Go," Mandy whispered.

Banyon and Eric exited the garage carrying the dolls as they ran. Eric pressed the button to open up the rear door of the SUV. They had the dolls spread out in the back and the SUV door closing in twenty seconds.

Back in the garage, out of sight, Banyon said. "Mission accomplished."

Heather immediately turned from the mail box, walked quickly back to the garage, and closed the door. The first phase of Banyon's plan was complete without a hitch. They returned to Banyon's place and began to pack. Heather went and changed into a buff colored jump suit and donned her blond wig.

Banyon found Mandy in the kitchen, rifling through Banyon's freezer. "I'm hungry. We need to eat something before we go," she said with her head in the freezer. Suddenly, she squealed. "I've found a coffee cake. I love coffee cake." *So does Loni*, Banyon thought.

"Leave it," Banyon ordered. "Loni will notice. We'll stop at someplace along the highway and get food." He then opened his phone and called his cleaning service. He told them to come and completely clean the house. He didn't want any scent of Mandy in his house, or especially, in his bed.

"Let's make sure to not leave anything behind," Eric quickly told the girls. They rushed off to make a last sweep.

They brought their luggage into his garage and opened the door. They made sure the watchers saw they were loading their luggage and would not return to the condominium. Then they piled into the Escalade. Banyon had them roll down the dark windows of the SUV to make sure the watchers could identify them as they passed.

Twenty minutes later Banyon told Eric to take the exit ramp and hit the fast food place was just off the highway. While the others went inside to grab some take out, Banyon addressed Wolf.

"Wolf, is there anything new to report?"

"I think that Mr. Carlos is in for a bad day," he replied.

"Where is he now?"

"He is in a suite at the Stratosphere hotel, but has only had about an hour of sleep, he is not going to be in a good mood when he gets the phone call from Miguel, telling him they have to go now," Wolf laughed.

"Will they have all the men that we expect?"

"Yes, and he has the vehicles too. Colt, please do remember to bring water. It will be over ninety degrees in the valley, you will lose water fast."

"Will Carlos bring water?"

"He doesn't have time to think about it."

Banyon immediately went into the restaurant and bought three bottles of water for each person. They returned to the SUV, with their food and were back on I-15 in just a few minutes. The watchers were right behind them. Mandy said she could see one of them was on a phone.

Banyon quickly called Rebecca and told her he expected the hit team to be on the move very shortly. He asked if everything was prepared at the Valley of Fire. She said it was and she would have two FBI men, dressed as rangers, to let them in; all the tourists had been evacuated. He said they would be there in less than an hour. She thanked him for the update and hung up.

"So tell me more about this Valley of Fire?" Heather asked from the front seat.

"Well, the first thing I'll tell you is it is a fine place for killing someone."

65

"Get your lazy asses up," screamed Carlos as he threw the phone down on the bed. He had just gotten off the phone with Miguel, The news wasn't good. His five men were asleep in various places around the suite. They had stayed up with Carlos, almost all night, while he had lost fifty thousand dollars, at the blackjack tables. They were all still drunk.

"*Senior,* it's too early," one man moaned as he looked at his watch and realized that it was only ten-thirty in the morning. "What's the problem?"

"The problem is our targets have left the house. They took their suitcases and are heading out into the desert, you idiot. We need to go after them." Carlos was very mad and was not helped by his large hangover.

"Where are they going amigo?"

"All I know is they are headed up I-15 North. There is nothing out there for hundreds of miles, except Indian reservations," Carlos muttered.

"Maybe the *gringos* are tourists today," another said.

Carlos thought about that for a second. "You know. You could be right," Carlos said as he rolled out of bed still dressed. "I know of one place they might visit."

"What place?"

"The Valley of Fire," Carlos answered. "It would be a fine place for killing someone," he said at almost the same time as Banyon had said it.

"I don't like the name," one of them said as he crossed himself. "It makes me think of the devil."

I don't care what you think," Carlos fired back. "Get your lazy asses up and be ready to go in five minutes. Miguel will pick us up in front of the casino."

66

Banyon started talking about the Valley of Fire. He had been there several times during his lifetime. He had also done research on the Internet. "The Valley of Fire is one of our oldest National parks. It was the first one dedicated by the state of Nevada in 1935. It was formed over 150 million years ago. It is like another world."

"I never heard of it," Eric chimed in.

"It is a big oval basin. It is something like four miles across one way and six miles the other way, with only one main road that runs east to west and feeds all the parking lots. Most people haven't heard of it, because it butts up to Lake Mead and is at the end of the Grand Canyon. They are much more popular parks. But it contains many unusual windblown rock formations. They have names like 'The Elephant', 'The Beehives'', 'The Seven Sisters' and more. The rock formations are stunning."

"Most of this desert is flat. Why aren't there formations like it in other places?" Heather inquired.

"Well, I'm not a geologist, but it was once a sand dune desert. Then it was part of an inland ocean and finally it was once part of a tremendous faulting and shifting of the earth's crust. The sandstone rock, which is very soft, eroded over time and what are left are the formations."

"Why is it called the Valley of Fire?" Mandy quickly asked.

"Because, when the sun is strong and the sky is clear, like it is today, many of the rock formations reflect sunlight. They look like they are on fire. The majority of the rock for-mations are red. But you will see other colors are well."

"How does that help us?" Mandy asked.

"Actually, none of the formations I mentioned helps us, but there is one more rock formation that will be very useful to us." Banyon said dramatically.

"Which one?" Mandy demanded.

"It's called Petroglyph Canyon," Banyon said slowly to let it sink in.

"Wait; aren't Petroglyphs figures drawn on cave walls?" Heather said.

"Your right, Heather," Banyon replied with a smile. "Petroglyph Canyon is near the middle of the park. It is a huge rock formation which is riddled with canyons. It is like a big maze. There are many windblown and carved caves in the walls where the ancient Indian tribe called the Anasazi lived. They drew on the walls and outside the caves. Many people think the caves are haunted."

"So, we are going to lead the hit men into a maze, is that right?" Mandy asked. "Then what?"

"That's right," Banyon told them. "But not just any maze. We are going to lead them to 'The Mouse's Tank'."

"What's the Mouse's Tank?" Mandy asked with frustration in her voice.

"It's actually a depression in a rock. It's a pothole that looks like a bowl and is under several other rocks and not easily found. Most of the year, there is water in the depression. There is no other water available in all of the rest of the Valley of Fire."

"Do mice live there? I hate mice," Heather said as she squirmed in her seat.

"No," Banyon replied. "The story behind the name comes from an Indian named Little Mouse. In the 1890's he supposedly killed a local man and a posse chased him into the rock formation. For six months, they could not find him and thought he was dead, but one day he emerged and they caught him. He showed them the pothole and said he lived on the water, so they named it after him."

"But why set our trap there?" Mandy persisted.

"Well," Banyon continued. "It is at the far end of a dead-end canyon. It has fifty foot walls on one side and many caves on ledges above the path. It is high ground. Second, there is a picnic table at the end of the canyon. It would be perfect for our dolls. Third, the way to Mouse's Tank is well marked by signs and easy to follow, and finally, the way out can be easily blocked. Once they go in they are not coming out."

"I see a road sign. It says The Valley of Fire next exit. There is an exit coming up," Eric yelled.

"Take it and go right. There are no other signs or billboards for the park," Banyon told him.

Mandy swiveled her head back and forth. "I don't see anything. It is all just open deserts. All I see is those mountains way off on the left," she pointed.

"Across those mountains is Death Valley in California," Banyon told them. That got him a punch in the arm from Mandy.

"Know it all," she muttered.

Eric took the exit and headed up a nondescript road which led slightly up hill. He eventually came to a sign that said they were entering the Valley of Fire. There were two Park Rangers standing by the side of the road. They waved them to stop.

"Parks closed folks," the Ranger said. He wore dark sunglasses with his hand on his gun.

Banyon rolled down the window and said, "I'm Colton Banyon. We are expected."

"That will be six dollars, to enter the park," the Ranger replied with his hand out. Then a smile crossed his face.

"There is a blue ford with two Mexicans in it. They will be here shortly. Let them in too," Banyon told the officer.

"When will the rest of the bad guys arrive?" the Ranger asked.

"Probably within the hour," Banyon estimated. "But be careful, these guys are very dangerous and usually don't leave anyone around to identify them."

"No problem, when we see their caravan we are out of here until they pass. Then, we will be back on duty. By the way Rebecca Smith, with the FBI, and the troops are following them about a mile behind. I just talked to her." He then waved them through.

They drove about a hundred yards and suddenly they could see Lake Mead shimmering in the distance. There was also a sign which said steep slope. Eric crested the rim and the view took their breath away.

"It's stunning," Heather uttered.

"See the rock formation there on the left. Head for it," Banyon told Eric. The basin was like a crater on Mars. They could see the entire valley.

"That's easy," Eric replied. "There is only one road."

"Several movies were filmed here," Banyon said, then protected his arm from another punch from Mandy.

They could see several cars situated around the parking areas. Banyon guessed they were there to make the park appear open. Eric maneuvered the Escalade through the entrance ramp and into the parking lot. He pulled up as close to the entrance to the canyon as he could. They quickly piled out and began lugging the dolls, water, and several guns, to the final site. They all had handguns but also strapped HK417 assault rifles to their backs. The last item they carried was a box of ammunition. They were prepared for a war.

"I see the watchers cresting the ridge," Mandy yelled just as they were turning the first corner.

"Then we'd better hurry and set up the dolls," Banyon yelled back. They began to jog through the thick soft sand. It took them five minutes to reach the canyon where the Mouse's Tank was located. As they entered the canyon Heather spoke.

"This is very creepy. Look at all the caves. You can clearly see the petroglyphs on all of them. I wouldn't want to be here in the dark."

"Don't worry, we'll be gone long before night," Banyon told her. "Look there is the picnic table," he pointed to the end of the canyon. "They'll have to get real close before they recognize the hoax."

They quickly set the dolls up at the table and began searching the overhead ledges and caves for the best places to set up their guns. Banyon noticed his shirt was soaking wet with perspiration. When he checked out the girls and Eric, he saw that they were all losing a lot of water already.

"Make sure to stay hydrated," he warned them.

Eric, the former SEAL, picked the sniper holes. He told Banyon and Mandy to take the spot on the left and he and Heather would take control of the one on the right. Climbing the canyon walls was not easy, but eventually they were in their chosen spots. They still had their earpieces, so they could communicate.

"How can we be sure the watchers realize where we have gone," Eric said into his earpiece.

"Good question," Banyon replied.

"Why don't I go find them and lead them here?" Mandy suddenly said. "I'm the fastest runner and can act like I forgot something in the SUV. Give me the keys Eric."

"Mandy, they could have guns," Banyon protested.

"There job is to follow us. Even if they have guns, they have no idea that we know about them. I'm sure they will just follow," she replied logically.

"All right, go then. But be careful," Banyon said.

Mandy quickly climbed down the canyon wall. She waited for Eric to throw her the keys. As soon as she had them, she turned and sprinted out of sight. Banyon took the opportunity to check in with Wolf.

"Wolf, do you have an update?"

"Carlos and his men are only ten minutes away. The FBI is still one mile behind them. It looks like everything is on plan. But please check in frequently until this is over."

"Thanks, I will," Banyon replied and then opened his phone to call Rebecca, only to find he had no cell phone reception in the valley. He wondered if it was going to be a problem for them.

Meanwhile Mandy rounded the corner and jogged into the open parking area. She saw the blue ford parked about halfway up the parking lot. Both men were still in it. She opened the rear door of the SUV and pretended to be looking for something. The men were suddenly out of the car and headed toward her. This made her a little nervous, but she waited until they were only a few yards away before she calmly closed the SUV door and turned to head back to the canyon.

"Hey, where you going little *Chiquita*," one of them said.

She stopped in her tracks and looked at them. "My friends and I have having lunch at the Mouse's Tank," she said with innocence as she scanned the men for weapons.

"Where's that?" he asked in broken English.

"The path is clearly marked," she pointed to the sign and then began to run. The Mexicans scared her, but she knew they would follow. She raced back to the Mouse's Tank area and scaled the canyon wall like a monkey. She then plopped next to Banyon and picked up her gun. Banyon could see a river of sweat running down her small back.

"They'll be coming around the corner soon," she said into her earpiece. "So, we had better hide."

Soon one of the Mexicans peeked around the corner of the canyon, Heather spotted him immediately. "Mexican coming our way," she whispered into her earpiece. The man took a quick look, he then disappeared. He had seen the group of people having lunch around the picnic table; that was all he needed to know.

"They'll go and wait by their car now," Mandy said. "Then they'll lead the hit men in. I'm going to hide by the entrance so we will know when this party will get started." Before Banyon could protest, she once again came off the ledge and sprinted around the corner, but this time she had her HK417 with her.

"Mandy. As soon as you see the hit men, you get back here," Banyon screamed into his earpiece. *God, she is as impulsive as Loni,* Banyon thought.

"I guess we can relax for a few minutes," Eric said and leaned back against the rocks and closed his eyes.

"Wolf, do you have an update?" Banyon whispered.

"Everything is on plan right now," he replied.

But things were about to change.

67

Carlos sat in the front seat of the first van; there were three more vans behind him. He held his head in an attempt to stop the throbbing from his hangover. Miguel had picked the hit men up right on time and they sped off to kill Colton Banyon. Carlos had dispersed his men in the vans so he could communicate with them. The last stolen van was running low on gas, so his man called him and said they had to stop at the next exit. Carlos told his driver to head to the gas station. When they stopped, he went into the convenience store and purchased a coffee to help clear his head.

As he headed back to his van, he noticed several police cars parked just up the road, behind the gas station. He suddenly became suspicious; something didn't feel right to him. He returned to the convenience store counter and asked the clerk if it was normal for so many police cars to be congregated nearby. The clerk shrugged and told him he didn't know. This told Carlos that something was up. When he returned to the van, he told the men in the rear van to see if the police attempted to follow them.

When they were back on the highway, his phone rang. "The police cars are following," his man said without preamble. Carlos didn't know if the police had some inside information, or if they were setting up a speed trap, or maybe they just decided to follow sixteen hard-looking Mexicans in four vans, but he decided he had to do something. They were only a few miles from the exit for the Valley of Fire.

He said to his driver, "Speed up, I want to pass those two tractor-trailers before they get to the overpass up ahead," he pointed. He then called his man in the last vehicle and gave him instructions.

The four vans whizzed past the huge trucks. When the last van was near the front of the second truck, gun fire erupted from the windows of the van. It blew out all the tires of the truck. It immediately began to jackknife and pushed by the momentum of its weight, the truck began to roll over in the road. Soon the first truck was also rolling over as well. Both came to a stop just before the overpass and completely block the highway.

Carlos smiled for the first time that day. His goal was to stop the police from following him, but he unknowingly stopped the thirty SWAT members from continuing after him. He didn't know how lucky he was. He just knew the police would stop and help the victims. It was always their first priority.

"Exit for the Valley of Fire is coming up," his driver announced.

68

"No," The President of the United States roared. He and Marlene Moore were sitting in the situation room watching the action on the big monitor. They had moved a satellite so that they could follow the hit men into the park. They could also see the SWAT convoy a few minutes behind. They watched in horror as the semis rolled over and one exploded, completely blocking the highway. His cell phone immediately ran. It was Rebecca.

"We are in trouble," she started. "It is going to take us at least thirty minutes to get around this mess," she complained. "I can't even call Banyon to let him know. There is no cell reception in the valley."

"So, he has no idea there is no help on the way?" the President screamed into the phone.

"No, sir. They are on their own until we can get there. We have only two men up on the ridge to stop tourists from entering the park and they need to protect the populace. "

"Get there in ten minutes," the President ordered and hung up.

"Mr. President, Nellis Air Force Base is not too far away. Maybe we should scramble a jet and put a couple of missiles into the vans?" The National Security Advisor said.

"I can't lose Banyon," the President moaned. "And we can't shoot the vans. It would be political suicide."

"We have some Marines on the base. Can't we helicopter them into the valley?" Marlene asked, remembering that there was a group just in from overseas.

"Get them there as soon as possible," the President ordered. The National Security Advisor immediately called the Pentagon.

"It'll take ten to fifteen minutes. Do we have your approval?" he quickly asked the President.

"Do it." He answered. "I just hope Banyon can hold out until then."

69

Banyon suddenly saw Mandy sprinting into the canyon. He knew the hit men would be right behind her. So he decided to check with Wolf.

"Wolf, any updates?"

"Yes," Wolf quickly replied. "The entire SWAT team has been delayed by an accident caused by Carlos. Two trucks are involved and two men died. The SWAT team won't get to your location for at least thirty minutes. The President has scrambled some Marines from Nellis Air Force Base, but they will take almost as much time to get there."

"You mean we are on our own?" Banyon screamed as panic filled his body. Sixteen armed killers with machine guns against the four of them were not good odds. Their odds of survival had gone way down.

"It can't be helped, Colt."

"Should we abandon our position and hide?" Banyon was a veteran of gun battles. Over the last few years, he had been in many. But this time he only had one person, Eric, that he knew would perform. He was not sure about the women. He thought it might be prudent to wait for another day and a better plan.

"No, hold your ground" Wolf came back. "We need to rid the world of these vermin, today."

"But once the shooting starts, they will find us and there are a lot more of them. We'll be able to pick off some of them, but once they pin us down we'll be doomed. What happens then?" Banyon asked as Mandy climbed over the ledge.

"Don't worry Colt. I have a little surprise planned for them." Wolf went on to explain his surprise.

Banyon quickly activated his earpiece and told the others about the situation. Mandy looked at him with nervous eyes but said nothing. Eric and Heather were silent as well. "We have a backup plan in place. Just make sure you shoot as many of these assholes as possible, as quick as possible."

Carlos and his men marched into the canyon. He was in the very back of the group as he decided he didn't need to do any killing today. His head hurt too much and he was already dying of thirst. He had enough men with him to do the killing, even though his information about Colton Banyon had said he was very resourceful.

"When we reach to picnic area, I want you all to take them fast. Run in and kept shooting until they are all dead, and then we need to get out of here as soon as possible, before anyone else shows up. We'll take the back entrance out of the valley and be back in the city in less than two hours. The casino owes me some money. I intend to get it back." He told his men with confidence.

"We are here," one of the watchers said and pointed to the turn in the canyon. Carlos noted that the walls suddenly were very high in the canyon.

"We go on three," Carlos said. "One, two, three, go."

"Here they come," Mandy announced with a little panic in her voice. She cocked her gun and took aim.

"Wait until they start shooting," Eric said. "Shoot a man behind the front line. The men in the front won't know that the men behind them were hit, because of the noise. It will give us a chance to get a second shot off before they spot us. Heather and I will shoot the men on the right. You guys take the men on the left."

"Roger," Banyon said like a professional.

The hit men were pouring around the corner now in a full run. They had spread out and covered the entire walkway. There was no screaming, no yelling; just the sound of their feet pounding the sand.

Suddenly, machine gun fire filled the canyon. The noise was deafening as the sound bounced off of the canyon walls.

"Fire," Eric yelled into his earpiece, immediately four of the hit men fell backwards dead. The men in front kept firing at the rubber dolls, even though they had all been blow up in the first volley. It was blood lust at its worse, as often happens in gun battles, they couldn't stop firing. The next four men went down.

Carlos had already identified the shooters and peppered the ledge where Mandy and Banyon crouched. His remaining men soon followed his example. Banyon and Mandy hunkered down behind a large rock and were protected from the hail of bullets, but Banyon knew if one of the Mexicans was able to get on the ledge, he would soon be dead.

Right now the firepower was too strong to prevent that. Luckily, the hit men had not discovered that there were two groups of shooters. Eric and Heather suddenly popped up and raked the canyon with suppressing machine gun fire. The hit men dove to the ground, some hiding behind the dead bodies of their friends. Carlos could see the enemy had high ground and his men didn't have any cover.

Carlos now knew he was in real trouble. The people on the ledge could hold his men off for some time. He was sure that the police were not far behind. They could trap him in this canyon. The whole operation was a set up. He decided his only choice was to retreat. They needed to get out of the canyon and fight another day.

"*Vamos*," he yelled and waved his arm in retreat. He slowly began to back out of the canyon, firing at the sniper holes.

But that's when the surprise happened.

Suddenly, the canyon was filled with moans and sounds like Indians chanting. Everybody stopped firing and looked around to find the source of the noise. The chanting grew louder and louder until some of the men dropped their guns and covered their ears. The Mexicans were confused and then scared as smoky apparitions appeared at the entrance of each cave in the canyon. They looked like ancient Indians, in loin clothes and they carried spears. When the Mexicans turned to flee, the apparitions leaped from their caves, quickly gliding over the killer's heads and came to the ground, blocking the exit. The apparitions then started to move forward, pushing the Mexicans back into the line of fire. Sheer terror appeared on the killers faces as they reluctantly moved back into the canyon.

"Fire," Banyon screamed. Four more men went down before the remaining killers could grab their guns and return fire. The apparitions continued flowing deeper and deeper into the canyon. Carlos was one of the remaining four killers left alive. He decided he desperately needed to get away somehow. He thought the way out was to run through the ghost wall. He could clearly see through them, they were just ghosts. He could do it. He let out a blood-curdling scream and charged the wall of smoke, firing his weapon to punch a hole. One of the ghosts suddenly morphed into his mother. She stuck out an accusing finger at him. The superstitious Carlos stopped dead in his tracks. He could not run through his mother. He realized if he was going to get out he would have to get over the wall of the canyon. He then screamed. "I am Carlos *the matador*. You cannot stop me," he roared.

Turning on his heel, he rushed the back of the canyon. He wanted to get up on the ledge and then shoot everyone he found. His three remaining men joined him in the charge. They ran firing from the hip and screaming like madmen. Carlos almost made it to the back wall when a bullet from Colton Banyon's gun entered his heart. His three other men went down at the same time.

Suddenly, the canyon was eerily quiet. The chanting was gone, the ghosts disappeared, and no shots were being fired. It was like all sound was sucked from the canyon. There was only the smell of gunpowder and the hot unrelenting heat from the sun. The rocks looked like they were on fire. Mandy now understood where the place got its name.

Banyon took a deep breath. It seemed like it had been forever since he had taken his last gulp of air. He turned to Mandy and saw a look of feral terror in her eyes. Tears streamed down her cheeks. She dropped her gun and threw herself into his arms. Her whole body shook from fear and loathing. But she had held it together when it counted.

"I never killed anyone before," she wailed into his shoulder.

Banyon stroked her hair. "We did great, kid. I'm proud of you Mandy," he said softly.

Meanwhile, Heather and Eric had leaped down into the canyon. "Cover us," Eric yelled. "We need to make sure they are all dead." Banyon pushed Mandy back and picked up his gun.

It took them only a few minutes to confirm that all the hit men were dead. Colton Banyon and his team had taken on the most wanted hit squad in the entire world, just the four of them, and they had survived. "Thank you Wolf," Banyon said out loud.

"Who are you talking to?" Mandy asked as she stood up and stretched. Her clothes were filthy and sweat soaked, her hair was all over the place and her face was blackened. He realized that he must look the same way.

"I'm thanking the big guy," he replied. He didn't tell her the big guy in this case was Wolf.

Suddenly very serious, Mandy asked. "What just happened? I mean did you see the ghosts too? Where did they come from? Why did they help us? How did you…"

Banyon cut her off. "My guess is that are the ghosts from the Indians who used to live here. I told you, many people think they still haunt the place. Maybe they were protecting their homes."

"I think you had something to do with them," Mandy said accusingly.

"Remember Mandy, you can't tell anybody about what happened here," Banyon calmly replied.

"I think you are very special Mr. Banyon. You knew they would come. They were the surprise," she said. "And how come you always seem to know things that no one else does?"

"I talk to dead people," he answered deadpan.

"No, I mean, really, how do you know these things?" She asked.

But before he could formulate a plausible answer, Banyon's earpiece suddenly erupted. It was Eric.

"Someone is coming" he yelled as he and Heather scampered up onto the ledge. They were all back behind their rocks with guns aimed out when they spied a group of Marines rushing into the canyon with their guns aimed straight and the fluid motion of men that have gone into danger before.

When they got to the dead bodies, the leader suddenly raised his fist. The men immediately stopped and went to one knee. As he reviewed the carnage he said, "What happened here?"

"We are up here on the ledge," Banyon yelled down.

"Are you Colton Banyon?" The Marine leader was told to locate and protect him first of all.

"I am," Banyon announced and stood up. Mandy, Eric and Heather dropped their guns and showed themselves with their hands in the air.

"We were ordered here to protect you, but it looks like you handled things yourself," the Marine said with admiration.

"They were all contract killers who murdered many innocent people. They all needed to die," Eric said. He helped Heather down from the ledge and joined Banyon and Mandy near the picnic table.

"You four took down all these killers?" The Marine asked. He was surprised that two of them were young women.

"We didn't have a choice, our backup got delayed," Banyon replied.

"Well, we have only one thing to say about that," The commander said as he turned to his men.

They all yelled at the same time.

"Ooh-rah."

Epilogue

It was well after mid-night when Banyon parked his Jaguar back at his home in South Barrington, Illinois. He and Eric made their way into his house. They were exhausted, but knew Loni and the Patel sisters were due home in less than an hour and they needed to be ready for them.

The last seven hours had been a whirlwind of activity. As soon as the marines had secured the killing area, Banyon's group was allowed to drive over to the camping area in the park, with an armed escort, of course. They pulled their suitcases from the SUV and took warm showers, ridding themselves of the scent of killing. By the time they were finished, the SWAT teams showed up and took control from the marines, who promptly jumped into their choppers and returned to base without comment.

Rebecca surveyed the killing area and apologized to Banyon for being late. She handed Banyon a secure satellite phone and he was surprised when the President asked him if he was unhurt. When he said he was fine, the President asked him what happened.

"Marlene and I were watching a satellite feed in the situation room and had a clear view of the canyon. It looked like you were going to be overrun and all of a sudden the hit men went crazy. What happened?"

"I think they became dehydrated and disoriented," Banyon replied smoothly. "We had plenty of water, they had none." Banyon quickly realized the satellite camera had not pick up images of the ghosts.

"Oh," the President replied. "Will you be in the office tomorrow?"

"I think I'll take the rest of the week off. I need a little rest," Banyon quickly answered. "Why do you ask?"

"Our crisis with Mexico is over," he replied. "The Mexican President gave a speech a couple of hours ago and blamed everything on the drug cartels, so we decided to not mention the Effort plan. By tomorrow everything will be back to normal."

"So, why do you need me?"

"In his speech the President of Mexico brought up the name of Danta Lopez. He said Lopez was the new *Zorro*, wiping out corruption in Mexico. The people now see him as a new super hero."

"So?" Banyon cautiously asked.

"Well, I kind of told him, I could help communicate with the new *Zorro*. I expect I will be hearing from him soon."

"Even *Zorro* needs a vacation," a weary Banyon said.

Rebecca had two of her men drive the Banyon team back to the airport and they quickly boarded their plane and headed back to Chicago. Everyone was too tired to even talk. They all slept for the three hours it took to reach home base. When they landed, Banyon gave each of the women a big hug and told them he was taking several days off.

"When will we be paid?" Heather asked, "And how much?"

"I'll call Bart in the morning and tell him to release ten percent of whatever we made. Is that fair?"

On the drive home, Banyon and Eric talked. "What do you want to tell the girls?" Eric asked.

"Well, we need to tell them about the bomb because I was on camera," he calculated. "Let's tell them the rest of the time was spent bringing down Slezeck, but it is top secret. They should know about that part anyway. I wouldn't mention anything about bodyguards, okay."

"They performed well, when we needed them," Eric said.

"It was certainly a memorable event," Banyon replied.

"They sure were fun, too," Eric added. Nothing more needed to be said.

The women returned home at a little after one o'clock in the morning. Banyon and Eric were asleep on his couches, with the TV on, but bounced to attention as all four women flowed gracefully through the kitchen door from the garage.

"We're back," Loni announced. Each woman was dressed in loose-fitting colorful cotton sundresses and they brightened up the room like sunshine. Previne carried a small wooden box and placed it on the kitchen island.

"Look what we have," she exclaimed cheerfully, her arms open in an invitation to look.

Loni immediately ran at Banyon and leaped onto his body. He thought she seemed a little heavier than Mandy. She kissed him hard on the lips and Banyon immediately felt the urge to carry her directly to the bedroom, but she dropped down and went and gave Eric a non-brotherly hug. She was immediately replaced by Previne, who gave Banyon a kiss on his lips and then wrapped her arms tightly around him.

"I missed you most of all," she purred into his ear as she gripped him tightly.

He was shocked and aroused by the time Maya got to him.

When Pramilla came close for her hug, Maya flicked her eyes south for Pramilla to see. She immediately began grinding on the aroused Banyon. "I haven't felt one of those for a while. It feels good," she whispered into his ear. When he looked for Loni, he saw she was still hugging Eric. *Oh my God, what went on between these women on the sailboat,* he thought. *They are all as horny as a cat in heat.*

"We need to go and let these guys get some sleep," Eric urgently said. The three Patel women looked at him like hungry lions.

"We are going to leave the box here, for tonight," Previne announced. She wanted to be sure to have an excuse to come back tomorrow. "We'll come by around noon."

"We have some urgent business in the bedroom," Banyon leered as soon as the door closed. He picked Loni up and carried her like he was on a honeymoon. She giggled with delight and started unbuttoning his shirt.

The next morning, Banyon got out of bed around ten o'clock because he needed to use the bathroom. When he returned, Loni beckoned him to her side of the bed. She threw back the covers and lay naked as he sat down on the side of the large bed. She didn't have any tan lines on her small body.

"I feel guilty about having so much fun while you had to work and deal with a bomb in your office. Is there anything that I can do to get rid of my guilt?

Banyon thought for a minute. "Go put on your maids outfit. You have to wear it all day, even if we have company. You will do everything I order you to do, for the whole day."

"Really, that's pretty harsh, don't you think," she exclaimed as her eyes lit up. Banyon knew that above all things, Loni hated to be domestic.

"Then I'll forgive you," he said.

"Underwear or not?" she asked.

A few hours later, Colton Banyon sat at his desk. He decided to write a short list of their accomplishments, just as he had for all his previous adventures. He began to write:

Stopped a war between Mexico and the United States.
Saved the Presidents granddaughter.
Rescued two kidnaped girls.
Stopped a multi-leveled plot by the Effort.
Brought down Paul Slezeck.
Found another old Nazi—Walter Klotz.
Started a new position.
Prevented a bomb threat at Dewey & Beatem.
Eliminated a feared Mexican hit team.
Make some new friends?

He didn't want to write anything more, just in case Loni ran across the list in the future. She would have a bunch of questions about the mystery and especially the women. He put the list in his desk draw where he kept all the lists from previous adventures. He then sat back and thought about

Mandy and Heather. *What am I going to do about those two?*

Around noon the Patel sisters showed up with Eric in tow. They were all dressed in skimpy white shorts, halter tops and flat sandals. Eric was in his usual grubby attire. When they saw Loni in her, black, short, maids garb, complete with a little white apron, they gave a questioning look at her.

"I'm being punished," she acknowledged with a smile. "The man is such a brute."

Previne quickly played along. "Colt, can you have your maid bring me some coffee?"

"Bring Previne some coffee, wench," Banyon ordered.

Loni pouted, but did as he asked. "Here is your coffee, ma'am." This, of course, riled Previne. She hated to be called ma'am.

"Let's get to the treasure," Banyon said. They all gathered around the island in the kitchen and Previne expertly divided up the loot. She said that some of the items could be traced and put them in another pile.

"I know where to take them. I'll do it later today, Loni do you want to come?" She said with a bright smile.

"No," Banyon responded. "She is being punished. What are you guys going to do with your shares?"

"Didn't Loni tell you?" Pramilla asked.

"I have been kind of busy, you know, doing domestic things," Loni said, seeming a little embarrassed.

"Then I'll tell him," Previne announced. She turned to Banyon and said, "We are buying into your detective agency and moving it to a new location in town. We are all going to have private offices and maybe a sauna. If you don't want to sell us some of your shares, that's okay. Loni has already agreed to sell us some of hers." Previne's long term plan to capture Colton Banyon had taken another step closer to her goal.

Author's Notes

This book is, of course, pure fiction. Any resemblance to any person is coincidental, unless they have agreed to let me use their name. You know who you are. Other names are picked at random.

However, many of the events and places described in the book are very real. Of special note are the events that take place on our border with Mexico. The trafficking of human beings into the United States is one of the biggest problems we face in America, both socially and economically. It is also bigger than anyone admits. Last year, in a one hundred and sixty acre stretch of total desert near the border in Arizona, volunteers cleaned up forty-two tons of garbage left by the illegals.

The killings of newscasters, kidnappings of young girls, cartel gang wars, and even bombings are straight out of the headlines of several newspapers. The strangle-hold that the drug cartels are putting on Mexico is also true. Unfortunately, there is no real Danta Lopez, the new *Zorro*, around to control them.

The Sinarquistas movement mentioned in the Prologue was and is a real organization that still lives today. There are even chapters in the Southwestern United States. They became controlled by the Spanish *Falangists* and ultimately the Nazis during the period before World War II. The Nazis had something like twenty thousand spies along the Mexican border. When they took control of the Sinarquistas movement, they had the most powerful anti-American force in the western hemisphere. When Mexico entered the war on the side of the Allies, the entire organization was doomed, even though Mexico provided less than fifteen thousand troops to fight. However, about one hundred and fifty thousand workers flooded to the United States, to work in the factories that were now depleted of American men.

There are a number of secret government "Black Ops" groups that have been used around the world to fight injustice. They do much good work and you never hear about them unless there is a problem. But the SEAL team described in the book does not exist.

The Las Vegas part of the novel contains many real facts that are also true. Places such as; the Naked City, the supermarket style adult amusement stores, and of course, The Valley of Fire are real. The Valley of Fire is almost exactly as I have described in the book. It is a fascinating place to visit and is truly breathtaking. Petroglyph Canyon and the Mouse's Tank are must stops if you go there. However, I will tell you that the rock caves do feel haunted.

Author's Acknowledgements

Ever since I began writing several years ago, my son, Kris, has helped me develop several characters and plots. His view point is different than mine and he offers insight into subjects that I haven't mastered. He has more knowledge about the internet than anyone I have ever met. I am happy to co-author the continuing Colton Banyon series with him.

My books are turning into a family affair as another of my sons, Jonathan Kubicki, has helped me design the current cover for this book. Jon is a web designer with a long history of artistic successes.

I also want to thank Kathy Mayeda for her continued involvement in making my books successful. She reads, criticizes and pushes me towards better writing.

Brittany Walters-Breaden has edited several of my books, including this one, and it is time that I recognize her for her efforts. She has a long history in the publishing business and is always quick to help when I need it.

I research and qualify all of my own work, so I can't blame anyone else if I have made any errors. I am constantly amazed at the speed and the depth of data found on the Internet, but offer one word of caution; it was something I learned decades ago when studying history in college. Everything that is written and spoken comes with the slant of the author. Their ideas, beliefs and morale convictions are embedded in their work. Mine too.

Bonus Reading from my next book:
A Dubious Curse

1

It was early March in Las Vegas which meant spring was already in full bloom. Trees had leaves and bushes were budding with new branches, it was as green as the desert city would get before the hot sun began to dry out everything. UNLV was bustling with activity. Students were hurrying to classes at the main campus, just east of the famous Las Vegas strip. The students carried backpacks, computers, and food. Many clutched term papers, recently completed, to hand in to their professors. Everyone wanted to get their work done and up to date so that they could go on spring break. It started that evening.

One of the last scheduled classes for some students, going on break, was a history class in one of the main lecture halls. While several underclassmen blew off the class, the hall was still filled to capacity, even though no one took roll call. Attendance was not mandatory. More than two hundred and fifty students crowded the lecture hall. That was because the speaker was not only very entertaining, but her lectures were very thought provoking. It didn't hurt that she was quite beautiful and spoke in a voice which sent tremors of lust through most of the young men who attended.

Professor Lisa Lange stood at the podium. Today she was dressed in a long, flowing, multi-colored, cotton, dress, with a slit on the right side running to mid-thigh. The slit allowed for a considerable view of her long leg as she walked. Buttons on the front of the dress ran the entire length of her five foot seven, lean, athletic, body. She had opened the top buttons of her dress; a hint of cleavage was visible. Her golden blonde hair flowed to the middle of her back and she used it like a weapon, to get, and keep attention. She flicked her hair when she attempted to make a point. She always wore five inch high heels, todays were red.

She was not a traditional lecturer and did not stay in one place to speak. She roamed the room, often climbing the stairs between rows, to be near to her students, much to the delight of the young men in the room. She did this on purpose, to keep them motivated, and interested in her lectures. She often felt like her classes were more theater than lecture. She had a good record of success with her style and students flocked to her lectures.

Professor Lange was in her mid-thirties and had been teaching at the university for two years. She was a military brat raised by her single mother who had served in Iraq, in the first war. Her mother spent most of her time abroad, but Lisa had always lived in Las Vegas. Her mother had instilled in her daughter the importance of education with a love of reading, which led Lisa to studying history. She not only loved history, but she was also very good at piecing historical information together to prove her points.

Sometimes, her conclusions were very different from traditional historians. She could put a spin on most subjects. Her lectures sometimes sparked controversy, and good discussions. She liked it that way. Today's lecture was one of those.

When it was time to start her lecture, she cleared her throat to get everyone to quiet down and take their seats. She lowered the lights in the hall from buttons on the podium. She then started.

"I'm going to put three pictures up on the screen. I want one of you to tell me how they are connected. You can ask me any questions needed, to connect the pictures," she told her students. She pressed a hand held remote button and three pictures appeared on the big screen. While the students studied the pictures, she moved from behind the podium, gliding up the steps and stopped halfway to the back of the big hall.

The three pictures were side by side on the big screen at the front of the lecture hall. The first picture was of a book written by Edward Bulwer-Lytton. It was called *The Coming Race*. Below the book the date of publication was listed as 1871. There was also a caption that said, "This was the original title". It was a hint for an observant student.

"It was one of the first science-fiction books written," she tossed out as an additional hint to the many science fiction buffs in the audience.

The second picture was of a very beautiful woman. She had features which resembled Lisa Lange, high cheek bones, perk nose, blonde hair, and eyes that a man could get lost in. She stood about five foot six and was slender. The real difference in appearance from Lisa was the woman in the picture had very long hair. It almost reached her ankles. The date of the photo was written as 1919.

"She was the leader of a secret society," Lisa offered. "She may have been one of the original hippies, or at least a groupie."

The third picture was a rough drawing of something which looked like an upside-down tea saucer, with a hump in the middle. It looked like the drawing was made by a child. The date under the picture was also 1919.

"The drawing was not made by a child. The person who drew it was in a trance," Lisa explained.

After waiting for more than five minutes, Professor Lange threw out. "Can anybody identify any of the pictures?" She searched the crowd. One student raised his hand. She pointed to him to speak.

"The woman in the picture looks like you," the student observed.

"I assure you, it is not a picture of me," she quickly replied. "You will note, the picture was taken in 1919. There isn't enough makeup in the world to correct the lines I would have by now," Lisa said with a throaty laugh. Several students chuckled. "Come on people," she clapped her hands, "Think."

Another student raised his hand, she gave him the floor. "The third picture looks like a flying saucer. That leads me to believe this has something to do with World War II, but the Germans didn't work on saucers until the nineteen-forties," he said.

"Very good, Tom," she replied. Lisa prided herself by knowing the names of many of her students. "It is a crude drawing of a flying saucer, but was actually drawn in 1919. It was drawn by the woman in the second picture. I'll give you a hint," she added. "She was a median."

A murmur quickly rose in the gallery. "That's science fiction," a student yelled out. "No one can talk to dead people."

"Who says they were dead?" Lisa shot back. "And she didn't speak to them. She would write and draw what she received by telepathy, during her sessions."

"What did she write?" another asked.

"The drawing was one thing," Lisa confidently answered. She knew she was gaining their attention. "She also wrote long passages in an early German script and even ancient languages which she knew nothing about. Her writings were translated by other members of a highly educated group."

"But who was she communicating with?" asked a girl right next to Lisa.

"She told people they were the original inhabitants of earth." The professor let that sink in. "She was the leader of a very secret organization. It still exists today. It is called the 'Vril Society'," the professor added as another hint.

"Can you tell us more about the woman?" another student asked as confusion filled her eyes.

"She was the original flower child," offered Lisa. "She would have fit in nicely in the 1970's. She sought a society, a utopia, where everyone worked together and life was easy. She believed such a place existed."

"Can you tell us anything else?" The young girl next to her asked.

"She unfortunately she lived in a devastated post-World War I Germany," the professor added grimly.

Suddenly, another student raised her hand. The professor acknowledged her.

"If she was head of the Vril Society, then the book must have something to do with the flying saucer."

"Very good Stefanie," Lisa said. "Now connect them."

"So, the book was written about the Vril and the median followed the principles in the book, right?"

"Now we are getting somewhere," Lisa Lange announced. She paused for a second before she continued. "But Vril is not a person or even a people. It is an alternative energy source. It is an energy source unlike any known to man. It combines electricity, gravity, and several other energies to create the ultimate weapon. It was a tool for a maintaining a utopia. The Vril was the alternative science which led to a Utopia. It allowed for space travel, time travel and eliminated the cost of producing energy."

"But isn't the book, in the picture, a work of fiction? You already told us that." A student asked.

"It was more like a bible to the Vril Society," Lisa responded quickly. "Many things in the bible have not been proven, yet people still believe," she reasoned. "Star Wars is complete science fiction, yet many people follow the series like a cult."

"Does this have something to do with the Third Reich in Germany?" one of the smarter students asked.

"It most certainly does," Professor Lange replied enthusiastically. Before she could continue another student asked a question.

"Why did Hitler call his regime the Third Reich?"

"That's a very good question," she replied. "Hitler believed Germany had three golden ages. The first was the Holy Roman Empire. It ran from 962 AD to 1802 AD. The second Reich ran from 1871 to 1918, when Germany was defeated after World War I. The Third Reich was expected to last for a thousand years, but only lasted twelve, monstrous, years. Some believe a Fourth Reich is coming, but may not be in Germany. It will however, be as oppressive as the Third Reich.

Another student blurted out a question. "So, are you saying the Third Reich was based on a fictional book?"

"Well, yes and no. Part of Hitler's ultimate plan for the world, was based on the book," She quickly replied.

"That's ridiculous," someone said.

"No it's not," responded an angry Lisa Lange. "Think about it. Hitler believed he was an Aryan, a superior race. He also believed in the occult. He sent out many expeditions to find objects with supernatural powers. He believed in wonder-weapons that were undefeatable and he believed, one of those weapons, was saucer shaped. In a way, he searched for the power of Vril."

"Are you telling us, Hitler was so crazy, he based his regime on a book of science fiction?"

"You need to decide that," she quickly replied. "And your assignment during the holidays is to make the connection with Hitler, the Third Reich, and with each of the photos. In a paper to be submitted, two weeks from today, I want you to explain what he expected to discover from the Vril Society and the effects on his war efforts. You will have to read the book and study up on the Vril Society."

"Another hint please," a girl yelled out.

"The name of the medium was Maria Orsic."

Several large groans came from the student crowd. "But it is spring break," someone yelled out.

"All right, I'll give you three weeks and I am always available for consultation. My schedule is on my office door."

"Thanks for being reasonable," the girl next to her said.

"If there are no further question, class is dismissed," Professor Lange said officially.

Lisa Lange made her way back to the podium and began to pack her small briefcase with her notes as the students filed out of the lecture hall. When she looked up, she spied an older man slowly heading down the steps towards her. She didn't recognize him. When he reached her he spoke.

"I would like to know more about your premise concerning the mediums," he said in a mid-west accent. He was well dressed and handsome for his age, which Lisa judged to be well over forty years old.

"Are you a student here?" she quickly asked.

"No," he simply replied.

"Did you attend today's lecture?" She inquired as she flicked her hair.

"I did."

"Then you know as much as any of my students. You can find the answers on your own," she said, thinking this was some kind of a ploy to get more information out of her. *If only her students worked as hard at doing the assignments as they did at avoiding the work, most would be very successful*, she thought.

"I know much more than your students," he replied.

"Like what?" Lisa's interest was now growing. She cocked her head and took a half step forward with her right leg, causing the split to reveal her toned bare leg. She noticed when he took a quick look.

"I know you are a member of the Vril Society, your real hair reaches your ankles, and you still are searching for the book of The Vril," he replied.

Shock registered on her pretty face. She began to turn red, telling the man that what he said was true. "That's absurd," she said forcefully. "Please leave," she continued nervously, "before I call security and have you thrown out of the building."

"I mean you no harm. In fact, I may be able to help you," he calmly replied. "You are in imminent danger. Your life will soon be threatened because of what you know. My team can protect you. But you will have to come with me."

"Wow, that's one hell of a pickup line," she laughed as she threw back her head in defiance. "What do you want from me, for all your protection?"

"I just want to discuss a few things with you. I need to get up to speed quickly on the Vril Society."

"Why do you even care?" Lisa Lange asked suspiciously.

"This isn't about you, it is about the future of the world," he replied. "But you are the medium."

Gerald J. Kubicki & Kristopher Kubicki

"Who are you?" Lisa Lange asked in desperation. "Why have you made these accusations about me? I'm nothing but a humble teacher."

"My name is Colton Banyon," he told her. "I know there are two other women in your cell. They both live here in Las Vegas."

"How can you know this?"

"I have some abilities of my own," he simply answered.

"What do you really want?" The professor asked.

"I want to find the book of The Vril and protect it for you."

2

It had all started for Colton Banyon two days earlier, when he was relaxing on his couch, in his sprawling ranch home in suburban South Barrington, Illinois. Loni, his lovely partner, live in companion and best friend, was curled up next to him with her head on his lap. They were watching television on an eighty inch screen Loni had bought for him, to watch football. She was good to him in many ways.

A news flash suddenly filled the screen. The talking head announced that there had been another shooting in Mexico. This time seventeen members of a drug cartel had been dispatched by the side of a rural road. The cartel members had been traveling on a country road near the American border when all three trucks suddenly blew up, burning the seven million dollars of drugs, they carried. A few cartel members had made it out of the trucks, but were cut down by machine gun fire. A bloody note was found on the road. It read "Danta Lopez was here, be afraid, be very afraid"

"Did you have anything to do with that?" Loni quickly asked as she lifted her head and stared at him with her dark Chinese almond-shaped eyes.

"No," Banyon replied. "I've been with you all day. I wonder why the President didn't call me to help?" he added.

"Better ask Wolf," she said as she removed her toned athletic frame from the couch and stretched causing Banyon to take notice. She arched her back and undid the tie that held her long black hair in a ponytail. It cascaded down her back. She then went into a yoga position which reminded him of a ballerina. She kept one eye on him all the time.

"I think I will," he responded as he reached for her tiny body and pulled her onto his much bigger lap. "I'll do it in a minute," he added.

Colton Banyon was well over sixty years old, Loni was around fifty, but looked twenty-five and acted like it too. She kept him captivated and constantly interested with her seemly innocent, yet insatiable sexual presents. The night shirt she was wearing, flew off, Loni style, which meant she paid no attention to where it was going. It landed on top of a lamp. Neither of them noticed. An hour later, Banyon finally addressed Wolf.

"Are you there Wolf?" Banyon asked into the air.

Wolf was actually Wolfgang Becker, but had lived most of his life as a man named Wulter Pierce. When he learned he was dying, several years ago, he arranged for a friend in India to cast a curse on him. The curse allowed Colton Banyon to talk to the now dead Wolf whenever he wanted to. Banyon had to ask a question, and could not ask about the future, but could otherwise talk normally, although no one else could hear the spirit, even in public. All Banyon had to do was ask a question.

Colton Banyon didn't consider himself as having special powers. He saw Wolf as his eye in the sky. Wolf was also his researcher and could find out anything in history, given enough time. All history was visible to Wolf, but he had to sift through it. Wolf had explained, all history left a timeline of energy. Wolf could track the timeline and follow the path to see the actual history. He could then report to Banyon his findings. They had solved many mysteries and recovered several ancient artifacts over the years. Banyon was at first frightened by and very concerned about the spirit, but soon understood Wolf was there to help him. Banyon was also there to help Wolf.

Wolf hunted old Nazis and artifacts, his curse would end when the last Nazi died. They had solved many Nazi mysteries together, while bringing down many old Nazis. Banyon and Loni had formed a detective agency, as cover, and had become wealthy along the way. The only other people who knew about Wolf were the Patel clan, whose grandfather had placed the curse, and the President of the United States. He often used Banyon's ability to solve problems he could not solve himself.

Danta Lopez was a creation of Colton Banyon. In Mexico, he was known as the new *Zorro*. But he was actually a team of Navy SEALS, working with the Mexican government, to rid the nation of the many drug cartels. Usually, Banyon was involved in any Danta Lopez operation, but this time he had been excluded. Banyon was included because Wolf could watch and inform Banyon of anything affecting their operations, in real time. The operations had to be done clandestinely and could leave no trace.

"I'm here," the spirit replied in a culture voice.

"Why wasn't I included in the recent cartel takedown in Mexico?" Banyon asked the spirit.

"It was not sanctioned by the U.S. government. They are as unaware as you are," Wolf answered.

"Then who did it?"

"Another drug cartel took them out. They wanted the turf."

"Should I be concerned?"

"No, your plan is actually working. The cartels are eliminating each other. They all believe Danta Lopez is one of their competitors. They want to eliminate him before they themselves become a victim." the spirit answered rather happily.

"So, we are good then?"

"Yes, on that subject. But I do need your help," Wolf added.

"What do you need? Is there another Nazi for me to take down?" Banyon and his group were always ready to bring down some evil swine.

"I'm afraid it is more sinister than that."

"How could that be?"

"There is a disturbance in the force which surrounds me."

"What does that even mean?"

"In the past, whenever there was a disturbance, someone new eventually joined the group up here. It has happened about twenty times since I have been here," the spirit told Banyon. "We have become accustomed to the event."

Gerald J. Kubicki & Kristopher Kubicki

"So, why is this time different?"

"This time the new spirit will be a threat to you, Colton."

"Why?"

"The new spirit will be after the plans for the anti-gravity machine. Remember you were the last person to touch a working version." Banyon and his friends had found an actual working model of the machine, in a cave, in the Death Valley national park a few years ago. Wolf had made him destroy it.

"But that is the future. You can't tell me that, can you?"

"I can see the new curse surrounds the anti gravity device. Additional information is now blacked out to me. They will be after the plans."

"But there were no plans in the cave, don't you remember?"

"That is correct, but there is the original plan. The Nazis build their models from the plan which had been drawn by a medium in 1919. That plan still exists in a book. You must find the book, before they do."

"So, tell me where the book is and I will get it. You can do that, right?" Banyon had found many artifacts using Wolf's help.

"It's not that simple," the spirit replied. "The curse has already been activated, but won't take effect until the cursed person dies. It will be soon, by the way. However, none of us up here can see anything involving the new curse, the history is all blank. I am essentially blind on this one."

"Can't you go back in history to see where the book was located, years ago?"

"The medium that held the book also learned some curses and spells from the others. She eventually disappeared using a spell. She also put a curse on the book, so the Nazis couldn't find it. Only someone who knows the curses can find the book."

"But you know the plan exists, right?"

"The history of the device has been published for some time. The power source has not. It is part of the plan. The power source will change everything. It is both a weapon

322

and a blessing as the energy is limitless and cheap. It could be used to build a utopia."

"Is that bad?"

"In the hands of the wrong people, yes it is bad.

"That seems like a dubious curse," Banyon replied.

"But there may be a bigger problem," the spirit hinted.

"Uh, oh," Banyon uttered. If Wolf said it was a problem, it was a big problem. "What do you mean?"

"In addition, there will be a new person who will be able to talk to a spirit like me. That person is a member of the Effort. The person dying is also a member of the Effort. I'm afraid, there is trouble ahead."

"Oh, my god," Banyon suddenly yelled. The Effort was the modern version of the Third Reich. They had infiltrated America, starting in the nineteen thirties, and intended to turn America into the new Third Reich. Banyon had fought them before.

"Can you give me his name?" Banyon asked.

"My ability to see the history around the subject ended as soon as the curse was placed, so, no, not until the curse is completed, when the cursed person dies. But you must protect yourself Colton."

"Why?"

"The new spirit will quickly discover you have had a hand in the demise of several of the Effort plots and people. They will be able to see that you found the working model of the saucer. They will also find out about me and will surely come after you. You are in grave danger and you must act quickly."

"But where do I start?" Banyon felt the cold chill of fear, gripping his heart. His fear included the safety of his friends as well.

"First, you must have the Patel's find a way to neutralize the curse. If we can hinder the spirit from communicating, we can stop the plot."

"Will the new spirit have the same rules? I mean, will the spirit need questions to respond, like you do?" Banyon quickly asked.

"That is my understanding," Wolf answered.

"Do you know anyone who can give me a lead?"

"There is one person. She is a direct descendant of the medium who drew the original plans for the anti-gravity machine. Her name was Maria Orsic."

"What is his name and where do I find him?"

"He is actually a female and she is a medium too. Her name is Lisa Lange. She is a professor, of history, at UNLV in Las Vegas. She is a leading member of the current Vril Society. She is also in great danger. You must protect her as well."

"Do you think your plan will work? Can we stop their plans?"

"We have a good chance. We will also attempt to block the new spirit from learning how to research history. This position, up here, does not come with a procedure manual. You have to learn from others up here. My friends and I will surround the new spirit and attempt to block him from learning. They will still be able to see recent history though and communicate with their conduit on the ground. I will know more when they get here."

Banyon quickly turned to the wide-eyed Loni. "Call the Patel's. We need to have a meeting right now. Next book us on a flight to Las Vegas. Tell the Patel's they need to go with us. Finally, get me everything you can find on the internet about the Vril Society, and especially anything you can find about a woman named Maria Orsic."

Loni, who did everything a top speed, fled the room. "I have to pack first. It will be fun to be at our condo."

About the Author

Gerald J. Kubicki currently has additional sequels in the works. The books follow the continued adventures of Colton Banyon and his team of unique characters.

Gerald started writing fiction novels after a long career as a successful businessman. He has traveled the world and is an avid history buff. His writings contain large amounts of actual historical events and real places woven into the plots.

He currently resides in Las Vegas.

You can find out more about this author by visiting his website:

www.geraldjkubickibooks.com

Kristopher Kubicki has joined his father in writing the Colton Banyon series.

Kristopher has been writing articles for major magazines and trade publications since entering college. He currently owns a company that does research on the internet, but has collaborated with Gerald on several books.

He currently resides in Chicago.

You can find out more about this author by visiting his website:

www.geraldjkubickibooks.com

Made in the USA
Charleston, SC
23 March 2015